THE
ARIZONAN

The Bierman Saga - Book 3

A Novel

By

William Burgdorf

The Bierman Saga by William Burgdorf
Book 1: *The New Mexican*
Book 2: *Company A*
Book 3: *The Arizonan*

Fiction/Western/Historical Fiction

First Printing

Produced by Venture Galleries.com

Formatted by Enterprise Book Services, LLC

Dedication

This book is dedicated to the American Southwest and to those who settled it. It's also dedicated to writers of westerns who keep the love of the West vibrant, active, and alive. Last, but not least, to Nancy, who's ridden with the Biermans and me over every word.

Acknowledgement

I want to acknowledge the assistance, support, challenge, and friendship I received during the review of *The Arizonan*. I meet with a group of outstanding writers and we critique each other's work. This process is extremely beneficial. It allows me to become a better writer, and my work to become even more exciting and adventuresome. The comments and feedback shared in our circle sometimes requires thick skin and is always shared to make us better tomorrow than we are today. My thanks and appreciation to: Caleb Pirtle III, Linda Pirtle, Ryann Martin, Beverly McCay, and Richard Hollingsworth.

Table of Contents

1
HACIENDA

"It wants to kills us," says Guillo.

"What does, who does?" Byron quickly scans the horizon.

"This desert. It tries hard. Our water, it's gone; horse almost dead; *mi Companero*, Zep, and me tied together."

With relief, Byron realizes what Guillo is talking about. "I remember Pa telling about the time you both walked out of the desert."

Riding south from Lordsburg, Byron watches the Chihuahua Desert fill the horizon with vast stretches of desert piled with scrub brush and cactus. The rocky terrain is broken periodically when dust devils swirl around and quickly disappear. Heat waves quiver and rise from the dry arroyos of a land untouched by rain. Distant mountain ranges hide behind a mist of purple haze.

Guillo rides along staring vacantly into the distance, remembering.

"Was it a long walk?" inquires Byron almost reading Guillo's thoughts.

"*Si.* We come from Chihuahua, Mexico, and cross the desert. We needed water, food, and shelter."

"Why did you do it?"

"To escape *tres gringo banditos*, Mexican *soldados*, and an Apache ambush."

"Did the Indians follow you?"

"*Si*, uno Apache. We did not know then. We are too busy trying to stay alive. *Su Padre* does everything he knows to cover our trail."

"Pa never talks much about it. It's as if his life doesn't start until the *hacienda*."

"*Si*, one can say his life, it changes the day we arrive."

"How?"

"*Don* Louis de la Vieta, he takes us in, yes. We clean up, recover, eat, and in the evening, we sit on the porch of the bunkhouse. *Señorita* Alassandra de la Vieta steps onto the porch of the big house. *Su Padre,* he is a lost man from that moment." Guillo smiles at Byron.

"My mother." Byron smiles back.

"*Si, su Madre.* She captures *mi Compañero*, Zep."

"Do you want to ride hard and make it to the *hacienda* late tonight, or spend a night in the desert and arrive tomorrow morning?"

"We will be doing hard riding soon enough. Let's take it easy to the *hacienda*." Guillo shrugs.

They spend the rest of the day watching the landscape change from scrubby trees to manzanita, mesquite, barrel cacti, and scattered brush in a rocky, sandy soil. The horizon is populated with distant purple mountains. As the sun sets in the west, Guillo stops beside Animas Peak, a tall rocky mass thrusting up from the desert floor. Erosion and time causes an accumulation of loose scree at its base.

"We will camp in the open spot," says Guillo. Byron turns his horse towards where Guillo points. Dismounting, he strings a picket rope between two mesquite bushes and ties his horse and the two pack mules.

"Guillo, tell me the story about you and the mule?" Byron grins.

"*Ay, yi-yi*, he was the hard headedest animal *El Dio* ever creates," says Guillo unsaddling his horse and tying it to the picket line. "He always turns left when I want to go right. He almost kills me when Apaches are around by braying his *estupido* head off, and I couldn't ever had a better *caballo* than that mule." Smiling, Guillo looks at the two pack mules.

Byron is raised on Guillo's mule stories, and always likes hearing his uncle reminisce. Both men scrounge firewood and soon have a small blaze to cook over. Night drops around them like a dark blanket, and aside from coyote calls, the evening is quiet as they are bombarded with light from the millions of stars overhead.

Morning's sunlight scoots across the desert floor as the sun inflames the eastern horizon. Both men awake and load their gear before the sun springs over the horizon. With the light, they strike an easy trail to the *hacienda*.

Miguel *de la Vieta* begins this morning like every other; walking onto the front porch of the main house to watch the change of the *vaqueros*. A dozen mounted riders gallop through the open front gate with the rising sun to begin their day of managing the live stock herds of the *hacienda*. He waves and most wave back. Some branch off and begin work as sentinels to watch over the farmers and herdsmen of the *hacienda* going about their daily chores. Being watchful never changes in this land. Something or someone is always waiting for a slip up in vigilance, and Miguel is ever vigilant. As soon as the dozen *vaqueros* exit the grounds, another dozen enter through the open main gate.

He smiles, *the appearance of my 'night hawk' riders looks like it was quiet last night. They'll head for the cookhouse, then bunkhouses, and casas. It is good to have quiet nights; otherwise it means someone gets hurt. Today, maybe tomorrow, Guillo and Byron arrive and we have much to agree on and set into motion.*

Turning, he quickly scans the wall that surrounds the *hacienda* and spots men on guard at the parapets. He sees families come from the *casas* around the main house, children shout and run around. He watches the blacksmith fire up the forge, and listens to singing from the barns. He hears two *vaqueros* move around on the roof of the main house as they guard. As he observes, he thinks, *this hacienda is home to so many, a village made possible by the artesian well. My father was a wise man to build here, and it is my job to maintain all he started, making it stronger and better for everyone.*

He turns and enters the main house, walks to the patio and joins his *esposa*, wife, for breakfast.

The *vaquero* yanks his horse to a sudden stop beside Byron. His charge is unseen from behind a screen of manzanita bushes, and takes Byron and Guillo by surprise. His rifle points toward them.

"*Señor Guillo y Byron, estar usted, bueno.*" shouts the *vaquero* lowering his rifle. "I did not know it was you." A second *vaquero* pulls up his galloping horse and walks toward the others. Byron acknowledges his arrival with a nod.

"*Si, Gilberto*, it is good to see you again, and see you are on the job," says Guillo to the first *vaquero*. "You are upon us before we notice, *es bueno.*" Guillo grins at the mounted *vaqueros* who guard the *hacienda*.

The riders continue along the trail leading to the house in the distance. As they ride, the two *vaqueros* peel away and return to their assigned job of guarding the *hacienda*. They wave goodbyes. Byron waves back.

"Uncle Miguel doesn't take intruders lightly, does he?"

"No, he is very serious to make certain the *hacienda* and all who live here have protection. It is part of his responsibility as the *Hacendado.* All look to him for security and livelihoods." Guillo acknowledges. "His father, *Don* Louis, was also a very vigilant *Patron*, and Miguel learns from the best."

Their approaching the *hacienda* compound is noticed and the main gate opens as they ride toward the wall around the village. Riding through the portal, they acknowledge waves from friends and family, dismount in front of the main house, and Miguel de la Vieta comes through the open doorway onto the porch.

"*Buenos dias, mi familia*. I am glad you made it here so soon. No difficulties I trust?"

"None, Miguel. The train is real progress for New Mexico," Guillo replies with a smirk.

"It used to take us days to get here. Now, we ride on the train and enjoy the scenery. Yes, it is progress. Good to see you *Tio* Miguel." says Byron.

"This railroad has been good for our cattle business, no? Now, we drive herds to Lordsburg and ship them to Las Cruces where your ranch hands pick them up, corral them, and fatten them for market. Our losses are small, no Apaches to deal with, and that means more livestock for our customers. Come in, clean up, and meet me on the patio. There is much to discuss." Miguel turns and walks into the house. Stable hands lead the horses and mules to the barn as Guillo and Byron grab their saddlebags and rifles.

Entering through large wooden doors into the long central hallway, the temperature cools to comfortable. Four arched doorways on each side of the long central hall allow access to bedrooms, office, workspaces, and storage. *Don* Miguel's office is through the entrance vestibule on the left. Guillo and Byron follow a servant to a bedroom in the rear right corner.

In the room, Byron sees colorful blankets hanging on smooth adobe walls. Tossing their saddlebags and rifles on the beds, both men wash the trail dust from their hands and faces with water from a pitcher and basin sitting between the beds.

From a cut glass decanter, Guillo pours two fingers of the clear liquid into two glasses and offers one to Byron.

"*Mi Sobrino*, my nephew, to your health," Guillo raises his glass in a salute to Byron and tosses the liquid into his mouth. "Ahhh, nothing like Tequila to cut the dust."

Byron raises his glass and throws the liquid down his throat. He bursts into uncontrollable coughs as the Tequila sears his esophagus and tears well up in his eyes. Whispering, he squeaks out, "This is good stuff." Guillo is already leaving the room with a big smile on his face. Byron rushes to catch up, still gasping for air.

Both men exit the main house and see *Don* Miguel sitting at a round table amid lush plants, blossoms, vines, and potted plants, which comprise the patio gardens.

Miguel's stepmother began many of the plants once the *hacienda* was built and it's been maintained and increased over the years. Byron's mother was introduced to his father in this garden years ago. He remembers all the stories.

"I know you just arrived," says *Don* Miguel, "But we must talk about the herd for Arizona. My *vaqueros* round up the livestock and hold them in a temporary corral west of the *hacienda*. Eight *vaqueros* agree to accompany you to Arizona. Some will stay, others will return because their families live here."

"It's more than I was expecting," says Guillo.

"I correspond with *Señor* John Slaughter in Arizona," says *Don* Miguel. "He says land is available north of his property and I have arranged for its purchase."

"Slaughter is selling us some of his ranch?" asks Byron. "I understand he has 65,000 acres purchased from the old Perez land grant. Isn't two-thirds of his land in Mexico?"

"*Si*, my well-informed nephew," says *Don* Miguel. "He leases additional acreage on the U.S. side of the border to continue expansion of his *rancho.* He is not selling us any of his land."

Guillo adds, "Texas John Slaughter acquires land on the south end of the San Bernadino Valley. So, it is our plan to acquire land further north, *si*?"

"*Si*, Guillo, I already have papers for 30,000 acres in the San Simon Valley. This land separates the Chiracahua, Dos Cabezas, and Pinaleno Mountains on the west from the Peloncillo and Whitlock Mountains on the east. The San Simon River flows northwest through the valley and joins the Gila River," replies *Don* Miguel. "Let's go to the front porch." Rising, he walks quickly through the house and steps onto the front porch. Guillo and Byron follow closely behind. Miguel points west toward the purple hazy shape of mountains on the horizon.

"The tallest peaks you see to the west are the Chiricahua Mountains. North of that mountain range, the San Simon Valley runs north and south. On the north end is a small village called Solomonville, Arizona Territory. We will ranch the valley from there to San Simon at the south end. The Southern Pacific Railroad can load cattle at San Simon's train stop. A ranch headquarters somewhere in the middle would be the best."

"*Tio* Miguel, I can barely see the mountains you point out," says Byron. "You talk about them like they are next door."

"*Si*, they are next door to me, Byron. I've thought about this venture for many years. It is the only way to continue to grow our cattle business. With *ranchos* in Arizona, Animas, and Mesilla, we will have grazing in both Territories with each location supporting the other in good times and bad, and all connected by the railroad.

Do you understand why you need to make sure the Arizona *rancho* is successful?"

"It looks like a long way, *Tio*," says Byron. "What about Mama, Adeline, and Billy?"

"Not to worry, *mi Sobrino*. *Vaqueros* already ride to Mesilla to help manage the *rancho*. *Su madre, hermana, y hermano* will not have to work the *rancho* unless they want to. I will see to their safety and welfare. You go make the *rancho* in Arizona successful, *si*?

Giving his concerns one last thought, Byron replies, "When shall we leave, *Tio*?"

Clapping his hands together, Guillo says, "It had to be his choice, Miguel, but now that it's made, we are ready to ride."

All three partners walk back to the patio. A meal waits for them.

"*Bueno, bueno,* you leave in the morning, *mi Compañeros*. Arizona is waiting." Miguel digs into his meal.

2
ARIZONA TERRITORY

Brax and his three travel companions ride in a Pullman railroad coach from Deming to Lordsburg. No attention is paid to the landscape or surroundings they pass. The conductor walks through the car to announce arrival into Lordsburg. Kicking Hayes seated across from him to wake him, Brax says, "Lordsburg; wake up the others."

Hayes rubs his eyes and takes a look out the slow rolling railcar window. "Yep, peers to be Lordsburg." He commences waking the other two.

"We need to grab some grub?" says Gregory.

Brax replies, "Yes, you three find a cafe close to the depot. Get a table away from the door, and wait for me. I need to check on a few things." Rising, he quickly moves to the platform between the rail cars and prepares to step down the stairs toward the ground. As the train comes to a slow roll, he leaps off and walks rapidly toward a bulletin board that hangs on the side of the depot. In the upper right corner he sees a posted handbill, a wanted poster, with his name on it.

"I expected it. Not a surprise to see it," he says to himself. "I knew Pa's killing would draw attention. This poster will turn bounty hounds loose on me. Can't stop in Lordsburg. Got to get out of this territory, quick."

Turning away from the bulletin board, he sees Hayes lead the gang up the street away from the depot. Shouting at them, they stop, turn, and look.

"Get back to the train, we're pulling out of here." Brax points toward the railcar.

"Aw, boss, I need something to eat," squalls Gregory with Vern bobbing his head in agreement.

Brax shifts his hand toward the pistol on his right side. "You have a problem with what I told you to do, Greg?"

Grabbing Vern by the shoulders, he holds him between Brax and himself, Gregory moves towards the railcar. "No problem with me boss. Maybe Hayes can get us something while we wait in the coach."

"Hayes, round up some grub for us and get back here, pronto." Brax thumbs two silver dollars to him. Herding Gregory and Vern, Brax moves back to the depot and quickly purchases four tickets for Benson, Arizona Territory. He boards the railcar behind Gregory and Vern. Hayes shows up twenty minutes later with a sack of sandwiches from the mercantile and four bottles of beer. He sits beside Gregory and Vern out of earshot of Brax.

"There's a handbill on the bulletin board at the depot that says Brax is wanted dead or alive. A reward could carry us a long way. I'm tired of bein' bossed around by him and say we take him. Are you with me?"

"Have you plain lost your mind?" Gregory says. "He'll kill us."

"No. Look, when he's asleep, grab his gun arm, hold him, and I'll go get some help to tie him up," says Hayes.

"Wait, I hold him while you run around and try to find someone to help? You have lost your mind. Get away from me. Leave me alone," Gregory shoves Hayes away.

The train whistle shatters their conversation and people climb aboard the railcar and jostle for seats. Shortly, a second whistle sounds and the train moves.

Byron rides beside twenty-five hundred head of cattle as they plod across the Animas Valley. Dust swirls and billows upward. The desert of scrub brush, cactus, and rocky terrain the herd covers from Animas to the Arizona border has his attention. He knows the dust announces a large, slow moving herd.

Looking around, he watches *vaqueros* push the cattle. One rides point, two are swing riders, two flankers, and two ride drag as they prod, shout at, and harass the cattle to keep them on the move. A *remuda* of spare horses trots beside the herd as the dust cloud billows high overhead. Guillo and Byron ride with the point man.

"There's no hiding where we are, is there?" asks Byron.

"No, we are much too big to hide, and I worry about that."

"We have been five days since the *hacienda*, and with luck in six more will be in San Simon. What's worrying you?"

"It's been too easy. Someone watches out there, and I wonder when they will act," says Guillo.

Off to the left rolls the *carreta*, chuckwagon, ahead of the dust and looking for a spot to set up camp.

Byron quietly rides beside Guillo and watches the landscape change from mesquite, creosote, manzanita, and barrel cactus to ocotillo, yucca, Palo Verde, and saguaro cactus. The once distant Chiricahua Mountains become more and more noticeable.

"When you see how rugged and ragged the buttes, canyons, and valleys of the Chiricahua Mountains are, you understand why the Apaches use it for their sanctuary,"

Byron says to Guillo, "It's sure different country than around Mesilla."

"It is Arizona Territory, *mi Sobrino*; you would expect it to be different, *si*?" replies Guillo.

"Do we keep pushing today or circle up the herd and bed them down?"

"We push for a few more hours. The sooner we are into the foothills the better; I want to be off this plain and out of this desert as quickly as possible."

Guillo spurs his horse and moves to the point man gesturing where the herd is to move. Both men nod their heads and the cattle plod on. He rides over close to the chuckwagon and talks with the cook, points forward, and waves the *carreta* off into the distance to make camp. Returning to Byron he looks around for any signs of problems.

"You do suspect something, don't you?" Byron asks.

"*Si*. Your *Padre* talks about 'his tickle' when things don't feel right. *Ay, yi-yi, madre mia*, I think I have 'his tickle' now. Something, does not feel right."

Early dusk, Byron follows as the point man turns the lead bull; the herd follows and flows to a slowly circling stop. The cattle look for comfortable ground to bed down. Ground without rocks, thorns, and rattlesnakes is hard to find. Most cattle simply sleep standing up. The *vaqueros* move toward the chuckwagon in search of coffee and grub. Two remain and slowly ride a circle around the herd while they sing softly assuring the animals everything is all right.

Byron holds a tin cup full of coffee while he stands beside the chuckwagon, smells the mesquite wood smoke, and watches the *vaqueros* quickly claim tin plates of frijoles, tortillas, and sliced beef. They carefully claim spots around the fire as they load their tortillas with beef and beans, wrap them, and devour the *burritos*. They wash everything down with hot strong coffee. A guitar appears from the wagon and soon a soft melody drifts over the camp. Byron smiles and looks for Guillo.

Standing outside the circle of firelight, Guillo surveys the surrounding countryside.

"When, where, and who?" asks Byron while approaching Guillo.

"Morning, *aquí*, three or four *hombres*," says Guillo.

"How do you know?"

"I see their dust wisps this afternoon. They will hit in the morning, because it is the best time to strike. It's what I would do," Guillo answers without turning to look at Byron.

"How do I learn what you know?"

"Experience, *amigo*. No other way to learn, and experience, the teacher, is *la perra,* a bitch. Your *Padre* teaches me much, now you listen and learn. *Si*?"

"How do we prepare?"

"Tonight only two of us sleep at a time, only a little whiles. The cook keeps the fire burning and coffee hot. We ride around the herd and wait for morning. I think they will ride from the east to use rising sun to blocks our seeing them, but we will be ready."

"What do I need to do?"

"Nothing yet, maybe plenty later. Get some sleep now, I will wake you at midnight."

"What if nothing happens?"

"Then nothing happens, yes? But, if we are not ready we can lose a herd." Guillo shrugs and smiles a big grin. Byron can't keep but laugh out loud.

"*Si, mi Tio*, all we can lose is a herd. But, not on our watch, *right.*"

"*Si, mi Sobrino*, not on our watch." Guillo mounts his horse and rides off to tell the *vaqueros* how to prepare.

Byron stops by the *remuda* and swaps horses. Switching his saddle to a fresh mount, he moves to the chuckwagon, collects his bedroll, and dismounts. He shakes out his bedding at the edge of the fire-lit circle, and ground ties his horse beside him. Morning will come soon enough.

A brilliant sunrise is precipitated by a soft predawn filtering onto the desert. Sunrise spills its light, and four horsemen gallop out of the east yelling and shooting their pistols. Startled cattle immediately begin to bawl, scramble to their feet, and mill around.

Byron watches as a cow dashes out of the herd. The rest follow and a stampede is underway. Two *vaqueros* quickly ride up beside the breakout leader and start to turn the runaways. Guillo and the other four riders gallop toward the rustlers shooting their handguns.

It's apparent their surprise is lost, and the rustlers yank the reins on their horses to ride back into the sunrise.

Guillo waves for the four *vaqueros* to dismount to steady their aim. All four crouch and fire a rifle volley at the rustlers. Two drop from their saddles.

Byron, rides up, draws a bead with his Winchester .45-40 rifle, and knocks a third would-be thief from his horse.

Guillo gallops hard, gains ground on the fourth rustler, takes out his lariat, spins a loop over his head, and flings it at the escaping rider. Softly, easily, the loop drifts over and drops around the rider's shoulders. Guillo ties off his end of the lariat to his saddle horn and yanks his horse to a sudden stop. In a fraction of a minute the lariat snaps taut and the rustler and horse separate. The horse continues its break-neck gallop into the sunrise while the would-be thief collapses into a heap on the ground.

Guillo, two *vaqueros*, and Byron ride up.

"*Señor*, you make a wrong decision this morning," says Guillo to the man on the ground.

The terrified thief stares up like a small captured animal at the riders that surround him. Wide-eyed and frantic, he scrambles around only to be pushed back by booted feet to the center of their circle.

"How did you know? We waited for the right time." the rustler shouts.

"There is no right time, *amigo*," says Guillo. "Only a time to live and a time to die. You chose the wrong one, yes?"

"The mercantile in Lordsburg. He hired us to rustle your herd. Figured it was a quick way to get beef."

"But he is not here, *amigo*, and you are. That does not sound right, no?"

"Cowboy, you picked the wrong employer," says Byron. "What do we do with him now?"

Guillo asks the *vaqueros* to return to the herd. With one foot in a stirrup, he throws his other leg up and around his saddle horn, leans forward, and levels his Henry rifle at the man on the ground.

"If I want you dead, you would be just like your *amigos*, yes?"

The rider rapidly nods his head in agreement with Guillo.

"What you will do, *amigo*, is to bury your *amigos*. Pile rocks on them to keep coyotes away. Nobody wants to be chewed on by coyotes. Then you will ride the *carreta* with cook. We are going to Arizona Territory. Maybe you live, maybe I kill you later. We shall see, *bueno?*"

Guillo leaves his lariat around the rustler and pulls him up to his feet. Walking their horses behind him, they hike to the chuckwagon where Guillo shakes loose the rope.

"*Señor* cook, keep your pistol ready. Watch to make sure he buries his *amigos*. If this man jumps off the wagon shoot him, don't wait, don't worry, just blow a *grande* hole in him." Guillo watches the cook nod his head in acknowledgement and give Guillo a big grin. The rustler knows the cook will shoot him and enjoy it.

Byron rides to the rustler he shot and looks at the dirt-covered lump lying lifeless before him in a pool of blood. Guillo rides up.

"You do what you must do, *mi Sobrino*."

"It doesn't make it easy or what I want to do."

"No. It must be done. *Si?*"

"I understand, *Tio*. It's just this is the first man I've ever killed."

"It may not be your last, *mi Sobrino*."

"I don't like it and shouldn't have to do it."

"*Si*, I understand. I am glad you don't like it. Remember always. It is not something ever done lightly."

"Yes, I will remember."

"Don't forget you are responsible for those who look to you to take care of them. Then, you do what you must do and do not worry about it. *Si?*"

"I will remember." Byron slides his Winchester into its scabbard.

"Good, let's take these cattles to Arizona. We have been too long in the desert. Tonight, we will be in the foothills and a few days from now we will be in San Simon Valley."

Guillo rides off to find the *vaqueros* and get the cattle headed up and on the move again.

Byron looks around at the land behind them, *like Guillo, this may be my last look at New Mexico Territory. Once I cross that invisible line, I will be in Arizona. From there forward, for the rest of my life, I'm an Arizonan. What that means and where it leads, I will find out.*

Byron sits on his horse at the side of the canyon between the Peloncillo and Chiricahua Mountains and watches the wave of brown cattle slowly and steadily climb up from the plains and into the foothills leading into Doubtful Canyon. He's aware this pass between the mountain ranges serves the old Butterfield Stage route as well as other emigrant trails entering Arizona Territory. It also is known to be an Indian ambush spot, along with Apache Pass located to the west in the Chiricahuas.

Two *vaqueros* rode out early in the morning to sweep the area for Indians prior to the herd's approach. The way appears clear.

Ripple after ripple of the wave of cattle crests midpoint in the canyon, begins to disappear over the top, and descends into the San Simon Valley. Guillo rides up beside Byron.

"The peak over there?" he points to the northeast. "It's called Steen's Peak for some loco U.S. *soldado* who wanders around out here too much, I think. It is on the New Mexico Territory line, and we are west of it. We are in Arizona."

"Then, we've made it, *Tio*."

"*Si*, we are making it. Tomorrow we cross the Southern Pacific railroad and head to new grazing land."

"We'll begin the B-Z ranch."

"*Que es,* B-Z, *mi Sobrino*?" asks Guillo.

"Uncle Miguel and I talked about it before leaving the *hacienda*. A new ranch needs a new name."

"A new name is good, *bueno.* But what is B-Z mean?"

"The Bierman and Zapato ranch," says Byron smiling.

"*Ay, yi-yi.* How can I be part of such an important *rancho?*" asks Guillo.

"You have been for years, *mi Tio.* Now, we are partners, *si?*"

"*Si, mi Sobrino.* We are now partners, just as your *Padre* and me once were." Guillo flashes a smile of agreement and remembrance.

"*Tio* Miguel sent a telegram to Tucson to register our ranch and brand with the Cattlemen's Association."

"It is a good name, yes? It has a nice sound to it...Bierman *y* Zapato *Rancho.*"

Together they ride over the crest into Arizona Territory followed by the *remuda* and its *vaqueros*.

3
TOMBSTONE

Not now, not here, thinks Byron riding at the front of the herd. *We haven't driven this herd over one hundred and fifty miles to lose them. It's not gonna happen.* Byron helps push the cattle north through the San Simon Valley. It is very evident there is a lack of water for livestock. It appears the land advertised to his *Tio* Miguel is not what it is. Byron shouts to Guillo, "Fan the *vaqueros* out to ride in an arch in front of the herd and find water. We're not losing them now."

Guillo gestures ahead.

"*Agua, agua*, water, is ahead. A spring. It bubbles from the ground."

"The *vaqueros* find it?"

"*Si*, they are preparing for the herd's arrival. They have already named the spot, *Tanque*."

"Circle the herd, water them, and bed them down, this is the spot we stay." Byron replies.

"We are close to the Gila River and Solomonville," says Guillo.

Byron takes stock of where they are and what they face. Brush, grasses, cactus, ocotillo, and Palo Verde cover the landscape. It appears the land is watered from rains and runoff from the mountains, but surface water flow is unseen. If the spring is any sign, the water table below ground could be close to the surface. The valley stretches in a gentle swag between the Pinaleno Range and the Peloncillo Mountains. Byron studies the mountains on either side and spots green forests atop each. Guillo rides slowly toward him.

"Ah, Nephew, the neighbors announce our arrival," he nods toward the south.

Byron twists around in his saddle to see what Guillo gestures at. From the foothills of the Dos Cabezas Mountain tendrils of smoke snake upward.

"It appears we are newsworthy," says Byron. "Do you think they are Chiricahua Apaches?"

"More than likely," says Guillo. "They cover this area from Mexico to the White Mountains, north of the Gila. Those White Mountain Apaches there don't like us either."

"Are the *vaqueros* aware of the neighbors?"

"*Si*, Byron, they are the ones who pointed the signals out to me." Guillo sits with his arms folded over his horse's neck and watches the distant smoke swirl upward.

"Since they know we are here, we might as well make ourselves at home," says Byron. "Do you think we should dig deeper to find more water and start building water storage tanks?"

"The *vaqueros* already begin," Guillo smiles. "They do not want to run out of water either."

"What if we send riders to scout both sides of the valley for water," Byron suggests.

"*Si*, it is a good idea. I will send out riders."

"No. I'll do it," says Byron. "They need to hear from me, not just you."

"*Bueno.* Is good. They hear me too much already."

"You know, for an uncle, you are right many times," laughs Byron as he rides over to the nearest *vaqueros*.

Guillo grins and continues watching the smoke signals in the south.

Brax steps off the train at the depot in Benson, Arizona Territory. He's rail-worn and sore from the continual pounding of the train since Lordsburg, New Mexico. The whistle stop is brand new with tents, wooden shanties, tarp buildings, damaged railroad cars, piles of cross ties, and iron rails. This spot is built about a mile from a traditional crossing of the San Pedro River on the site of the Butterfield Overland Mail depot. On the train, he heard it is only twenty-five miles from Tombstone.

Hayes, Gregory, and Vern straggle off the railcar and wait beside the tracks for Brax's instructions.

"Well, I suppose you'd like to ride a horse from here to Tombstone instead of walk, right?"

Vern chances an answer, "Yep."

"Get the horses and tack out of the livestock car, check them over, saddle 'em, and get back here. MOVE." The three scatter toward the boxcars.

Brax mutters to himself, "I don't know why I've stayed with them; in Tombstone I'll go my way, and they can go theirs."

He finds a shady spot beside the depot and waits. Eventually, he hears hoofbeats approach. Pushing his hat from his eyes, he sees the gang with his saddled horse in tow.

"Did any of you think about how we're gonna eat and where we're stayin' in Tombstone?" Brax asks the gang.

"Nooo. No, sir." Vern says looking at the other two for answers. Gregory glances away and studies the sky. Hayes glares hatefully at Brax.

"Figures," says Brax as he steps into his saddle.

He shouts over his shoulder, "Let's go, Tombstone's down the road." He spurs his horse into a gallop through Benson.

Brax and gang ride through the desert from Benson, onto a flat mesa, and into Tombstone. Darkness greets them but they still see construction everywhere. Lumber is stacked up against buildings; and partially erected stores, saloons, and warehouses line the main street. Tents seem to sprout everywhere. Even though it's night, people wander about like midday. Lantern lit saloons operate at full tilt. The town is above The Tough Nut silver mine, announced the sign alongside the road coming into town. Finally, in front of a saloon, Brax dismounts and ties his horse to a hitching rail; the gang follows his actions.

Stepping to the batwing doors he looks into the establishment. Along the back wall, a bar of planks lays on upended barrels. On a shelf behind the bar, he spots bottles of Old Overholt, Old Crow, and Old Grand Dad whiskey. A piano player bangs out racket in the right corner of the room. He counts fifteen tables with chairs scattered around them. A small stage uses the left side of the building. Faro dealers operate at three tables, and five tables have participants clinging to cards with multiple combinations of fifty-two chances to win their poker games. Across the room, a roulette game clatters as the ball bounces from pocket to pocket on the spinning wheel. Cheers rise as fortunes are won and lost. The thick crowd of hard-rock miners, cowboys, and barflies shuffle around the room while six skimpily dressed whores slide through the crowd seeking their next mark. A pallor of blue-black smoke hangs over the place and the odor of stale beer, vomit, and body odor assaults his nostrils. Brax smiles to himself.

"My kind of place," he mutters while he shoves the swinging doors open and walks inside. He moves toward the bar when the doors swing open again.

"Good evening, Marshal Earp," a Faro dealer speaks to a gentleman dressed in a black sack coat buttoned by the top button to show off his light gray vest. Earp reaches into a pocket and pulls out his watch, takes a quick look, and returns it to the pocket. The chain drapes across the vest.

"Evening, Harvey," says U.S. Marshal Virgil Earp as he looks around the saloon from under his black wool Homburg. After a quick survey, he exits into the night.

Brax makes a snap decision, spins around, and almost collides with Hayes, Gregory, and Vern swaggering into the saloon. He steps around Hayes and quickly rushes into the street to catch Virgil Earp.

"Pardon me, Marshal," says Brax. "I've just ridden into Tombstone. I'm from--back east."

"Well, everybody has to be from somewhere," says Virgil without breaking his stride.

"Yes, sir," says Brax. "My point is I'm here. My money's back there."

"Where?"

"Don't remember. One poker table looks like another."

"Tough situation to be in."

"I'm looking for a job, Marshall Earp."

"What are you good at?"

"Most anything, I imagine. I need to earn a living and find a place to stay?"

Virgil stops and turns to Braxton. "If I was down on my luck, I would seek out the best source of information in town, namely me. Having done that, my suggestion is for you to go to the Oriental Saloon down the street and ask for my brother, Wyatt. He deals Faro there. Tell him I sent you, and you want to deal Faro. Ever done that before?"

"I'm willing to learn."

"I'll look in on you later." Virgil Earp continues his walk along the main street of Tombstone.

Braxton looks down the street to locate a sign hanging above an entrance with the name Oriental Saloon. He moves toward it.

The Oriental looks similar to the saloon Brax just left, only this emporium has a large mirror suspended on the back wall behind a finished, ornately carved mahogany bar. On the wall above the piano hangs the large picture of a nude female lounging on a sofa with pendulous bare breasts and only a shear scarf draped across her lap.

Brax walks to the bar and motions to the bartender.

"What'll you have?" asks the barman.

"Beer will do me just fine," says Braxton. "Oh, could you point out Wyatt Earp?" Brax leans his back against the bar and waits for the man to identify Earp.

"Who wants to know?" asks the barman.

"Not your concern, friend. His brother, Virgil, sent me."

"Okay. Since Virgil sent you, he's dealing Faro at the table by the roulette wheel."

"Much obliged."

Picking up the served beer, Braxton drinks deeply, sits the glass down, pushes back from the bar, and approaches the Faro dealer.

"Excuse me, are you Wyatt Earp?" Brax watches money scoot across and stack up on playing cards painted on the tabletop. The dealer watches every movement on and around the board like a hawk.

"If I am, what's it to you, stranger?" The dealer doesn't even look up. Cards continue to be dealt.

"Virgil told me to find you." Brax glances around at the unruly crowd of players laying down bets, cursing, shouting, and shoving to get to a better position at the table.

Earp kicks an empty chair towards Brax. "Sit down. When this boot's empty, I'll take a break." The dealer nods his head toward the chair.

Brax sits and watches Earp's every move.

The Faro dealer's well-manicured hands move rapidly across the table. He collects coins and pays out money. His black frock coat, white shirt with stiff celluloid shirt collar, and a silk cravat style necktie with stickpin distinguish him from miners, cowboys, and drifters hoping to beat the house. His blond hair is short and carefully combed. Heavy eyebrows rest above piercing blue eyes and a full handlebar style mustache rests above his upper lip. Wyatt appears at ease and friendly as he deals Faro.

The game wraps up. Wyatt stands up, clears his money from the table, and motions another dealer to take his place. He moves to a nearby table, and signals for Brax to join him.

"So, my brother sends me another stray puppy," says Earp. "He always finds one or two of you wandering the streets of Tombstone and sends him to me like I can do something."

"Well, sir," Brax replies. "He did say he would stop by and see me later after you teach me to deal Faro."

Laughing out loud, Wyatt continues, "What makes you think I'll teach the likes of you?"

"If not Faro, then I guess I just have to become a cowboy."

Wyatt's expression changes dramatically; he leans forward on both elbows and stares at Brax. "Let's be real clear, tender-foot, about what a cowboy is in this territory. Texas waddies trailing cattle from south Texas to Wichita and Dodge City are legitimate cowboys, drovers, and cow punchers. These Arizona cowboys, led by Curly Bill Brocius, are rustlers, killers, thieves, bushwhackers, and the lowest vermin on earth. Be real careful to call anybody a Cowboy around Tombstone unless you are well heeled, can draw faster, stay calmer, and shoot straighter than the poor son of a bitch standing in front of you." He pats a Smith & Wesson .44 American revolver holstered at his side.

Taken by surprise, Brax replies, "I don't mean any disrespect to anyone, Mister Earp. I am just saying I need work."

Wyatt rests back in his chair and slowly looks Brax over. "If you ever hear of someone named McLaury, Clanton, Ringo, Pony Deal, or Frank Patterson, walk away. They're part of a gang of over three hundred who extort a living from Mexico to Tombstone. They ride roughshod over everyone and everything. Since my brothers and I moved here, it's been right ugly with them. Walk a ways around them. No, run away. Do you hear me? They are evil amblin' around on two feet."

"Yes, sir. I only want to learn to deal Faro. Will you help me?" Brax implores.

Wyatt eyes him curiously. "Sure, I'll help you. By the way, you got a name?"

"I'm Braxton Bierman," pausing, he adds, "From back east."

"Well, Mr. Bierman, I'm Wyatt Earp, from back east also." He grins from under his mustache. "What say before we start we go down the street for a bite of dinner at the Frisco's cafe?"

"Hungry caught up with me about ten miles outside of town." smiles Brax.

"Drop the Mister, Brax. Just call me Wyatt. I like you Braxton Bierman. Looks like we might make a Faro dealer out of you."

The returning *vaqueros* report their findings.

"*Don* Byron *y* Guillo," says one rider, "The mountains, they rise gently from the valley and on the slopes I see a group of hot springs. They are hidden by trees and plants around them."

"About how far is it to the hot springs?" asks Byron.

"*Don* Byron, the ride is about *dos* hours," answers the *vaquero*.

"*Gracias, amigo*. Find cook and get something to eat." Byron turns to Guillo.

"If we base here and put a line cabin at the springs, a few *vaqueros* can live there. What do you think about that?"

"*Si, Amigo*, it sounds like a good idea, but remember our Apache neighbors. We can't spread ourselves too thin. *Si?*"

The second rider reports other springs are about three hours the opposite direction. Both Byron and Guillo acknowledge his report and send him to the chuckwagon.

"So, we spread one half of the herd north and the other half south, or keep all 2500 head of cattle together," says Byron. "What do you think is the right way, partner?" He looks at Guillo.

"Well, *Sobrino*, it would be better to keep the herd together I think. We should not divide our *vaqueros* or cattle. Does this not work for you?"

"*Si*, Guillo. That is the way we will do it." Byron nods his head and rides toward where the *vaqueros* complete a stone lined water tank.

Brax sits at a table off the hotel lobby while Wyatt goes over the rules for Faro.

"All right, you know this game is more popular than poker and came to us from Europe?" says Wyatt. "I've been playing Faro ever since I could count cards."

"Well, that's my good fortune. Let me go over the game again. The table has one suit of cards, almost always spades, Ace to King lie face up on it. There's a separate black square on the table for betting on the high card. Most of the tables in the saloons have the cards painted on them."

"Yep, those are called the dealer's 'board' and every good dealer has his own," smiles Wyatt. "Also, when someone says he's 'bucking the tiger,' it means playing Faro. The original playing cards used to have tigers on the back and the expression stuck."

"Great, fifty-two cards are 'bucking the tiger' and I've got to watch every hand on the board to make sure nobody moves bets, changes amounts, or steals from the dealer, right?" Wyatt nods in agreement. Brax had no idea this game moved so fast or the dealer must constantly pay close attention.

"You got it," grins Wyatt. "Some of those jasper's hands move right fast too."

"Okay, there's one dealer, or banker, and any number of players. Each player places his stake on one of the thirteen cards on the board. Every player can place bets on the same or multiple cards when they slip their coins between them or sit on the edge of a card. They can also place a bet in the high card box. Good gosh, hands and coins move everywhere on the board, and as a dealer, I've got to eyeball all of them?"

"Yep, you're beginning to get the drift," grins Wyatt.

"All right, a full deck is shuffled and placed in the 'shoe,' a dealing box, to keep me the dealer, honest. I draw two cards out of the shoe. The first card is mine and goes to the right side of the shoe. Everyone who bets that card on the dealer's board loses their money to me, the bank. The second card is the player's card and is placed on the left side of the shoe. Everyone who bets that card is paid dollar for dollar. If anyone is playing the high card box and the player's card is higher than the banker's they win also."

"Friend, if you can keep all this straight in the heat of the game, you might just make a dealer." Wyatt rises from the table and slowly walks into the lobby.

"Well, I appreciate your providing me a hotel room, and giving me some basic training, Wyatt. I know I have to practice and practice. Oh, damn, I forgot about 'coppering.' Let's see, when a player wants to reverse the meaning of the banker and player card they put a copper penny on their wager and the win/loss piles are reversed. That one's sneaky; I've got to watch that move," mutters Brax to himself.

"Keep up the good work," Wyatt says over his shoulder as he exits the hotel.

Brax sits back in the chair with a sigh, looks over the table and Faro layout. Suddenly, he remembers and mutters, "When three cards are left in the shoe, I 'call the turn' and a special bet can happen with those remaining cards. The players can predict and bet the exact order of those cards. If all three cards are the same, the bank wins it all, if the players call the cards correctly the pay out is four to one. I see why Wyatt didn't want me to interrupt him when we met."

Leaning on the table and shuffling the deck, Brax begins to deal another practice hand. Hayes, Gregory, and Vern walk into the room and sit at his table.

"So, you're fixin' to deal Faro?" asks Hayes.

"Nope, I'm just lookin' to cover the top of this table with cards. What do you want?" Brax asks annoyed by their disturbance.

"Well, you left us last night. We didn't know where you went to and it took us a while to find a spot to sleep," Hayes says.

"We ain't ate nothin' today neither." Gregory blubbers out.

"So, what's that to do with me?" asks Brax. "You're all grown men and I ain't your mama."

"Well, we kind of figured you might want to hear what we found out last night," offers Hayes. "It can put us in some money easy like."

"Easy money?" Brax shakes his head. "You boys are heading for disaster."

"Anyway, we was talkin' with some fellars, calls themselves Cowboys, about a wagon load of silver leaves out from Tombstone headed for Benson and the railroad tomorrow morning."

Hayes, Gregory, and Vern sit with smiles like drunken children.

"Ike Clanton, a right good fellar we met last night, says we can jump the wagon a few miles outside of town and clean it out. He said some Cowboys can ride with us to back up our play." Hayes sits back in the chair proud of his discovery.

"So, you are going to try to rob the silver from the wagon, right?" Brax asks. "Do you think they will hand it over to you when you ride up?"

"Well, Brax, there will be three of us and them other Cowboys to back us up." Hayes defends his plan. "Besides, why would they want to die over silver that ain't even theirs? It belongs to the mine owner."

"Boys, you have to do what you have to do, but I'm staying here. So, good luck to you. I'll look you up on Boot Hill." Brax shakes his head in disbelief.

"What's that there Boot Hill?" asks Vern.

"The locals call the cemetery outside of town, Boot Hill," smiles Brax.

"We just wanted to let you in on our sure thing, Brax. Since you've turned us down, I reckon we'll throw in with Clanton and the Cowboys. They seem to appreciate men of action like us." Hayes stands up and, in indignation, stomps out of the hotel. Gregory and Vern watch him leave, and nodding to Braxton, scuttle along after him.

"If I say something to Wyatt, then Virgil and others will think I'm squealing on my own. If I don't say anything and they tie the bunch back to me, they'll think I'm holding out on them. If any of that miserable bunch gets caught, they will flip on me in a heartbeat. I'll ride there in the morning to make sure I can eliminate any possibility of my involvement," Brax mumbles under his breath. He gathers up his deck of cards and climbs the stairs to his room.

4
AMBUSHED

Brax stirs from sleep as the sun slips through the cracks around the window shade. Remembering Hayes, Gregory, and Vern will attempt to rob the silver wagon headed for Benson this morning, he jolts awake. *Am I too late? Who's going to die this morning?*

Racing downstairs, out the front door, he circles around the hotel to the livery, saddles his horse, and rides rapidly out of Tombstone. "I don't know what's going to happen," he whispers aloud and he knows none of it can be good.

Brax rides around a bend in the road halfway to Benson and hears gunfire up ahead. He spurs his horse to go faster.

Quickly, the gunfire volume increases as he turns into the brush off the roadway, dismounts, crouches, and climbs to the edge of the hill. He overlooks the gunfire.

"Not possible. Just not possible," he mutters. Before him, four men stand on one side of a buckboard firing their rifles around strongboxes stacked in the bed. Three men scramble around the hillside in front of them, sporadically returning pistol fire.

"I knew it, I just knew it. Those three can't do anything right. Now, I've got to go bail them out, and probably get shot in the process. I should have left them in New Mexico." Brax says out loud overcome with frustration.

Suddenly, three mounted riders charge the four men by the wagon from behind. Quickly, the men by the buckboard spin and return fire. Three fall quickly, the fourth breaks out and runs toward Hayes, Gregory, and Vern. The men on horseback catch up and shoot him in the back. Then they turn their guns on Hayes, Gregory, and Vern and shoot them where they stand beside the road with their mouths agape and stunned.

Brax rolls over on his back and quietly cusses a blue streak. The Cowboys use his acquaintances and then eliminate any connection to the robbery. Wyatt told him they were all about murder and killing. He sees it here today.

"Too late, too late, too late." Brax laments aloud the death of Hayes, Gregory, and Vern. "They didn't deserve to be treated like this," he whispers. "I'll find the Cowboys who did this. They are dead men walking."

Rolling back over, he looks at the road below him. The strong boxes are gone as well as the riders. Only an empty buckboard, a team of horses, and seven still men lie on the ground to tell the tale.

Brax quickly slips down the hillside and walks from body to body checking for a pulse or any life. He confirms that all the men are dead and slowly returns to his horse.

"Got to find Wyatt and tell him what I saw regardless of how it implicates me," says Brax aloud. "He'll know what to do."

The sun beats down on the foothills of the mountains as Gilberto and Raul ride slowly through the brush to flush out cattle. They are part of the group of *vaqueros* who push the herd from New Mexico to Arizona. Gilberto knows they plan to stay and make Arizona their home. In the past, they guard the *hacienda* and work the *de la Vieta* herds. Today, their sombreros shield them from the intense sun and their short-waisted jackets and tapered trousers are dirt covered. Their pullover shirts are sweat stained down their backs and under their arms from many hours in the saddle.

Gilberto catches a swift movement from the corner of his eye, and yanks his horse quickly to the right. An Apache warrior narrowly misses grabbing his horse's reins and falls in front of Gilberto. Another brave springs up to pull Gilberto down as he spins his horse around.

Digging in his spurs, the horse leaps into a full gallop escaping the Indians. Grabbing the saddle horn to stay aboard, he sees Raul is already slightly ahead of him.

Five Apache warriors break from their cover in an attempt to capture the fleeing *vaqueros*. They stop and launch a flight of arrows toward their targets.

"Ride, Raul, ride." shouts Gilberto, lashing his reins back and forth across his horse's withers. Two arrows strike Raul squarely between his shoulder blades. His eyes stare at Gilberto in disbelief as he slowly loses grip of his saddle and slides off.

Raul strikes the ground and rolls into a human dirt ball before coming to a stop. Blood pools around him.

"NO. *Madre de Dios*, NO." Gilberto screams. He lies over his horse's neck attempting to meld into one animal.

The Apaches are on top of Raul almost before his body stops it's roll. Screaming, shrieking, and scalping, they yank off his clothes, stop, and fire another flight of arrows.

Gilberto clings to his horse, hurls prayers skyward, and races toward the new *rancho*.

Byron rides with Guillo to Fort Bowie in Apache Pass to submit a bid on the government contract to supply beef for army posts in Southeastern Arizona.

Since arriving in San Simon Valley, the herd prospers. We ship cattle regularly to Miguel in New Mexico. Now, it's time to sell cattle here, Byron scans the landscape. *Riding this valley, I'm seeing ways we can use it in the future.*

He spots the fort.

"Over there, Guillo, on the plateau, see the buildings?"

"*Si, muy casas,*" says Guillo. "An adobe wall connects them all, yes?"

"Yep," replies Byron. "The California Volunteer Brigade built the first fort."

"It is the same *Californianos* that chases *su Padre* and his Arizona Rangers back to Mesilla, no?"

"The one and same soldiers. They fought Apaches here while they marched to New Mexico during the Civil War. Been military here ever since."

"Everybody fights here because of the spring, yes?"

"Yep, there's a spring in the pass. Butterfield Stage Lines used it when their changing station was here."

"*Si, Señor* Butterfield, he goes everywhere," Guillo grins.

Riding into the fort, Byron surveys the post. Adobe barracks and buildings surround the large central parade ground, a two-story hospital is on the far side, the trading post and sutler are on one side, officer's houses, and the headquarters building are on the other side. People mill across the grounds and around the buildings. Infantry squads drill on the open parade field. Behind the sutler are large corrals and stables. Mounted cavalry practice maneuvers on the roadway around the grounds. They stop and dismount in front of the headquarters.

"This is a real busy place," Byron observes as he ties his horse to the hitching rail.

"There are more *soldados* here than out chasing *indios*," replies Guillo. "Maybe they wait for *indios* to come here. It would be easier to catch them that way, yes?" Guillo grins beneath his drooping mustache. Byron nods his head.

As they climb the steps to the front door, a sentry steps forward.

"State your business and who you are here to see." He stands at port arms and awaits their answer.

Byron replies, "We're here to see the quartermaster about the beef contract. I have cattle to sell. Do we go into the building with you or through you?"

"Easy, rancher, the soldier boy is just doing his job."

Bryon turns around and sees an older gentleman with white hair. Facial whiskers connect to a full mustache. He wears a canvas jacket, silk vest, white shirt, black trousers, and black boots. His thumbs hook over his holster belt that carries one ivory handled pistol turned backward for cross draw.

"I didn't mean any disrespect, sir. I just want to talk to the proper party for purchasing cattle." Byron answers.

"Well, so do I," the gentleman says with a smile. "I know for a fact the party will not be here for another hour. How about we adjourn to the sutler and let this soldier boy go about his business? I'm buying."

"It has been a dusty ride; a drink, it sounds good, yes?" Guillo forces a cough.

Byron smiles. "I agree. Lead the way. I'm Byron Bierman, and this is my partner, Guillo Zapato. We have the B-Z spread in San Simon Valley."

"My acquaintances call me Texas John Slaughter," he answers. "Glad to make your acquaintances. B-Z, you say? Bierman, you say?" John Slaughter turns and walks across the fort's parade ground in route to the sutler.

Byron looks at Guillo, shrugs, and they hurry to catch up.

Walking into the store, Byron sees stacks of uniforms, clothes piled neatly on tables, bolts of cloth, canned goods on shelves, firearms, ammunitions, pots and pans, and practically anything you could want.

Slaughter makes his way to a bar set up in the back of the building. There are five tables arranged in front of a plank bar. He sits at one with four chairs around it.

The bartender comes over, and Slaughter orders whiskey all around. He leans forward on the table and looks at Byron.

"Your spread in San Simon Valley with your ranch house at Whitelock's *cienega*, is that right?"

45

"Yes, sir. We have twenty-five hundred head in the valley and an artesian well. The *vaqueros* call it *Tanque*."

"Well, sounds like you've arrived with intent to be in the cattle business," says Slaughter. "You related to any Bierman from Texas?"

"Yes, sir. My pa was Zepaniah Bierman from Mesilla, New Mexico. Well, he was born in the Texas hill country and eventually made it to Mesilla. Why the interest?" asks Byron.

"Years back, I was a Texas Ranger. That's why I've been hung with the moniker, Texas John. My brother and I went into the cattle business after we mustered out of the Confederate army. We're from down around San Antonio. The hill country is where we flushed out mavericks to build our first herd. While down there, we met a mustanger named Zep Bierman. He knew his horses and traded on the square. The man had grit and integrity. Both are hard to come by on the frontier. So, he was your pa?"

"My pa was in that business. It may have well been him."

"Blue eyes. He had the bluest eyes. They could cut right through you like a knife," John Slaughter says, remembering.

"*Señor*, you have just described *mi compañero*, Zep," said Guillo. "His eyes, *mi amigo*, could cut you six ways from Sunday by just staring at you."

"That's the man I knew," says Slaughter.

Byron sits back in his chair surprised. This man before him, in the wilds of Arizona, did business with his pa."

"Where is he today?" questions Slaughter. "Is he above the snakes?"

"Pa was killed a year ago," Byron somberly replies, "My brother shot him."

"Well, I'll be," says John Slaughter. "Killed by one of his own. Life is sure full of mysteries."

"Is no mystery, *señor*. Zep did it to save my life. *Mi compañero* died for me." Guillo stares at the table with moist eyes.

"Sorry to hear all that. I didn't mean to dredge up bad times or hurt, my friends, but that's the Zep Bierman I knew. He kept friendships. They meant more than life itself to him." Slaughter slowly sips his drink. "Why, there was a time in *Las Cornudas,* east of the *Hueco* Mountains, old John Chisum and I was in the thick of a poker game. We got to spittin,' cussin,' and sputterin' about our cards, and I thought we was goin' to kill each other. Your pa steps in between us, pulls pistols, points one at my chin and jams the other against Chisum's forehead and asks 'you want it together or separate?' Why, we just busted out laughing so hard we fell down right there on the floor." Slaughter begins to chuckle and then laughs out loud.

"He never talked about Mr. Chisum or you, Mr. Slaughter." Byron sits back in his chair.

"Son, my acquaintances call me Mr. Slaughter or Texas John. My friends call me John H. You can call me John H."

"Thank you, John H." Byron smiles.

"That was your pa, son. He never was someone to drop names. He was a friend, and for most of us, it was more than enough. He traded horses with John Chisum and me. Never was a better man to know horseflesh."

"Your ranch is south of here isn't it, John H.," asks Byron.

"I got a piece of property in the San Bernadino Valley, southeast corner of Arizona Territory, it's both above and below the border. Been running cattle there for a while. How's San Simon Valley treat you?"

"We're starting to agree with each other. A little rough to begin with, but we're coming to terms. My uncle, Miguel *de la Vieta*, arranged for the land without verifying surface water."

"*Don Miguel de la Vieta* is your uncle? By all that's holy, son, you do get around. I've been in correspondence with *Don Miguel* for a while. I knew he was looking to expand ranching to Arizona Territory, and now here I sit with you two in Fort Bowie."

"I've heard him mention your name," says Byron. He looks at Guillo who nods in agreement. "He has respect for all you've accomplished in this territory. I hope we can be as successful."

"It ain't easy between the *bandito* and Apaches in Mexico and the Cowboys and Apaches this side of the border."

"I thought cowboys punched cattle," says Byron.

"Almost anywhere but here," says John H. "In this territory, Cowboy is a curse word. They make up the biggest gang riding both sides of the border. They rustle, murder, and destroy.

They're bad medicine. If they show up on your range, shoot first, and ask questions second."

"None came by our place. The only things we've seen are Apache smoke signals."

"Where there's smoke, you'll see Apaches pretty quick. You got a couple of options: kill them and kill them all, or provide some beef occasionally. They're starving, and the government doesn't give a damn about them. They're just trying to live the only way they know how. You don't have to like them, but you do have to respect them. They've been here a long time before us, and this land used to belong to them. Sometimes change just goes down hard."

"What are you doing at Fort Bowie, John H?" asks Byron.

"I'm fixin' to take the quartermaster's contract for beef to supply the army," says John H. He smiles.

"Sorry you rode all this way for nothing," smiles Byron.

"Knew I could like you, son." Slaughter laughs. "May the better man win. Bottoms up."

The men down their whiskeys.

Rising from the table, they walk from the sutler and begin crossing the parade ground. Slaughter reaches out, grabs Byron, and roughly drags him back. A company of cavalry thunder past with their sabers, canteens, and harnesses jangling as they pass.

"Glory be, that was close," sputters Byron.

"Yep, you were almost pounded into pulp," replies John H.

"Thanks, for pulling me back in time."

"You'd have done the same for me. Let's get across and out of harm's way."

The company quickly disappears down the road and out of the fort.

Slaughter waves down a passing soldier.

"What's all the rush about," he asks as he points at the disappearing troops.

"We just got a telegraph message about an Apache outbreak from the reservations," the soldier says. "It has something to do with arresting a medicine man at Cibeque Creek on the White Mountain Reservation. The Apaches jumped the reservation and are attacking every white on their way south. The company is fixin' to deliver a big surprise to those injuns."

Guillo and Byron stare at each other, realize the direction the Indians are headed. In one motion, they sprint to their horses. Their feet hit each of their stirrups at almost the same moment, they fling themselves into their saddles, spin their mounts around, and race after the disappearing cavalry.

Slaughter stands in the roadway, shoves his hat back on his head, and watches their departure. "Ride fast, my friends," he mutters.

5
ATTACK

It's a hard ride to catch up with the fast traveling Cavalry Company. Their route is into the San Simon Valley. The young lieutenant signals halt when he notices Byron and Guillo charge to the head of the column.

He turns with a scowl, stares sharply at Byron, and says, "Gentlemen, this is a military mission, and you are asked to return immediately to Fort Bowie. I will have troopers escort you if necessary."

"Lieutenant, our ranch lies directly in the path the Apaches are sure to take, and we're headin' there as fast as possible," says Byron.

"Gentlemen, if your home is in the San Simon Valley, you are undoubtedly too late. Apaches jumped the reservation two days ago. A delay in notification because of downed telegraph lines means we'll probably meet them in the next few miles. You're welcome to ride wherever you choose, but our orders are to join with a detachment from Fort Apache heading toward us. Good day." The Lieutenant signals forward, and the detachment rapidly moves forward.

"Hey, *Compañero*, looks like we're on our own, *si*? says Guillo. "Let's get home quick." He turns his horse north and spurs it into a gallop.

"I'm right behind you," shouts Byron, lashing his horse.

They quickly cover territory they slowly rode through the day before. Shortly, gunfire sounds followed by screams and shouts. Coming to a rise, they stop below the crest, slide off their mounts, and creep to the ridge top. Below them are the partially constructed adobe walls of the ranch. The main house's walls are complete, the bunkhouse has walls four to five feet above ground level, and the barn is only framed.

Byron sees livestock mill frantically around the corral. Some cattle and horses lie dead in the enclosure. Indians creep through brush and grass toward the adobe walls. The *vaqueros,* sheltered in the structures, defend themselves with effective gunfire.

"Look to the far left," Guillo whispers. "On the hilltop. Three Apaches watch what is going on below."

"I see them," Byron replies.

"What if we go give them a visit? I don't think they expect one," says Guillo moving back to the horses. Byron follows.

They mount, circle away from the gunfire, and move toward the hilltop on their left. Byron knows full well the urgency of helping their *vaqueros*. When in position behind the hilltop, Guillo pulls his revolver and charges his horse toward the ridge where they saw the Indians. Byron moves beside him.

Nobody. To his right, Byron sees a small dust cloud as the Apaches ride into the valley.

Guillo points toward the ranch and spurs his mount in the direction of the sputtering gunfire.

Byron pulls his rifle as he rides up to the bunkhouse, springs from his horse, vaults over the partially constructed adobe wall, and quickly crawls to the adjoining wall. Guillo is one moment behind him.

Byron glances at the vaquero beside him. Blood oozes freely from a wound in his thigh.

"Gilberto, what happened?" Guillo questions.

"*Jefe*, Raul and I are surprised by Apaches while we look for cattle. Raul is *muerto*. I ride here firing my *pistola* to warn everyone. The Apaches, they attack us. That is all."

Byron suddenly realizes a whiskered old man hugs the wall beside him. He's not one of the *vaqueros*.

"Who are you, mister?" asks Byron.

"Jacob Weitzer. Headed to Tombstone. Been prospectin' up in the mountains. Got flushed out by them Apaches. Was up at Solomonville just a day back, heard the ruckus about Apaches jumpin' the reservations and figured to make tracks to get ahead of the free-for-all. Figured wrong. It caught up to me about a mile from here. Sure am glad y'all have this ranch or I would've been catched out in the open. A goner for certain."

Byron looks the prospector over. Jacob Weitzer appears to be a middle-aged man under layers of dirt, wearing a worn-out plaid shirt, threadbare denim pants held up by wide suspenders, and the cuffs stuffed into worn mule-ear brown boots. He has a flat crowned soft felt hat jammed down on his head and a weatherworn face full of gray whiskers.

"What's got the Apaches riled up?" asks Byron.

"Them Apaches are lookin' for revenge for past wrongs. It's time to go to ground, dig deep, and expect the worst because it's comin'," says the prospector.

"Looks like we've already got it here with us, old timer," replies Byron as he rises and snaps a quick shot with his rifle. Dropping back down beside the prospector, he asks, "What's got them on the warpath?"

"Them injuns got all fired up by Nock-ay-det-klinne's ghost dancin' in his village on Cibeque Creek," Jacobs says.

"Ghost dancing? Cibeque Creek?" what's that to us, Byron asks.

"It's a religious, spiritual thing for the injuns," Jacob answers. "They're fed up with reservation life, don't want to be farmers, don't want the government starvin' 'em, and just plain hate white men."

"Okay, but jumpin' the reservation, that's a big thing. What caused it?" asks Byron.

"The damn fool Army went on the reservation to arrest the medicine man, Nock-ay-det-klinne. Them Apaches weren't about to let him be taken without a fight."

"Makes sense. Why'd they do it?"

"Town folks in Fort Apache, Globe, and Tucson figured it was only a short time before the medicine man whipped up the injuns into a killin' fit. Course, the ghost dancin' been goin' on for a month or better."

"Couldn't the Army have captured Nock-ay...what's his name?"

"Oh, them bright-boy soldiers tried that. They went on the reservation, right up to the medicine man's Cibeque Creek camp, with Apaches Scouts. Them are injuns the Army has workin' for it."

"Apaches capturing Apaches doesn't sound like too good of an idea."

"Well, it weren't. Them Apaches Scouts turned on their officers and commenced to shootin', and troopers, scouts, Apache warriors, and the medicine man all die in the ruckus. Them soldiers that survive skedaddle to Fort Apache for protection. The reservations, White Mountain and San Carlos, explode into a breakout."

"Damn. Sounds like some mix up."

"Oh, it were, it were. That shoot-em-out at Cibecue Creek launches warriors led by Naiche, youngest son of Cochise, Juh, and Geronimo off the reservations. Southern Arizona, New Mexico, and Mexico are in a fix now."

The prospector heaves a sigh and slides lower on the wall. Byron clinches his teeth and grips his rifle. The Apache path of blood and destruction goes directly through them en route to the Sierra Madres Mountains in Mexico.

A sudden silence settles as Byron realizes the shooting stops. Slowly, he rises up, and looks over the wall. All he sees are two thrashing horses and three cows lying still around the ranch grounds. There are no Indians.

"Gilberto, do you know how many *vaqueros* are here," asks Byron,

"Si, *Patron, cinco vaqueros esta aquí. Dos* at the hot springs cabin, and Raul *es muerto.*"

"Horses. Cattle. Any idea about them?" Guillo questions.

"No, *Jefe*, the Apaches hit us so quick it was all we could do to find cover," Gilberto answers.

"You're hurt," Guillo points to the leg wound. "Others may be wounded, too. Let's find out."

"I tried to outrun a bullet. The bullet, she is faster, no?" the *vaquero* grimaces.

"*Si*, the bullet is much faster. Next time get a head start," Guillo replies with a grin.

Guillo tightly bandages Gilberto's leg wound, stands, and supports Gilberto's weight. They leave to check on the other ranch hands.

Byron sits beside the wall to catch his breath. Jacob Weitzer's sharp green eyes stare intensely at Byron.

"Consarn it. I've seen you before, feller. I can't put it exactly where, but your face is nigh on familiar."

"I've got a familiar face?" asks Byron.

"You ever been down Tucson way? Maybe, in Benson? I know'd I seen your mug before."

"Nope, just been here," says Byron.

"Got it. By jingo, got it. I've seen you in Tombstone. You been there, right?"

"Can't say I've ever been in Tombstone, old timer."

"I know'd I seen you in Tombstone," Jacob is adamant. "It's you, by jingo, or you got a doppelganger. You know, somebody who looks just like you."

"I ain't got a doppelganger, but I do have a twin," says Byron.

"That's it. That's it then. Your twin's in Tombstone." Jacob relaxes knowing he has solved his mystery.

Byron gazes off in the distance. I wonder if the old prospector can be right.

Braxton steps into the Oriental Saloon in search of Wyatt Earp. Taking a quick look around, he doesn't see him but spots John Holliday dealing Faro. Braxton pulls up a chair next to the Faro table to wait for the hand to end.

Brax watches Holliday's skill with the cards.

"Doc, dealing like you do makes it hard to believe you're a dentist," says Braxton.

"That was a lifetime ago," says Doc without any decrease in his deal or losing concentration. "I practiced dentistry from Atlanta, to Dallas, to

Las Vegas, New Mexico. Wyatt convinced me to come to Tombstone."

"Why not hang out a shingle for dentistry here?"

"I get more pleasure out of Faro, and don't have to listen to complaints and caterwaulin' after pulling teeth. Besides, I enjoy the notoriety of my gun reputation and being a professional gambler."

"You've known Wyatt a while?"

"Since Texas days. We met in a saloon incident. I protected him from back-shooters. We've done that for each other since then."

Doc suddenly breaks into a deep, violent hacking cough. Holding out a hand, he stops card play, pulls out a silk handkerchief from his coat pocket, dabs his lips, folds up the now blood-red spotted kerchief, puts it back into his pocket, and signals for card play to continue.

Braxton doesn't call attention to Doc's consumption.

Doc finishes his deal and sits in a chair across from Brax.

"So, Mister Faro dealer, what brings you into the Oriental this morning," he asks.

"I'm looking for Wyatt and watching a genuine, professional dealer at work."

"It takes time and experience to perfect this game, and you're coming along real well. Just keep your eyes more alert. You have to know everything going on with the bets on your board," says Doc.

"You're trying to tell me something, so spit it out, Doc," says Braxton.

"I saw a couple of jaspers move bets the last time I watched you at your Faro table. Didn't say anything then. Wasn't much they moved, next time could be different."

"I'll be more careful watching the board," says Brax. "Do you know where Wyatt is this morning?"

Doc points towards the doors of the Oriental as Wyatt steps into the saloon.

"Thanks, Doc." Rising from his chair, Brax follows Wyatt to an open table against the back wall.

6
AFTERMATH

The sounds of thrashing, dying horses, and the acrid smell of burnt gunpowder linger as Byron slowly stands up to look over the arrow speckled adobe wall.

Gone.

As silent as the wind, the Apaches disappear.

He watches Guillo step over the wall, mount, and slowly ride out searching the area in front of the ranch buildings.

"Put down those horses and butcher the cattle," he orders.

"*Si, Patron.* We will save the meat, yes?" asks a *vaquero.*

"Yes, save what you can. Salt it to keep it from spoiling."

"*Si, Patron.*"

"Hey, junior, you seen my mule," Jacob shouts as he walks up to Byron.

"Why do you use a blamed mule anyway, Jacob? Donkeys are more even tempered."

"Oh, I've had a mule for years. They're great for packin' loads, and a decent ride, if necessary," Jacob replies. "I'm kind of partial to my mangy old mule, Arbuckle, cause we've been through a lot. Hate to lose him to a thievin' Apache who's gonna eat him for tonight's supper."

"While we were fightin' for our scalps, your old mule probably wandered off lookin' for water and forage. Take a look over in the draw behind the well house." Byron smiles as he hitches his thumb over his shoulder.

Byron sees Guillo approach leading two horses. "Apaches left these,"

"What about cattle?" asks Byron.

"Two dead and partially butchered," answers Guillo. "Apaches were more interested in food than horses."

"They must be hungry to leave horses. We're lucky they moved fast and didn't stay around to finish what they start," says Byron.

"*Si, Compañero*, I think they're in a big hurry to reach Mexico."

"Don't think Mexico changed their minds." Byron points to the mauled Fort Bowie cavalry company slowly riding toward the ranch house.

Guidons drag the ground, wounded soldiers feebly stay in their saddles, bodies drape over some horses, and many soldiers ride double. Only a handful of troopers remain unharmed.

Their blue uniforms are stained and caked in sweat, blood, and dirt. The detachment comes to a halt in the open ground in front of the unfinished ranch house. Troopers drop to the ground, some lie still after they fall.

A sergeant dismounts and rushes to the Lieutenant to steady him in the saddle.

"Sorry, to inconvenience you," wheezes the Lieutenant weaving in his saddle. Byron stares at his blood soaked tunic. "They were on us before I even saw them." He topples forward from his horse into the sergeant's arms.

Byron shouts at the *vaqueros* to give all the help they can to the troopers. Men hustle to find shaded places to stretch out the wounded. Shirts are ripped into bandages, and all available medicines are brought out to share.

"Sergeant, bring the Lieutenant over here," shouts Byron. Two troopers run to assist the sergeant and after lying blankets on the ground they attempt to make him comfortable. Blood oozes scarlet from his chest wound.

The sergeant stands and turns to Byron.

"I'm Sergeant Brock, Sir. We missed meeting up with the company from Fort Apache. Lieutenant Kirby kept pushing us hard, and we rode right into the Apaches."

"What happened, Sergeant?" asks Byron.

"They flanked us, closed off the front, we rode into a shallow valley, and they slammed the backdoor. It was every man for his self."

"How'd you get out?"

"The Lieutenant called every trooper still mounted to charge the front. We broke through, but paid a price. Chaos, confusion, dirt, blood, screaming horses and men, and the God-awful Apache shriek is all we knew."

"Did the Apaches fair any better?"

"Don't rightly know. We gave as good as we got. Bullets and arrows were everywhere."

The Sergeant hides his eyes in gauntlet-covered hands. Byron places a hand on the soldier's shoulder, steadying the man.

He looks up with a tear stained face.

"But, I didn't see the Lieutenant flinch. He stands there in command and calls shots for his troopers. His horse is killed from under him in the charge, but he stands and keeps commanding. We rode into an ambush, but I'd follow him into hell and back."

They look over at the wall where the Lieutenant lies and watch two troopers pull the blanket up over his head. The Sergeant returns and kneels beside the body.

Byron helps a *vaquero* move another wounded soldier into the shade. He turns as Guillo rides up.

"*Compañero*, they are badly chewed up, *si*?"

"Yep. They've taken a lickin' but sounds like they hurt the Apaches too."

"What should we do with them?"

"We've got to help them get back to Fort Bowie."

"*Si*, but to move now might not be so good. Morning, she might be better."

"Can we get the stock watered, fed, and ready to ride?"

"*Si*, and the Apaches will take their wounded and dead and head south already. I think everyone should rest. Let's leave at sunup."

Byron walks to the Sergeant, who's helping other wounded troopers.

"Sergeant, how many mounts do you still have?"

"We managed to hang onto most of our horses, Sir. We should have more than enough to provide for your *vaqueros* and my men."

"Good, everyone needs to be ready to ride at sunup. We'll pack the dead with us."

"Yes, Sir." Sergeant Block turns and passes orders to his men.

Byron turns to Guillo.

"Have Gilberto get the *vaqueros* ready to ride. We'll help the wounded stay in the saddle and provide protection. Send a rider to find Raul. He needs to be buried tonight."

"*Si, Compañero...mi Patron.*" Guillo pulls his horse around and rides off to find Gilberto.

Byron stands surprised at Guillo's addressing him as *Patron*. He looks around the ranch at the aftermath of the Apache attack. Dead and wounded men and animals litter the ground.

Shaking his head, he moves to help a wounded trooper.

Hell of a way to run a ranch.

Sunrise explodes over the horizon and sends brilliant rays of light slicing through scattered clouds. From horseback, Byron watches the line of soldiers and ranch hands ride steadily south from the ranch compound.

"How many will make it," asks Byron to Guillo riding beside him.

"I do not know, *Compañero*. The strong will."

"How about the Apaches?"

"We'll have a safe ride to Fort Bowie," says Guillo. "The Apaches are near the border by now, I think."

Looking over his shoulder, Byron watches the sergeant shepherd his troopers along, both the wounded and healthy. Jacob brings up the end of the line, riding his mule. The *vaquero* ranch hands travel along both sides to provide protection and warning.

At midmorning a stop discovers two more dead troopers. They are wrapped in blankets and tied across their horses.

The noon stop allows time for the horses to be watered and grazed. Wounds are redressed and men rested.

"Let's get everyone remounted and move, Sergeant," Byron orders. "Fort Bowie is the next stop."

"Yes, Sir," replies Sergeant Brock. "Troopers mount up, we're burnin' daylight. You're not goin' to get home sittin' here."

The able and wounded remount and Byron watches them resolutely move forward. He kicks his mount and gallops to the front of the line.

By late afternoon, Byron shouts to those following, "Fort Bowie ahead."

Sergeant Block gallops up beside him.

"Yes, sir, that's home," he smiles. "Wasn't real sure I'd see it again."

"We'll be there before dark," Byron says.

Sergeant Block salutes Byron and returns down the line directing soldiers to make themselves as presentable as possible.

A mounted squad gallops out of Fort Bowie and heads their direction.

Guillo, rides up and points toward the cavalry unit, "More *soldados*, *Compañero*. Do they come for us?"

"Appears to be," says Byron. "I think they are taking a head count to see how many are coming back."

Byron watches the soldiers slide into line beside the wounded men to accompany them into Fort Bowie.

Passing through the gateway of the Fort, Byron's unit hears a cannon volley. He looks quickly at Sergeant Block, who nods his head and smiles.

"The post gives this unit 'Honors,' Sir. It's recognition for special units. I'm sure the post commander will have more to tell you. I have to leave you now and see that my men are taken care of. Your assistance is much appreciated." Sergeant Block spins his horse around and begins riding back down the line barking orders to his troopers.

Byron and Guillo dismount in front of the headquarters building, and motion for Gilberto to take the *vaqueros* to the sutler and mercantile. Walking up the steps, in the late dusk, they are stopped by a trooper with his rifle at port arms.

"State your purpose, and who you are here to see, sir."

Before Byron can respond, the door is opened and an army colonel steps onto the porch. "At ease trooper, and dismissed," he says. Turning to Byron, "I am Colonel Woodrow Galt, commander of Fort Bowie."

"I'm Byron Bierman and this is my partner, Guillo Zapato. We own B-Z Ranch in the San Simon Valley. Your troops were in a world of hurt and came upon our place. Their arrival chased off the Apache attack. The least we could do was get them back here," says Byron.

"We appreciate your assistance and recognize your cooperation with us, but you don't realize what you and Company C accomplished, do you?" The Colonel smiles, gestures for them to join him, turns, and reenters the building.

"Colonel, I don't really get your point," says Byron following behind the Colonel. "All I know is we were fighting for our lives, then the Apaches broke. Company C rides up looking like it's been clawed by a mountain lion, and today we're here. What else is there?"

"Come in, come in, gentlemen. There is much more to share." He waves them through the door. They move into the office past a corporal who jumps to attention as they enter.

"At ease, Corporal," says the colonel as they pass by.

Byron admires the office; a large map of Arizona Territory hangs on the wall behind the desk. The colonel motions them to two rawhide chairs haphazardly arranged in front of his desk. "Gentlemen, have a seat."

"Thank you, Colonel." Byron acknowledges the hospitality. "What is the rest of the story you mentioned?"

"Mr. Bierman, apparently without your knowledge, your actions and those of Company C blunted this recent reservation outbreak."

"What do you mean, blunted?" asks Byron.

"The renegades were in full flight south from the San Carlos and White Mountain reservations. They attacked homesteads and ranches with little or no resistance. When they fell on B-Z, your group put up stubborn resistance, and Company C took the starch out of their breakout. Now, the Apaches run for the shelter of the Sierra Madres. We telegraphed the Mexican army to prepare for their arrival."

"Taking the starch out of them cost dearly," says Byron. "Your Lieutenant Kirby and seven troopers along with my *vaquero* paid the price for this escape."

"Naturally, we are upset at the loss of good men and great soldiers, but what was done will ultimately save others who are more vulnerable and possibly unable to defend themselves." Colonel Galt sits back as he concludes his summation.

"If there are those who can't defend themselves and wind up vulnerable, then Arizona Territory ain't the place for them to stay." Byron rises and prepares to leave the office. Guillo stands and steps beside him. "Whatever happened with the quartermaster's bid to supply beef for the army?"

"The bid is complete. John Slaughter received the contract for next year." The Colonel reaches into his desk and withdraws an envelope. He holds it out to Byron. "John Slaughter left a letter for you pending your return to Fort Bowie. I guess he knows more than we do about your itinerary."

Taking the envelope, Byron pauses in the open doorway.

"Thank you for the 'Honors' volley, Colonel. It meant a lot to your troops. Good evening." Byron and Guillo move through the doorway, cross the reception area, and step onto the front porch.

"The Army sure has a strange way of looking at things," says Byron.

"*Si, soldados* do not think like we do. What do you mean about this Senor Jefe Colonel, *Compañero*?"

"It's how calloused he is about the troopers and Lieutenant dying. Seems like they are just calculated losses."

"*Si,* he didn't seem too troubled. He was more bothered by the Mexican Army catches the Apaches, *si*?"

"I don't pretend to understand it all. Let's go find our men."

Looking at each other, they set out for the post sutler across the parade ground.

Braxton sits at a table in the hotel dining room. He finishes dinner and sips at a cup of coffee. Doc Holliday told him not to run. Maybe Doc is right. *Once you start, you never stop, and your days are spent looking over your shoulder. This will be my life if I run, what might be left of it. Byron would never have let his life get into this position. He's always the smart one.* He finishes his coffee and makes his decision. It's time to find Virgil Earp.

Stepping out onto the boardwalk, Brax looks to his right and sees the Bird Cage Theater is running wide open and wild tonight. Folks are laughing, they enter and exit, and appear to enjoy themselves at the ribald, raunchy antics that go on in the establishment.

A smirk creeps across his face as he remembers a newspaper article he read about the Bird Cage. *The writer calls it "the wildest, wickedest night spot between Basin Street and the Barbary Coast." Sure looks like it's living down to its lowly reputation.*

Across the street, the Oriental Saloon appears to have steady business. He watches patrons rush in and out. *Tombstone is growing all around me. In the nine months I've been in this town it seems to have literally jumped out of the ground.*

His hearing is assaulted by noise from the silver ore crushing machines and stamping mill that pound relentlessly day and night. Its constant rhythm overwhelms the people living in Tombstone.

I'm sure Ed Schieffelin didn't think it would be like this when he named his silver claim 'Tombstone' after army scout Al Sieber told him that's all he'd find prospecting. This town never sleeps and it's too tough to die.

Braxton scans the street and sees the businesses: saloons, bordellos, Ever Cold icehouse, bowling alley, banks, bakeries, *The Tombstone Epitaph* newspaper, opium dens, Mabry's Ice Cream Parlor, dance halls, and gambling halls. *If this is progress, I'm not sure I like it.*

Shaking his head to clear his thoughts, he looks again for Marshal Virgil Earp.

In front of Braxton, three horsemen ride by momentarily breaking up the crowd of men jostling in the street.

A buckskin; I know that horse. Brax stops, turns, and stares intently at the horse and rider. *One of those holdup Cowboys has the same horse.*

Braxton scans the crowd of men exiting the Oriental who push, shove, and elbow their way along the boardwalks and into the road in front of him. He faces a dilemma. He has to find Virgil and not lose sight of the buckskin.

At the corner of the Oriental, hidden in the shadows, he sees Marshal Virgil Earp watching the three mounted Cowboys.

Braxton forces his way through the mob and crosses the street to the Oriental Saloon.

7
ALLIANCE

"I don't believe it. I just don't believe it." Byron sits at a table in the bar of the sutler's store in Fort Bowie.

"What's not to believe, *Compañero?*" asks Guillo. "What's going to happen now?"

Byron stares at the letter clasped in his hand. It's from John Slaughter, and awaited their return to Fort Bowie.

Standing from the table, Byron paces. He shakes his head, and continues to look at the message written on the paper.

"Do you know what that old Texas transplant did?" His blue eyes flash at Guillo.

"No, *Compañero*, I do not know, but if you don't tell me quick, I'm going to shake it out of you."

"He's told the quartermaster to purchase one half of the army's annual beef requirements from his ranch and the other half from ours." Byron stares at Guillo in disbelief.

"That's thousands of dollars he just gave us, *mi Sobrino*, nephew," says Guillo. ""Why would he do that?"

"He just met us and doesn't know us from a hole in the ground." Byron struggles to understand Slaughter's magnanimous gesture.

He sits down at the table, straightens out the wrinkled letter, and reads aloud.

> *Byron and Guillo,*
> *It's never a good thing to see cavalry heading for your ranch. Hope you manage to come out of the scrape okay with everything intact. I've met with the quartermaster for the U.S. Army posts in Southern Arizona Territory. We managed to work out a deal that favors all parties and have a contract being written up right now. The official paperwork will come from the Department of the Army with all the details. It suffices to say we ain't going to get hurt on the deal. I managed to get the contract away from Henry Hooker this time. If you ain't met Henry yet, you'll like him. His spread is west of you in the Sulphur Spring Valley. Some say his was the first by-God cattle ranch in the Territory. He grabbed up a Spanish hacienda and been in the*

territory cattle business since 1872. He constantly looks to expand his holdings. Between his, mine, and yours we have most of the southern part of the territory sewed up.

Now, here's the deal. I'm supplyin' cattle to the forts, posts, and reservations this next year. I've directed the quartermaster to accept one-half the annual beeves from me and the other half from B-Z. You boys are runnin' with the big horses now. Do the deal right, don't cut no corners, and we'll both profit. Henry will know you're on the map and look to cut into your business. Your Pa always did good by me, Byron. This is my simple way to repay a good remembrance. If y'all need anything just send word, I'll help out. Keep clear of trouble and them Cowboys, punch your cattle, and you'll do all right. Oh, you've bound to lost some cattle to the Apache, so, I've got a few head drivin' your direction. I'll settle up with you in the spring at calving.

Sincerely

John H. Slaughter

"*Madre de Dios.*" Guillo sits back in his chair. "John H., he's put us on the map, *Compañero.* It's like he says, 'we run with the big horses now.'"

"Pa sure made a positive impression on him," says Byron. "I know Pa was a good man, but this just gives me more notion of how others felt about him." Byron looks away from the table and stares out the front door.

"*Si, Compañero*, I knew your *Padre* for a long while. He is someone I will never forget," says Guillo, his eyes damp with tears.

"Virgil. It's them. They robbed the silver wagon and shot the guards and the others," whispers Brax as he steps into the dark corner beside the Oriental Saloon.

"I know, boy. I, know," responds the shadowed figure beside him. "I figured it was them from the get-go. Just didn't have solid evidence to go on. You've eye-balled them, and that's good enough for me."

"What do we do now?"

"*WE* do nothing," says Earp. "You go into the Oriental and leave this to me."

Virgil Earp moves from the shadows into the street and slowly follows the three riders as they weave through the Tombstone nighttime mob.

Reluctantly, Braxton turns and walks through the swinging doors into the din of the Oriental Saloon. He pushes his way through the crowd over to the quiet end of the bar to where Wyatt stands.

"I saw the three who held up the silver wagon."

"Where?"

"Here in town. I pointed them out to Virgil. He's followin' them."

Wyatt nods his head and quickly walks to the door of the Oriental Saloon and looks out. Braxton follows closely behind.

"Did he ask for help?" asks Wyatt.

"No, he told me to get in here."

"Well, you've done as you were directed. Now, we wait." Wyatt returns to his place at the bar, places one foot on the brass rail that runs the length of the bottom of the counter, and slowly sips his whiskey.

Braxton follows and stands beside him.

"Thought you'd be at Faro tonight," says Wyatt changing the subject to take Braxton's mind off of what is happening outside. "I assume you're here to stay and not running?"

"I'll not run, Wyatt," says Braxton. "I need to tell you I've seen paper on myself for the murder of my Pa in Mesilla."

"You shot your father?" Wyatt looks at Braxton with slightly wide-eyed expression. "He draw on you, hurt you, or do something to provoke your shooting him?"

"No," says Brax. "He stepped in the way of my shot to protect a Mexican I intended to shoot. There, you have it all."

"Well, that's some weight to carry around. You didn't stick around to square things up?"

"Nope, just left. So, now there is paper on me. Have you seen it?" asks Brax.

"Can't say I have," answers Wyatt. "Did you plan to murder the Mexican all along?"

"No, just got riled up, didn't think, used the gun, and now can't take any of it back. Wish I could, really wish I could," whispers Brax.

"Sounds like you mean it," Wyatt responds. "What's done is done. Hell, Virgil, Morgan, and I done things we wish we hadn't done. Even Doc has, too. Course he won't admit to it. What's done has consequences. You own up to the consequences, and life goes on. If Virgil needs to arrest you, he will. Until that time, get on with your life. You can't drag one day to the next. You understand what I'm telling you?"

"I appreciate your saying it. I'm here, not running. If Virgil needs to find me, he knows where to look. I'll be at my Faro table." Brax steps over and asks the bartender to pass him his game board. He moves to an open table, pulls out his deck, sets up the dealer's box, and commences to deal.

Three days later, at midmorning, Brax enters the Oriental and talks with the bartenders when he sees a young boy slap the batwing doors open, stick his head in, and shout.

"It's happenin', Gents. Earps and Clantons gonna have it out."

He disappears in an instant.

Braxton makes eye contact with the bartender, spins around, and runs out the swinging doors. At the far end of Fremont Street, he sees Virgil, Wyatt, Morgan, and Doc Holliday walk slowly down the road toward a group of Cowboys.

The rustlers stand in a vacant lot behind the O.K. Corral engaging in conversation with Cochise County Sheriff John Behan. Braxton knows Behan is a friend of the Clanton bunch, and many times looks the other way on Cowboy activities. He's heard barflies say he's Ike Clanton's handpicked sheriff.

Braxton draws closer and sees Ike and Billy Clanton, Tom and Frank McLaury, and Billy Claiborne. He's dealt Faro many times with these men at his table.

The county sheriff breaks from the group when he sees the Earps and rushes down the street toward them shouting something about how the Cowboys want to leave town.

Braxton has expected this day for some time. It's been building month after month with insults, taunts, hold ups, rustling, and malicious attacks escalating to the point where both groups look for revenge. Virgil, Wyatt, and Doc talk incessantly about the outlaws that make up the Cowboy gang. Braxton sits with them as they fume for hours about the Clanton crowd.

I remember, thinks Braxton, *Virgil's talk about the first encounter with McLaury over stolen Army mules. Tracked the Cowboys to their ranch, and found the rebranded mules. Frank McClaury laughs at the Earps and Army Captain searching for the livestock. The Cowboys come to town and belittle Virgil, Wyatt, and Captain Hurst saying if they follow them again they'll kill 'em.*

Then, Braxton recalls, *Wyatt arrests Curly Bill Brocius when he kills Marshall Fred White. He pistol-whips Brocius, and the Cowboys testify at the trial about Bill's innocence. The case gets thrown out of court. The Cowboys laugh and jeer at Wyatt over out foxing him.*

The final straw happens when Wyatt runs for re-election as Deputy Sheriff for Pima County. The Cowboys gather non-voters like children, Chinese, dogs, burros, and poultry and cast ballots in their names for Wyatt's challenger. The election board picks the competitor. The Cowboys harass, laugh at, and insult the Earps continuously, and make death threats daily against all of the Earp family.

Braxton hears some of the threats from the Cowboys themselves and recalls editorials *The Tombstone Epitaph* runs fueling the fire about who controls Cochise County...the Cowboys or law and order.

Brax isn't surprised to see today's confrontation, *but why didn't Wyatt let me know?* He shoves his way through spectators and tries to get to Wyatt's side as quickly as possible.

8
FREMONT STREET

As Brax breaks through the crowd on the boardwalk, time seems to shift into slow motion.

He hears Wyatt holler something to the Cowboys. They turn in response and shout back.

Virgil yanks his revolver, coolly aims at Billy Clanton, and fires. The slug lifts Billy up and slams him back against the barn wall behind him. Blood blossoms on his chest.

From under his duster, Doc Holliday sweeps out a shotgun and triggers both barrels. A massive cloud of gun smoke belches from the gun and Frank McLaury spins around as the buckshot pierces him. Struggling, he manages to stand his ground and return fire.

Doc reloads and fires his shotgun again into Frank McLaury. The force lifts and flings him onto his back sprawled dead on the ground

Virgil is hit in the leg by a handgun slug.

Sliding down the wall, Billy Clanton, mortally wounded, continues to fire his revolver.

Morgan is clipped by a shot across his back.

Braxton sees Doc grab his arm as a slug burrows into it.

Tom McLaury fires round after round from his gun until lead slams into his midsection crumpling him to the ground.

Braxton watches Wyatt stand absolutely still, coolly firing his pistols repeatedly at the Cowboys.

Ike Clanton and Billy Claiborne scramble from the corral, seek cover, and run for their lives.

Thirty seconds and the shooting's over. Black gun smoke dissipates and drifts towards Braxton.

Virgil, Morgan, and Doc Holliday all have gunshot wounds. Wyatt stands in the street unscratched. Billy Clanton, Tom and Frank McLaury are dying or dead. Braxton watches Johnny Behan run around screaming at the Earp brothers calling them murderers and threatens to get them tried and hanged. Spectators begin to stand up or creep out from behind protective barrels and boxes.

Dumbfounded by the shootout, the world returns to full speed, and Braxton's ears are assaulted by the cacophony of talk, screams, and shouts of the spectators.

He knows his world changed before his eyes. Mobs of bystanders flood the street to surround the Earps and Holliday. Others gawkers gingerly make their way toward the Cowboys' bodies.

Turning around, Brax slowly walks back to the Oriental Saloon.

In the weeks following the gunfight, things go from bad to worse. Braxton hears of Vigil being ambushed while on his nightly rounds of Tombstone. His arm amputation effectively ends his lawman career. A short time later, Morgan is murdered while he shoots a game of billiards, again an ambush.

To Braxton, it seems Wyatt goes berserk and accuses everyone of plotting against his family; he sleeps little, and evasively moves from place to place.

Everyone Braxton listens to claims the Cowboys are behind the attacks on the Earp family.

After Morgan's murder, Brax watches Wyatt move his family to Benson, where they prepare to depart Arizona Territory aboard a train for California. Braxton hears Doc Holliday rides with them to Tucson for extra protection. When they arrive, the Cowboys attempt another ambush at the depot.

Two weeks later, Braxton is dealing Faro when Wyatt walks into the Oriental. Several men Brax doesn't recognize accompany him. They take a seat at one of the corner tables, and Braxton quickly wraps up the Faro game, moves toward Earp's table, and pauses for Wyatt to motion him over to sit down.

"It's a while since I've seen you," says Brax.

"Been taking care of some loose ends," answers Wyatt.

"Looks like you keep other company these days." Braxton looks around the table.

"Yep."

"I wanted to be with you at the incident on Fremont, but you never said anything to me. Don't know what to make of that."

"Don't look too deep into it," says Wyatt.

"I could have helped."

"Virgil didn't want to pull you into something that wasn't your fight."

"I thought we were friends. It was my fight."

"He said you had enough with your New Mexico situation."

"What about these riding with you now?"

"These boys here are with me to take care of things that have gotten out of hand. I know where your heart is. You're not going with me."

"How can you just ride off chasing down those Cowboys?"

"I picked up my U.S. Deputy Marshal papers and badge. Now I'm on the hunt. Ike Clanton and his Cowboys will be finished when I'm done. Stay put, live your life, do what's right, and know it's been my pleasure to call you a friend."

"Wyatt, if it wasn't for you, I don't know what would have become of me. Why can't I go with you?" Braxton awaits Wyatt's reply.

"What I'm fixin' to do is wipe the board clean. I've now got the badge to take the war to those that have it coming. They've killed, maimed, murdered for too long. Their thieving, rustling, stealing days are done. Lightning is coming and it's called Wyatt Earp."

Braxton's not sure but he sees his friend's personality change. A strange, almost vacant, countenance comes over him. As he sits back in his chair, Wyatt's eyes take on a wide-eyed, trance-like, appearance when he says, "Yes, lightning's coming."

Wyatt suddenly stands, and the other men with him rise as well. Reaching out his hand he gives Brax a firm handshake.

"You've been a friend I won't forget. I doubt we'll meet again."

Wyatt walks across the Oriental Saloon, pauses at the doorway, and turns toward Braxton.

"Virgil said he sent some message to New Mexico on your behalf. Never did get it straight from him once all this mess got set in motion. Been my pleasure, Braxton Bierman. *Adios*."

Wyatt walks out the batwing doors followed by the others.

Braxton stands rooted in place as questions flood his mind.

What message did Virgil send?

Why does Wyatt leave me here?

Should I just up and go anyway?

Who are those other rough characters with him?

What does "lightning coming" mean?
Brax stumbles his way to the door and watches the mounted group weave its way through the crowded street. As Braxton watches, Johnny Behan rushes up to Wyatt and shouts about the need to arrest him for a shooting at the Tucson depot.

Wyatt calmly turns to Johnny and replies, "I'm not going to be arrested by you today or ever, Behan." He continues to ride away. Johnny Behan stands in the street shouting at the departing riders.

Braxton walks through the swinging doors of the Oriental and makes his way to a cafe a short distance along the boardwalk. Inside, he finds a table beside the window and orders coffee and a slice of apple pie.

What's next? He stares out the store window at the churning Tombstone street crowd and disruptive night.

9
RIDING FOR THE STAR

The morning rays of sunlight stream down the Main Street and alleys of Tombstone as Braxton walks into the lobby of the Grand Hotel. He takes a seat on the far side of the room so he can watch the front door and a small room beside the entrance. Shaking open the morning edition of *The Tombstone Epitaph*, he waits.

Within an hour, Captain John H. Jackson enters the lobby, looks around, locates the room, enters, and paces. He takes a letter from his coat pocket, reads, and rereads it while walking. Finally, he returns the letter to his pocket and takes a seat at the round table in the room. Braxton watches from behind his newspaper.

Jackson is medium height, black wavy hair, and wears a buckskin-fringed jacket. He removes his gray slouched hat and drops it on the table.

His face is weathered from too many days under the Arizona sun. A starched white high collared shirt is shocking against his tanned appearance, and his deep brown eyes miss nothing as they continually sweep the lobby. Brax knows he'll have to move soon or become a subject of investigation.

Men stop by to meet with the Captain throughout the morning, and engage in deep discussions. They wear everything from buckskin to frock coats, soft felt slouch hats to top hats, and every description in between. Young, old, slim, heavyset, trail worn, fresh to the west, any and all kinds roam the streets of Tombstone.

Brax overhears comments when men depart.

"That jasper's plumb loco," says one man.

"Maybe he ain't loco, but he's lookin' fer an early grave," replies the other.

"Why, them Cowboys will chop up whoever comes after them and feed them to the buzzards."

"I ain't hankerin' to leave this life just yet, hard as it seems."

"Let's go back to the Birdcage."

They exit the hotel.

Brax wonders, *what am I doing here?*

What can this man do for me?

Why was it recommended I talk to him?

Should I just get up and walk out?

Finally, he stands and walks across the lobby.

"I hear you're looking for a few good men." Braxton steps into the room. "I've traveled New

Mexico and southern Arizona Territories, lived by my wits, and am pretty fair with firearms."

Captain Jackson slowly raises his head and sizes him up with a withering brown-eyed stare.

"I've seen you sittin' in the lobby. Wonderin' who you are and what you're lookin' to do." He slowly leans back in his chair and lets his right hand drop to his side.

"I'm no difficulty, Marshall. My name's Braxton Bierman."

"How do you know I'm a Marshall?" questions Jackson.

"I've heard about you. Knew you'd be here today. John Clum told me."

"Clum, the editor and ex-mayor? He's good people. He sent you?"

"He said it would be in my best interest to stop by."

Quickly, Jackson reaches out, grabs Braxton's right hand, and rubs across it. "Your hands look mighty soft and smooth. Don't appear you've done much real work."

"Hands don't tell all." Braxton quickly yanks his away.

"You know what I'm looking for?" asks the Captain.

"I think so. Sounds like you're fixin' on proddin' a hornet's nest."

"You up for the task?"

"I can hold my own."

"Take a look at this before we go any farther." Jackson slides the letter from his pocket across the table to Braxton.

"It appears to be a letter from Territorial Governor Frederick Tritle." Brax scans the document.

"It is, and it authorizes me to create the First Company of Arizona Rangers."

"I heard of Rangers during the recent war. This like them?" asks Brax.

"Yep and nope. This new unit's gonna deal with lawlessness in the territory caused by the outlaw Cowboys and hostiles."

"That's a tall order. How many men you recruiting?"

"Twelve."

"Only a dozen." Brax repeats in shock.

"It's enough to start what needs to be done," replies Jackson.

Braxton shuffles uneasily while he stands before the 'law dog's' scrutiny. It's not something he relishes.

"Son, you think you're up to riding for days, living in the open, eating nothing but trail dust, and getting up to come back for more each morning?"

"Well, sir. I know the outlaws you intend to pursue."

"Tell me more," says Jackson.

"I've met most of them here in Tombstone. I know where they hide out and how to find most of their places. Their loose saloon talk told more than it should have."

"Could be useful."

"If you want to run them to ground, you could use my help." Braxton pauses. His piercing blue eyes size up the Captain.

The silence is deafening.

"Sorry to waste your time." Braxton turns to leave the room but is stopped.

"Well, well, well." The Captain leans back in his chair and grins broadly.

"I know John Clum. Publishes a fine paper, the *Epitaph*, and he's fought the fight to end lawlessness. Since the Cowboys have targeted him, he's got to leave Tombstone."

"He's concerned about his son and knows he's spent enough time here," replies Brax.

"Since Clum sent you, you must be all right. Have your horse and gear ready to ride in the morning. We'll meet at the Cochise County Courthouse at ten o'clock. If you're not there by then, don't bother showin' up."

Byron watches John Slaughter's ranch hands ride away after driving fifty head of cattle to the B-Z ranch headquarters. "John H. sure sent more cattle than I expected." He and Guillo sit on the ranch house porch, their booted feet rest on the porch rail, and they look out across the sweep of the land before them.

"*Si*, John Slaughter is *muy bueno amigo*," says Guillo.

"It is nice to have the house, barn, and bunkhouse finished."

"The *rancho* is beginning to look like something, no?"

"It's shapin' up real nice," Byron smiles.

"*Compañero,* do you think we should find out about Henry Hooker? John H. says his *rancho's* in Sulphur Springs Valley, *si?*"

"Since we and John H. bested him for the quartermaster's beef contract, maybe we should ride over and meet *Señor* Hooker."

"*Si,* I think that might be a worthwhile ride. We can stop and check out Tombstone as well. Maybe we can sees the place they calls the Birdscage, no?"

Brax rises early, gathers his belongings, puts them into his saddlebags, picks up his blanket bedroll, checks his pockets for personal items, and leaves his room at the Grand Hotel. Downstairs, he stops at the front desk.

"Herman, you're a good clerk. I'll not be back. I'm paid up, but if there's some left over, have a drink at the hotel bar. Just shove aside those Cowboys that hog up the joint, and have a stiff one on me."

He slaps his key on the counter, turns, and walks out. His horse is tied up to the front hitching post. A stable hand stands there stroking the animal's muzzle.

"Thanks for bringing my horse around," says Braxton.

"No problem, Mister."

"Here's for your trouble." Brax flips a quarter end over end into the air. The stable hand catches it easily.

"Thanks, Mister." He runs back behind the hotel.

Braxton throws his saddlebags across the back of the saddle and ties them down. He secures his bedroll behind the cantle, and looks down the street toward the county courthouse. He notices a crowd standing in front of the building. Gathering the reins of his horse, Brax quickly steps into the saddle, turns toward the crowd, and slowly walks his horse up the street.

Outside the courthouse, he sees ranch hands wearing denim jackets, well broken-in boots, plaid shirts and pullover cotton tunics, some have bib-front button over shirts, and most wear jeans. The townsmen wear frock coats, brogan shoes, button up cotton shirts, pinstriped trousers, colorful vests, and an assortment of hats. All carry holstered side arms.

He stops at the hitching rail just as John Jackson walks down the steps from the courthouse.

"If you gentlemen will make your way into the building, we'll get started." Jackson motions the crowd to the doorway.

Brax takes a good look at the building. It's two-story red brick; on top a one-story cupola wears a lacy gingerbread "widow's walk" that crowns the structure, and there are eight-pane double hung windows on both stories.

Braxton swings off his horse, ties it to the rail, and enters the courthouse with the other men.

The courtroom is rectangular with a raised judge's bench facing two tables, one for defense and the other for prosecution. A short rail fence, with a swinging gate in the center, separates the spectator chairs from the tables in front.

Jackson leads the way into the room, steps through the gate, and stands in front of the judge's bench facing the men. The other eleven men and Brax file into the front row and take a seat. At the prosecutor's table sits Johnny Behan, the County Sheriff for Cochise County.

"Gentlemen, you are here this morning because you've been selected. I know some of you personally, some by reputation, and a few of you are recommended by someone I respect." Jackson looks directly at Brax. "I've asked Sheriff Behan to join us this morning. He's an observer and witness to these proceedings." Jackson nods to Behan and receives a nod in return.

"I know some of you are in Arizona Territory because, let's say, situations forced you to come here. Let's be clear, I don't care. Others are here because you want to do something different. Still others are legitimately interested in correcting wrongs. I'm not naive enough to think y'all are here with altruistic thoughts regarding the law. But, you are here." Jackson pauses.

Brax wonders, *why am I here?*

Can I leave quietly?

What's Behan doing here? A witness to what? He hates the ground I walk on?

Brax glances left and right to read the faces of those beside him.

"Here's the deal," Jackson announces. "You're asked to accept the job of Arizona Ranger. The pay is almost non-existent, the food lousy, living conditions worse than the food. There's no thanks and plenty of lawbreakers. If you want to leave now, you know where the door is." Jackson stares at the line of men sitting in the front row. Nobody moves.

I can go now. Right? He just said we can go.

Why can't I move? Nobody else moves.

This is crazy: twelve men to tackle Arizona Territory.

There ain't anything out there but desert, cactus, rattlesnakes, Cowboys, and death.

This isn't rational. It ain't reasonable. So why can't I move?

"I don't care what you've been, who you've been, or where you've been. What I need now are men to ride for Arizona Territory and uphold the laws of the territory. If you do, we are good. If you take this job and violate my trust, break the laws of Arizona Territory, or cause harm to those you swear to protect, I will find you. When I find you, I will personally see that a deep, dark hole in Yuma Territorial Prison will be your home. I guarantee you will not like it."

Brax hears a quiet murmur among the men.

"I've heard about Yuma."

"Me, too. It's a stinkin' hell hole."

"You know Cap'n Jackson will hunt you down."

"Stick by him, he'll stick by you."

Jackson continues, "If you take the oath about to be administered and uphold the laws of this Territory, if you 'Ride for the Star,' you will have no better supporter and friend than me." Jackson stares down the line at each man. "You will have difficulty with local marshals and county sheriffs."

Behan starts to speak, but Jackson cuts him off.

Jackson says, "As long as I carry the letters and credentials from the Governor of this Territory, we are the sworn enforcers of the law. Marshals and sheriffs will work with us, but be prepared for resistance. Now, anyone who cares to leave, stand up and go. No one will think the worse of you."

Jackson pauses, and picks up a stack of papers from the defense table. He looks back at the men. "No one's left?"

"Stand up gentlemen, and raise your right hand." Jackson squares his shoulders as he raises his hand.

Repeat after me, "By the authority of the Governor of the Territory of Arizona, I, state your name," he pauses as every man says his name. He continues, "Accept the position of Arizona Ranger. I will uphold and enforce the laws of this territory whenever and wherever needed. To protect persons and property needing my assistance," Jackson pauses again for all to catch up. He continues. "I pledge my effort and if necessary my life. So help me God."

Brax hears everyone, himself included, finish repeating the oath.

Jackson reaches over and slaps the table with a resounding bang. Everyone jumps. With a big grin on his face he says, "Welcome, gentlemen, you are now Arizona Rangers. Step up and fill in your name, or make your mark, on the top of your form lying on the table. Sheriff Behan will sign as a witness. Leave the page on the table and see me at the outside door. I'll have your badge and instructions. We have work to do Rangers. Get the paperwork out of the way. We have to ride." He walks through the swinging gate out of the courtroom, turns, and waits beside the outside door.

One by one, each man steps forward, finds his form, signs the paper, hands it to Sheriff Behan for his signature, and steps out of the courtroom. John Jackson shakes the hand of each man, gives verbal instructions, and hands over an Arizona Ranger badge.

Brax overhears that some men are headed to McDowell, Tubac, and some to the border at San Rafael.

I wonder what hotter-than-hell spot the Captain has picked out for me.

He steps forward, signs his paper, looks squarely at Sheriff Behan as he hands it for signature.

In a low bitter guttural whisper Johnny Behan says, "I know you, card sharp. I know you are an Earp man."

"They're all gone, Johnny. I'm just gettin' on with my life," says Brax.

"One false step, one little fault, a simple misjudgment, and I'll have your hide, Faro dealer."

"I got no grudge with you, Johnny. Leave me be to do my job, and I'll leave you alone as well."

"I know you are an Earp man," Johnny says. "I'm watching and waiting for you to step out of line. The Earps got away from me. You won't."

He yanks the paper from Brax, grudgingly signs, and waves him away.

Brax moves quickly to the doorway.

John Jackson shakes his hand and glances at Johnny Behan.

"I saw Behan talkin' with you."

"Yep," says Brax. "He was wishing me well."

"You really got to be a better liar. Clum says you're good people. I accept that. I also know Behan wants to get his claws in you in the worst way."

"Johnny has some pent up bitterness," says Brax.

"This unit is riding for the border to stop the Cowboys and their rustlin'. I want to have my cases hold up in court, and with Behan gunnin' for you, it risks cases being tried fairly."

"It ain't anything I've done," says Brax.

"I know you've just got ahold of the short end of the stick. You won't ride to the border with us. I want you to head for the Tonto Basin. There's noise of two groups up there, the Tewksburys and Grahams, mixing things up in that part of the territory. Check it out, fix what needs a fix, and keep me informed. You've got the telegraph, so use it. I don't want to be blindsided by actions my Rangers take. Got it?"

"Yes, Captain. Tonto Basin, Tewksburys and Grahams. You want no surprises."

"You got it, Ranger. Now, get out of my sight. You've got work to do. Good luck." Jackson hands Braxton his badge. The round silver circle encloses a five-point star. On the top of the circle is written *'Territorial'* and on the bottom, *'Ranger.'*

10
COW COUNTRY

The brisk cutting wind sweeps down the *Pinaleno* mountain range and washes over Byron and Guillo as they ride south from the B-Z Ranch. Byron tugs his hat down tighter as his bandana whips around his neck.

"Not much farther to the pass between the *Pinalenos* and *Dos Cabezas* ranges," he says to Guillo. "It's the same pass used by the Southern Pacific Railroad."

"*Si, Compañero.* It's been a good ride this far."

"*We'll follow the rails west to cross from San Simon Valley onto the Sulphur Springs spread,*" says Byron.

While the cadence of the horse rocks him in the saddle, he wonders, *what waits for us at the end of this ride*?

Will this trip be a success or disaster?

What's Hooker like? Does he hold grudges?

Will we ride away from this visit or fill a hole somewhere on this spread?

They ride on.

"*Senor* Hooker's *Sierra Bonita rancho* is only twenty-five miles north of Maley, no?" asks Guillo.

"Yep. I hear Hooker drove ten thousand longhorns from Texas to the Territory in 1872," says Byron.

"It's a lots of cattles to drive a long way, *Compañero.*"

Byron nods and continues, "He stumbled onto Sulphur Springs Valley chasing a stampede. From what I've heard, he bought the Spanish *hacienda* and land grant, fought off Apaches and rustlers, and built himself a cattle empire."

"*Si*, the new ranch hands we hire speak highly of *Senor* Hooker," says Guillo. "They say he never dresses like a *Ranchero*, he always wears gentlemen's clothes. Some say he looks like an Englishmans. I'm not sure what that looks like, but I'm interested to see."

"Well, whatever he looks like, there's no denying he's successful, and that's what I want us to be. Besides, you might just make a great English-looking man." Byron laughs out loud while he enjoys his mental picture of Guillo.

"*Compañero*, what if this *Señor* Hooker no likes our being competition for him and makes trouble for us?" Guillo suddenly turns serious. "We have come too far to go back, and B-Z is not leaving San Simon, *si*?"

"We are not gonna go anywhere, *Compañero*. Let's just see what old Hooker is like. If he's an ornery cuss, then it won't be hard to dislike him. On the other hand, if he is a decent sort, then maybe we can learn more about this Territory."

The setting sun streaks the western sky with dazzling reds and orange colors as they ride into Maley. The town is another whistle stop on the Southern Pacific Railroad. Byron sees piles of creosote-covered cross ties, stacks of iron rails, baskets of spikes, and discarded railroad equipment sit beside the tracks as they ride into town.

The depot is a small, whitewashed, wooden shanty for the railroad agent. A sign hangs from the eve of the roof with the name *Maley, Arizona*, painted on it. A platform littered and stacked high with boxes and crates of every description wraps around the depot. Telegraph lines stretch from pole to pole parallelling the railway.

Multiple corrals butt up to the rails with inclined cattle chutes.

Guillo points out, "One of our hands says this spot is where herds they sell to buyers, load into railroad cars, and ships away, *si*. We needs to talk to someone about using this place instead of the San Simon railway stop. This one looks much better to load cattles, *si*?"

"You're right, *Compañero*. Sure glad we trailed down here to see it first hand. Who do you imagine we'd talk to about shipping our cattle?" Byron looks over the dilapidated boxcars, shanties, tents, and adobe huts that make the habitable hovels in Maley. He spots a new wooden building set back behind the corrals with a telegraph line run to it. " Looks like the place to start." He points out the building to Guillo. Both ride over, slide off their horses, and tie them to a post. Byron walks up to a window and peers inside. A man sits at a table and motions them inside.

"Come on inside and lighten your load," says the man as Guillo and Byron enter. "Too hot to stand outside and gawk through a window." He points at two chairs in front of his desk. "How can I help you?"

"We just rode into town, saw the corrals and loading ramps you have here. I'm looking for the person responsible," says Byron, settling in one of the offered chairs. Guillo slips into the chair beside him.

"Well, men, you've come to the right spot. I'm Harvey Skinner, a cattle buyer. I work for agents who broker the sale of cattle to eastern establishments and some new ranches in California as well." Skinner rocks back in his chair and props a boot up against the top edge of the desk. He wears well-worn jeans and a bib-front blue shirt. The red bandana tied around his neck splashes some color under a weather-beaten face. Dark brown eyes, above his handlebar mustache, quickly size up Guillo and Byron. As he talks, the telegraph key clatters in the box sitting on the desktop.

"Pardon me, men, this will just take a minute." Grabbing a tablet from the desk, he quickly writes down the message chattering over the telegraph. After the clickity clack stops, he reaches over, taps the buttoned lever on the device a few times, sits back in his chair, and again props his foot up against the table.

"Just my agent sendin' me the most recent order for beef." He wears a self-satisfied smile.

Guillo stares with rapt attention at the telegraph hardware and the man that operates it. *If I had not seen it work, I would not believe it. The man, he writes down what the chattering key tell him. ¡Ay, caramba!*

He asks, "*Señor*, how does the agent man tell you all this?"

With a smile, the cattle buyer says, "My friend, just sent me the message telling me what the order amounts will be. See I wrote it down on this tablet." He scoots the tablet toward Guillo.

"I see what you write, *amigo*. But, how does you knows to write that from the twittering thing?"

Guillo remembers, *Zep, Byron's padre, used to go to the telegraph office in Las Cruces. He says he sends messages about cattle shipment, but I never saw it in action before now.*

"Friend, it all has to do with dots and dashes, Morse Code. A quick click is a dot, and a longer click is a dash. Listening to them, you quickly understand the pattern, each combination of dots and dashes represents a letter, and multiple letters make words. Simple, you see?" The buyer's face crinkles in smiles as he enjoys his explanation.

"*Amigo, Ay-yi-yi*, you make my old head hurt. Clickity click and clackity clack is not something easy for this old *vaquero* to understand. I will leave it with you." Guillo holds his head with his hands as he shakes it from side to side.

Byron sympathizes with Guillo, but is intrigued by the telegraphed message. "So, your agent says the orders are up?" he asks.

"That's company business, Son, but I can tell you I'll pay top dollar for your cattle right here." The broker drops his foot down and leans forward. "You're selling cattle, ain't you?"

"Well, sir, yes, but not today. We own the B-Z over in San Simon and will have cattle to sell shortly."

"B-Z. Yep. I've heard about y'all. I'd be real interested to work with you when you get ready to sell your cattle."

The telegraph starts chattering again. The agent quickly turns and writes down a new message.

Byron and Guillo stand up and move toward the doorway. Turning, Byron waves to the buyer who gives a quick nod as he keeps writing. Both men step out into the street to collect their horses.

"He sure seems like a busy fella," says Byron as he gathers the reins and steps up into the saddle. "Looks like we'll need to spend some time with him come round up time."

"*Si, Compañero*, if we can pry him loose from his chattering box." Guillo, already astride his horse, slowly rides toward a nearby cafe.

The Southern Pacific train pulls out of Benson depot on time heading west. Braxton rides in a Pullman Railroad Coach, with a ticket to Maricopa. Captain Jackson's been very clear that Braxton's involvement with the Cowboy rustlers along the border would jeopardize convictions the Rangers badly want. Sheriff Johnny Behan's animosity toward anyone associated with the Earp family could taint any Cowboy arrest. Brax doesn't mind leaving Tombstone. *There've been plenty of changes to the town since I arrived; it's time to leave. Captain Jackson gives me a reason.*

The train chews up the miles and soon arrives in Tucson. Brax steps from the coach to find a cafe near the depot. He only has time for a cup of coffee and piece of apple pie before the shrill whistle alerts travelers to board. The train quickly departs.

Travel takes Brax past Picacho Peak, through Casa Grande, and stops again at Maricopa depot. Quickly, he gathers his saddlebags and rifle from the overhead carrier and departs the coach. He locates the station agent then retrieves his horse, tack, and pack from the livestock car. Saddling up, he turns north for Phoenix.

The Sonora Desert reaches deep into Arizona Territory with its hostile environment. Saguaro, barrel, prickly pear, cholla, and other cacti pepper the land. Rocky, rough, desert terrain scattered with buttes and hilltops fades into the distance. He marvels at the mesquite, yucca, and

Palo Verde plants that surround him, and above everything, the forever clear blue sky holds a fierce fireball sun.

An unforgiving land if I ever saw one.

Riding from the depot, he arrives at Maricopa Wells with its oasis of water. He stops to resupply with water and purchase provisions. Because of the reliable water supply, peaceful Pima and Maricopa Indians irrigate the lands. They turn a harsh place into abundant fields of corn, beans, and hay.

The road from Maricopa Wells to Phoenix appears well traveled and in good shape.

Why am I out here, he wonders?

What fool's errand have I gotten myself into?

I could be in Tombstone right in a Faro game instead of wearing out my back end on this horse.

What's driving me?

What am I gonna accomplish?

His horse continues its steady gait northward until Braxton sees the town of Phoenix on the Salt River.

His ride passes many irrigated farms and ranches closer to town, and the city looks well established. *The drummer on the train told me this place is growing steadily. In the newspaper he showed an editorial about how Phoenix seems to rise from the ground. Might not be long before it rivals Tucson.*

He spots the red brick courthouse; a cupola sits on top of its second story.

Single and two-storied adobe buildings, wooden structures, substantial brick homes, and a few shanties line both sides of Washington Street as people hurry along the boarded sidewalks shaded by overhanging porch roofs. He dodges buckboards loaded with fence posts, produce, and rolls of wire. Horsemen walk along the street. An occasional stagecoach jostles along the wide thoroughfare.

The newspaper article on the train said Phoenix is a city with almost twenty-five hundred people. Looks like most of them are out walking around this evening. They're scramblin' around like ants on an anthill.

Brax catches the attention of a boy hustling along with other pedestrian traffic.

"Hey you. Son. Can you tell me where I can find the marshal's office?" shouts Braxton.

"Sure, Mister. You got a nickel?" The boy stops and smiles.

"You selling information today?"

"Only to you, Mister. You seem to be the one lost, I ain't."

Brax fishes in his vest pocket, pulls out a nickel, and tosses it to the boy. "There, my dues are paid. Where's the office?"

"Right around the next corner, Mister. Thanks for the nickel." He races away.

"Been fleeced by a young shearing expert." Brax rides around the corner.

In the middle of the block he sees a two-story adobe building with barred windows on the second floor. A sign with *Marshal* painted on it hangs under the porch roof. Brax dismounts at the hitching rail, steps on the porch, and walks through the open doorway.

From his desk, the marshal glances up. His star glitters dangling from his vest. A droopy grey mustache covers a leathered face. Brown squinting eyes size Brax up as gnarled hands sort through wanted posters spread across the desktop. His white, cotton, long-sleeved, sweat stained pullover shirt is visible underneath a brown leather vest. Behind him a gun rack contains four rifles and two shotguns. A potbellied stove sits across the room with two chairs beside an upended crate that holds a checkerboard. The game's partially played with pieces scattered across the board. The smooth polished appearance of the game board makes Brax think it's seen a lot of use. A stairway in the back corner leads to a second floor.

"Howdy. Can I help you?" asks the Marshal.

"Who's winning the game?" Brax gestures toward the board.

"The judge is," says the Marshal. "But, he cheats."

Braxton glances at the posters on the desk. A fleeting thought about his picture being on one of them crosses his mind.

"Marshal, I'm Braxton Bierman, Arizona Ranger." Standing in front of the desk, he shows the badge pinned to his shirt.

The Marshal kicks back from his desk and reclines in his chair to get a better look.

With a smirk hidden by a quick hand swipe over his mouth and a mischievous flicker in his eyes, he says, "An honest, by-God, Arizona Ranger. Well, looky here. A real special one stands in my jail in little-bitty Phoenix." Sarcasm drips from every word. "I heared Governor Tritle done lost his mind and signed up a bunch of you Rangers to ride the territory. I guess you can get done what us Marshals can't. Is that the business?"

"Marshal, my name's Braxton Bierman, and I'm just doing my job. Not looking for difficulty or trouble, but would appreciate your assistance."

"My assistance is it? Well, here's my assistance for you: sit down and take the load off your feet." The marshal kicks a chair in Brax's direction. "In this territory, we can use all the help we can get." He smiles. "You do know old Governor Tritle ain't got enough money to pay y'all don't you? The legislature didn't give the old boy no money. He's climbed out on a limb with y'all, and he's trying to scratch up funds right now. They been talkin' about it over to the county courthouse. That's how come I know."

Brax sits down and thinks about what the marshal just said. *I just take a new job and lose it at the same time. What have I got myself into?*

Brax arrives at his moment of decision. "Well, Marshal, I gave my oath to protect those needing help in this territory, and I guess I'm honor bound to do that until I'm told otherwise. I appreciate your letting me in on the know about the finances, but I'm a lawman, and that's what I'll be doin'."

The marshal pauses, studies Brax's face, draws a long breath, pulls a cigar from his vest pocket, rolls the smoke slowly between his fingers, bites off one end, and spits it on the floor. He pulls a Lucifer from his other vest pocket, strikes it, and brings the flame close as he takes a deep draw on the cigar. He leans forward exhaling a cloud of smoke.

"By Glory. I like you, son. I think you might have the makin's of a real 'law dog' and I'll help. What do you need from me?"

"Well, Marshal, I need somewhere to stay for a day or two, some supplies, and then directions to Tonto Basin," says Brax.

"Tonto Basin? Why the heck are you headin'...Oh. You're going to wander into the Tewksbury-Graham thing, ain't you?" The Marshal looks shocked.

"My Captain assigned me to check it out, then I'm to let him know what's happening. It's a simple prospectin' job." Brax smiles.

The Marshal opens a lower drawer on the desk, pulls out a bottle of whiskey and sets it in the middle of his desk, reaches behind him, rummages around for two empty Mason jars, pours three fingers of whiskey into each, and scoots one over to Braxton.

"Son, you better drink this. You're gonna need it. Let me tell you about the hornets' nest you're fixin' to walk into."

11
SEARCHERS

The Sulphur Springs Valley stretches before Byron as he rides north from Maley. He thinks about the conversation with the cattle buyer.

How many cattle should we drive?

Where are the water holes?

How much grass will the animals need?

Guillo breaks into his thoughts.

"*Compañero*, look up ahead, it appears some ranch hands start an early round up." Guillo points toward the open pastureland before them.

Byron, squints into the morning sun and spots possibly twenty head of cattle driven their direction by three cowpunchers.

"Maybe they're driving a few head to Maley," answers Byron. "Let's find out where they're from."

Guillo stands in his stirrups, takes off his *sombrero*, waves it over his head, and shouts, "*Vaqueros. Vaqueros.*"

The three riders break from the herd, ease their mounts toward Byron and Guillo.

"A little early for a drive ain't it?" asks Byron.

A rider on a big buckskin horse answers, "Who's askin'?"

The three riders draw closer.

"Amigo, we sees you drives the cattles, *Si*?"

"What's that to you, Mex?" The buckskin rider slides his hand towards his holster.

"Easy, friend." Byron pulls his horse to a stop. "We're just bein' neighborly."

"Don't want neighbors, and we ain't your friends. Clear away before trouble starts." The two other riders edge to the sides of the small herd.

"All right. We're movin'." Byron turns his horse to the side and clears a path for the cattle to pass. His hand eases toward his rifle in its scabbard. Guillo follows Byron.

Seeing Byron's action, the buckskin rider suddenly pulls his pistol, and starts shooting at Byron and Guillo. The riders yank their horses around and scatter, riding off in three different directions.

Byron and Guillo fall forward over their horses' necks to make as small a target as possible. Pulling their Winchesters, they pause. To hit any of the quickly disappearing targets would require sheer luck as the spooked cattle rush toward them.

Trotting into to the milling cattle, Byron wonders why the drivers chose to fire at them.

"Doesn't make sense, Guillo. We didn't threaten them at all, and why ride off and leave their cattle? What is going on out here?"

"*Si, Compañero*, we no attacks them."

"Who were they? Where're they from? Who do they ride for?"

"Do these cattles belongs to them?"

"Good question. Take a look at the brand."

"*Compañero*, the cattles are marked with the letter 'H'."

"Probably Hooker's brand. Do the drivers ride for Hooker?"

"I don't know *Compañero*. Should we push the cattle back along the trail they left to see where they comes from?"

"Let's just edge around them and try to head them back up their trail. We can ride along to keep them moving. Maybe we will find out something," Byron agrees with Guillo.

Both men quickly gather up the scattered cattle. The valley is lush with grass and plenty of water. Small streams provide for the additional cattle they see scattered on the range.

Trailing the small herd, dust kicks up and Byron pulls his bandana to cover his nose and mouth.

"It looks like *Señor* Hooker has found the best land around, no?" says Guillo from behind the scarf he's tied over his face.

"It does looks like fine cattle country and I wish we had this surface water at home. Our tanks work okay, but the cattle can range further and feed better with more available water." Byron surveys the landscape around him with envy.

Over a small rise in front of them four riders rapidly approach. Byron motions for Guillo to stop and they pull their rifles. They aren't about to get caught without protection again.

The riders slow to a rapid walk, form a semicircle, and continue to approach scattering the small herd as they move forward. They stop a short distance away. Each rider has his rifle lying across his horse's withers. A rider with a full handlebar mustache, a tall hat, and leather chaps asks, "Where you Cowboys takin' this here bunch of cattle?"

"Who's askin'?" Byron eases his rifle around to point toward the mustached rider.

"I'm askin', and I won't repeat it." The rider nods and the other riders level their rifles at Byron and Guillo.

Byron suddenly realizes, *these men think we're rustlers*. He motions to Guillo to lower his rifle as he does.

"We spotted three riders south of here driving this bunch toward Maley. We called out and they opened fire on us. They're down that direction somewhere if you need to find them," Byran responds.

"If'n y'all will pull those bandanas offin' your faces we'd love to see your pearly whites," the leader says.

Byron realizes he still has a bandana over his face to keep out trail dust. He yanks his down and motions for Guillo to do the same.

"Sorry friend, just trying to strain the big chunks of dirt." Byron smiles at the riders.

"You say three riders?" asks the mustache.

"Yep. Pushing these cattle toward Maley."

"What kind of horses were they riding?"

Byron gives Guillo a questioning look.

"Two paints and a big buckskin," Byron replies.

"You sayin' one of those jaspers you claim to seen, rides a big buckskin?" the ranch hand on the right side asks.

"*Si, amigo*, one of the riders, he was on a big buckskin. He is quick to draw his *pistola* to shoots at us," says Guillo.

"I told you I saw him, Clint. I saw him a couple of days ago riding slow across the south pasture. It's got to be the same jasper," the rider tells the leader.

"All right, Mike. But what about these huckleberries?" he points at Guillo and Byron.

"If it pleases you gentlemen, we were on our way to see Mister Henry Hooker. If you know where he might be or if you can direct us to him we'd be much obliged." Byron removes his hat and wipes the sweat from his forehead.

"Quite a coincidence. We're going to see Mister Hooker. Why don't you boys ride up in front of us, and keep your hands away from your pistols, and stash your rifles. I wouldn't want you to come down with a sudden case of lead poisoning. We'll see you find Mister Hooker. Now. Ride." The leader moves aside and motions the four riders to flank them, two on each side.

"Y'all are ranch hands for Mister Hooker?" questions Byron.

"Yep," answers the leader.

"Is he a ways from here?" Byron tries to initiate conversation again.

"Nope," the leader says.

"Don't have much to say, do you?" Byron asks.

"You talk too much. Shut up and ride," says the leader.

The valley opens up and on a hill in the distance a *hacienda* is visible. *It's a single story adobe house surrounded by encircling walls that looks like a fort. This place is like my Tio Miguel's Hacienda de la Colina in Animas, New Mexico. It seems all the old haciendas are built for protection.*

"Mike, ride on ahead and tell the boss we are headed in with a couple of range riders," directs the mustached leader.

The ranch hand peels off from the group, spurs his horse, and races towards the compound.

Soon, they ride through an open gate and stop in front of the main house.

On the porch under an overhanging roof stands a gentleman of medium height with a full beard and mustache, dressed in a charcoal gray wool suit with jacket and trousers, white shirt, and black string tie. His polished black boots shine. Both thumbs are hooked over the pockets of his black vest. He has an air of power and assurance. He smiles at the riders.

"Well, Clint, what have you dragged in for me this time?"

"Mister Hooker, we found these yahoos in the south pasture drivin' about twenty head. They say they're looking for you. If they were tryin' to steal cattle, they sure had their directions mixed up. They also mentioned seeing the jasper on the big buckskin down in the south pasture. If it's the same feller, he's tied in with Clanton's bunch of Cowboys. You want one of the boys check out that pasture for a couple of days?"

"You are the *Segundo*, second in command, what do you think?"

"I'll take care of it," says Clint.

Hooker chuckles, "Well, Gentlemen, what do you have to say for yourselves?"

"Mister Hooker, I'm Byron Bierman and this is Guillo Zapato. We came looking for you, ran into three men in the south pasture who looked like they might be helping themselves to some of your cattle. One of 'em was riding a buckskin. They took off when they saw us. Your men found us and brought us here. That's about it." Byron takes a breath and waits for a response.

"Bierman, Zapato, from San Simon?" Hooker asks.

"Yes, sir. Our spread is in San Simon Valley."

"Well, come on in the house, both of you. Clint, see their horses are cared for and fed. It's a good idea to send someone to check out the south pasture." He turns and walks toward the front door.

The Phoenix Marshal's a big help, thinks Braxton. *Without his directions, I could be ridin' around here lost as a leaf in a wind storm. His directions to Tonto Basin are pretty clear:*

Follow the Salt River east.

Turn north where the Verde River enters the Salt,

Before you get to Fort McDowell, follow Sycamore Creek east.

When you get through the Mazatzal Mountains, drop into the Tonto Basin.

Why the Good Lord turned all this Mazatzal Range on its edge is beyond me.

Rocky buttes, sandstone and granite valleys, arroyos, canyons, and washes all jut jaggedly skyward. Saguaro, prickly pear, cholla, chaparral, agave, yucca, and century plants cover the landscape.

If there's a thorn to be found in Arizona Territory it's here.

He rides up one side of Sugarloaf Butte, slides down the other, and makes his way slowly along Sycamore Creek. The sandy soil at the bottom of the now dry wash is lined in many places with aged Sycamore trees. Rock pile upon rock pile makes up the Mazatzal Range.

Braxton and his exhausted mount stumble out of the mountains into an open field with four dilapidated canvas army tents arranged around a blackened fire pit. A grizzled sunbaked looking man in worn-out jeans, a buckskin shirt, and a cavalry hat with the front brim flipped up sits in front of a tent.

"Friend, where you headin'," the man asks.

"Anywhere I can sit a spell and recover," says Braxton. "By the way, what is this place?"

"You're at old Camp Reno on Tonto Creek. The cavalry cleared out a while back. There is a small general store still operating over there." He points to the only building in the field. "With the Apaches rounded up on the reservations, army don't see no reason to keep troopers stationed here any more."

"Much obliged. I'll head over to the store." Braxton walks the short distance to the clapboard weather worn building. He ties his horse up to the hitching rail in front of the store, steps onto the covered porch, takes his hat off, and slaps at his shirt and pants attempting to knock some trail dirt from himself before stepping into the mercantile.

"You just ride over from the Verde?" asks the clerk sitting in a chair behind the counter.

"If you call climbing up and sliding down mountains with my horse, riding," answers Brax.

"Figured as much," says the clerk. "Looks like you're wearing about half a hill of dirt." The clerk leans back in his chair with his mule eared boots resting on the counter. His long johns shirt hangs half in and half out of worn-out jeans held up by wide suspenders. He holds a fly swatter and uses it with deadly accuracy on swarming flies.

His white hair, full white beard, and sun wrinkled weathered skin indicate he's spent a few days in places other than in a mercantile.

"When I left Phoenix, the farms and fields gave me no idea I would have to climb over all the rocks in the world to get to Tonto Basin," Brax flops into a chair beside the potbellied stove in the middle of the store.

"Oh, Pilgrim, we hain't got but a few piles of rocks around us. Shucks, this is nothin' compared to the Rim. You just keep driftin' north from here, and you're gonna see a sight that amazes. The Lord Almighty done gone and shoved the earth right straight up nigh on hundreds of feet. Wheweeee, it's got the rocks, biggin's and littlun's to boot. The top and sides of the Rim's covered with the most beautiful Ponderosa Pine trees your eyes have ever seen. It is mighty special country, that's for certain. But, what brings you draggin' your sorry self into my store?"

Braxton begins to recover after sitting a spell. "I'm here to check on a couple of families, the Tewksburys and Grahams. My Captain of the Arizona Rangers sent me here to find out what's going on between them."

"You be one of those ranger fellers, then?" the clerk asks.

"I am," answers Byron.

"Well, water yore horse and head back to Fort McDowell. You're only goin' to find grief here, and you ain't appreciated."

"Whoa, hold on," says Brax. "Why grief, and while I'm not surprised, why not appreciated?"

"Ranger, you're a dang fool fixin' to walk into the beginnin's of a blood feud. Both these families are gonna be gunnin' for each other and those that ride with them. There is no stoppin' feuds, and when you get between them, why, they'll both grind you up like sausage."

"What's the feud over?"

"Who knows? I heard tell cattle and land are the main issues."

"Yeah, cattle and land makes for problems lots of times."

"It didn't start out that way. Those folks came to the Basin as friends, lived right well with each other. Why, Tewksbury invited Graham into the Basin."

"What turned the good feelings sour?"

"A big rancher, Jim Stinson, knows he's the 'he bull' in the basin. Seems he is playin' both sides against the middle. All that's certain is that it's comin' to blood lettin' and it's gonna do it quick like. It's damned stupid, but ain't no accountin' for stupidity, is there?"

"Why not just deal with Jim Stinson?"

"He's got some kind of clout down in Globe or maybe Prescott. Any way, too big to tussle with right now."

"So, nobody's trying to stop this or get either side to listen to reason before it blows up in their faces?" Braxton is shocked.

"It's a blood feud. Don't you hear right well? Once it starts, it has to run itself out. There's no stoppin' it." The clerk drops both feet to the floor with a thud, and stands up. He is a short man, well built and muscular. His fly swatter continues to extract a heavy toll on the fly population in the store. "Come on out to the porch. Let me point out a few things to you."

Braxton draws himself up out of the chair and walks onto the porch with the clerk.

"Did you ever see any land more beautiful than this here Basin? From Tonto Creek across them Sierra Ancha mountains plumb almost to Cibecue Creek and from the Salt River to the Rim." The clerk stretches out his arms embracing the panorama of the lush Tonto Basin in front of him. "This land can support cattle forever and a day. Such land is bound to create troubles, greed, and bloodshed. You just have to acknowledge it and stay out of their way. It might be a short-lived feud, or it might go on till everybody's dead. But, gettin' in the middle of it only means you lose and accomplish nothing." The clerk folds his arms and continues to look across the Tonto Basin. It appears his gaze is lost in the distant mountains surrounding the gently rolling grass covered hills.

Braxton gets caught up in the beauty all the while remembering the harsh rocky land he traveled to arrive here.

"Okay, I'll water my horse, but can't leave without finding out what's going on."

"Suit yourself, Ranger. It's your funeral, but before you go proddin' into somethin' you can't do nothin' about, how's about you ride north of here?"

"Why would I do that? The problem's here."

"Yeah, yeah, I know'd that, but I hear'd tell of a mighty fine spot up under the Rim called Green Valley. If I was a young man, I'd take some time, follow Tonto Creek up to the Rim, and sashay west a mite to Green Valley. Just to see what real beauty is all about. Then, if you have to mix it up with the Tewksburys and Grahams, well, you'll have seen a slice of heaven before they kill you. What about it? Will you give it a go?"

Braxton looks at the clerk.

"You ever been there?" he asks.

"Nope, never have, but always had a hankerin' to see it," replies the clerk. "Folks has told me about it, and it might be something for you to see. Give me your grub sack, and I'll fix you up with some supplies to get you there."

Braxton considers the clerk's offer. He thinks about the Marshal's comments about Rangering being unpaid and unappreciated.

What the hell, I can take a few days to see something special and then come back and deal with the feud. Might be kinda fun to see the clerk's 'slice of heaven.'

Both men go back into the store and prepare Brax for a ride to the Rim.

12
THE RIM

It's been four day's ride to the north end of the Tonto Basin. Braxton travels beside Tonto Creek and leaves behind desert vegetation. The land changes into forests as he continues to climb in elevation.

Before him, a line on the horizon runs from east to west as far as he can see. It morphs from indistinguishable shapes into rocky canyons climbing skyward. Sandstone and limestone strata buttes in soft shades of red and cream soar overhead. Granite outcroppings grasp upward to snatch at passing clouds. The Rim.

His path carries him through forests of short, stunted, twisted Junipers and Piñons that transition to towering Ponderosa Pines. The ground is covered with pine needles, which shower down from the trees.

He pauses often and stares up at the escarpment rising before him. Countless eons of erosion and faulting etch jagged canyons and stone formations into the face of the Rim. Miles of pine forests cover the slopes and crown the mammoth stone wall. Braxton is amazed at this wonder of nature.

The old clerk at Reno wasn't kidding.

He periodically breaks out of the forest and moves into mountain meadows and open valleys cut by streams. The temperature cools, and the air seems cleaner to him. He rides into a sheltered forest valley at the base of the Rim. Carefully arranged log cabins spread around a large meadow with corrals, barns, and foraging cattle.

Braxton senses someone watching him. He approaches a nearby cabin and shouts, "Hello, the house. Is anybody there?"

All he hears are songbirds in the trees. He hollers again, "Hello, the house."

"What the Sam Hill you shoutin' about? You think we're deef?" A man with a felt hat pulled low on his brow, long brown hair hanging to his shoulders, dirty and worn bib overalls, a red plaid shirt and scuffed up brogans leans casually against a huge Ponderosa Pine close beside Braxton. He cocks both hammers of the shotgun he holds, and points its barrels at Brax.

"No, sir. Didn't think anything of the kind. Just didn't' want to get shot riding up on a place unannounced."

"Well, consider yourself announced," says the man. "What in tarnation do you want?"

"I'm looking for Green Valley," says Braxton. The meadow, cabins, Rim, and forest provide him a sense of serenity in spite of the aimed shotgun.

"Looks like you found it, stranger. Now, what do you want with it?"

"Mind if I step down; it's been a long ride. Left Reno a few days ago to look for this place." Brax stands in his stirrups and begins to swing his leg over his horse.

"Slow down, stranger."

Braxton pauses in mid-dismount.

"Mind tellin' me what you come lookin' for?" asks the shotgun man.

Brax resettles himself in his saddle. "I'm looking for a 'slice of heaven on earth'."

Shotgun man laughs out loud. "You been talkin' to Old Clute down to the mercantile in Reno, ain't you?"

"Well, yes sir. He did steer me this direction. Mind if I step down, now?"

"Suit yourself. Ain't nobody stoppin' you."

"I was a little edgy because of your shotgun. You mind pointing it away from me?" Brax swings off and stands beside his horse.

"Ain't loaded anyways, stranger." Shotgun man raises his weapon, points it away from Braxton, and pulls the trigger. A massive blast discharge shatters the mountain quiet and startles Brax's horse. He quickly tightens the reins and steadies the frightened animal.

"Well, I'll be. It 'pears Ma or Becka done slipped a load in this while I weren't payin' attention." The man shakes his head in disbelief.

Braxton is dumbfounded realizing he could have been filled with shot.

Shotgun man points the way to a cabin located mid-meadow.

"You can turn your horse loose with the others in the corral. Put your tack in the barn and find a soft spot in the loft. Supper should be ready soon. Ma will give a holler from the porch when vittles 'er ready." He walks off heading past the cabin and into the forest. Over his shoulder he hollars, "Name's Billy Jewel, and I suppose you know your own." A loud laugh echoes around him.

Damned fool could have blown me away, thinks an exasperated Braxton looking toward where Jewel points.

Brax walks to a single story log cabin with covered front and back porches, a large two-story log barn, and two corrals. Six horses nervously stomp around the corral as Brax unsaddles his mount and turns it loose in the enclosure. Slinging his saddle over a divider wall in the barn, he tosses his bedroll, saddlebags, and rifle into the hayloft.

Walking out in front of the barn, he watches chickens skitter around their coop. A water trough has a woodpile stacked next to it with an ax sunk into a large chunk of split wood. He sits on an upturned stump, pulls a packet of cigarette paper, and a pouch of Bull Durham tobacco from his jacket pocket. Cupping the paper between his thumb and finger, he shakes out fixings for a smoke, carefully rolls the paper around the tobacco, and licks the paper to close it. He retrieves a Lucifer from his pocket, lights up, and takes a slow drag. A steady cool breeze wafts down from the Rim and crosses the meadow. He looks again at the mammoth rock buttes and craggy outcroppings rising high above him. He's dwarfed by their height and size.

It's a quiet place, peaceful, and nice. "A 'piece of heaven'," He murmurs to himself.

As he watches the clouds drift across the top of the Rim, he notices a woman wearing moccasins step onto the back porch. With one arm wrapped around a porch post, she watches the clouds drift over the edge of the escarpment. Her lithesome, flowing, sensuous movement entrances Brax as she walks from post to post along the porch. Her blue gingham dress with short sleeves hugs her well-tanned, curvaceous, perfectly proportioned body. Brax gazes and enjoys running his eyes over her. Long blonde hair pulled back into a ponytail sways as she walks. Braxton is captivated. She turns suddenly and with her crystal clear blue eyes bores into Braxton's stare almost knocking him off the stump.

A middle-aged woman with greying hair and stooped shoulders steps out, grabs a dangling iron rod, and begins beating on a metal triangle. "Supper's waitin.' Come and git it." she hollers.

Braxton gathers his wits about him and walks toward the porch.

The woman stands suspiciously watching his approach.

"Who might you be? Are you another one of them drifters my no-good husband dragged home?" She stands with hands on her hips.

"Ma'am, I'm Braxton Bierman, an Arizona Ranger. I met your husband when I entered the valley earlier today. He met me with a shotgun."

With a look of alarm, she reaches out, grabs Brax, and begins turning him around. "I know'd that no-good would end up shootin' a lawman one day, I just know'd it. Oh Lordy, son. Do you got buckshot in ya? I forgot to tell that worthless man I loaded the gun the other day to do varmint huntin'. Turn around. Do ya got holes in ya?"

Braxton stops, takes the woman's hands, and eases her agitation.

"Ma'am, I'm fine. Your husband offered your barn and a home-cooked meal. How could I turn down either?" Braxton smiles at her.

She stops, grabs the corner of her apron, pulls it up to cover a smirk, and wipes it across her cheek.

"Well, Mr. Ranger, it ain't much, just biscuits and beef stew. Course we do put lots of vegetables in the stew. Grow 'em ourselves. You're welcome to join us, call me Maud." She looks across the meadow. "If that no-good man don't come when I slap the angle, he can just go without."

Maud turns to re-enter the cabin and abruptly stops. "Mr. Rangerman, I plumb forgot. I apologize." She points to the girl. "This's my one and only, and her name's Rebecca. We call her Becca. Come on over here girl and be civilized." The woman reaches over, grabs Rebecca by the arm, and moves her to face Braxton.

"Pleased to meet you, sir." Rebecca says.

"Likewise, Rebecca." Braxton replies. "I don't want to seem forward, but I noticed you looking at the Rim earlier. See anything in particular?"

"No, sir. I come out in the afternoon to watch the clouds swirl over the Rim. They're almost magical. I just like to see 'em."

"I like them as well. I agree they're magical." Brax smiles.

"Y'all come onto the porch and wash up, I'm setting the table right now. Come on. Hurry up." Maud rushes back into the house.

Across the meadow, Billy Jewel hurries their way.

"Rebecca, would you call me Brax. I'd be more comfortable and hope you will too."

"If you'll call me Becca." She smiles a huge smile. He's stunned by the warmth, friendliness, and openness the smile conveys. It swamps his emotions.

"Becca it is. Looks like your Pa doesn't want to be late for supper." Brax points over her shoulder.

She turns, looks, and laughs, a jingling, melodic, laugh that grabs at Brax's heart.

"Let's scrub up, and I'll get a fresh pan of water for him," she says.

Becca pumps a fresh pan of water, and they wait on the porch as Becca's father arrives.

"Good to see you've met Becca, lawman. She is the best thing that's happened in this valley. Becca, tell Ma we're ready to eat." He scrubs his hands and arms, and sprinkles a few drops of water on his face.

"Pa, she is ready and waiting on you. Now, let's just go in and not make a ruckus tonight at dinner. Be on your best behavior. We have company." She smiles at Braxton.

He grins back and steps toward the doorway.

Feral-like ebony eyes sweep the open meadow taking in every movement. Smoke climbs slowly skyward from the chimneys of the scattered cabins. The scent of evergreen engulfs the meadow. Na-tio-tish lies at the base of an ancient Ponderosa Pine. He knows his White Mountain Apache warriors conceal themselves in the forest. His survey of the meadow community assures him this will be another easy kill. Na-tio-tish waits. *We've killed many whites in the Tonto Basin, burned farms, killed their livestock, but more must die along the Mogollon to satisfy my warriors. I know the soldiers chase us.*

The glowing, glittering morning sun streaks rays of light between the silent sentinel trees into the meadow. With an upraised arm, he motions for warriors to move into the meadow as two braves rush up to him.

"Na-tio-tish, the pony soldiers and their scouts have cut our trail and now follow," says one of the men.

"How close are they?" Na-tio-tish questions.

"They are but three hours away and coming fast," the tall brave wearing a bloodied blue army jacket says.

"How many soldiers and their Apache-dog scouts?" Na-tio-tish asks in disgust.

Why would any of my people scout for our enemy? I do not understand. Those Apaches who do are without honor and will never be one with The People.

"It is a group they call a company. There are four Apaches scouts and the 'white devil' Sieber rides with them," the blue coat brave answers.

"It is time for the old white-eye scout, Sieber, to die," says Na-tio-tish.

"Yes. He knows too much about *The People*, and is too dangerous," agrees the other brave with black and whites stripes painted on his face.

"The meadow will be here; it goes nowhere. We will come back for it. Now, we ride to prepare an ambush." Na-tio-tish rises and moves toward where the horses are held. His warriors melt into the pine forest following him. *We will go to the top of the Rim. There are many canyons and gorges that provide good ambush spots.*

Mounting, they ride silently through the forest along the base of the Mogollon Rim away from Green Valley.

The rain runs under the slicker and down Brax's collar. He listens to the thunder roll through the clouds that cover the Rim. He shivers.

All three times I've ridden into the Basin I've been rained on. Seems to be a message hidden in there.

Brax ties his horse and pack mule under a tall Oak in a stand of trees surrounded by a sea of grass.

I've ridden this Basin from West to East and North to South during the last two months. Seen cattle and a few cowboys, but no signs of a feud. I wonder if Ol' Clute is just imaginin' things?

The rain slackens and Brax sees a single mounted cowboy slowly wending his way toward his clump of trees. The cowboy's slicker collar is turned up and his hat pulled down to shed as much rain as possible. The water sluices off the front and back of the hat brim. As he draws into shouting distance Brax gets his attention.

"Friend, come on over and get out of the drenchin'."

With a jerk, the cowboy glances around to find where the voice came from.

"Over here. Under the big Oak," says Brax.

Seeing Brax, the cowboy's hand slides to his right side and slips under his slicker.

"Who are you? Who you ridin' for? What'cha doin' on this range?"

"The longer you ask questions, the wetter you're gettin'. Pull up under this cover and I'll be happy to palaver with you," says Brax.

Carefully, the cowboy approaches the tree, dismounts, and ties his horse under the covering branches. He shakes the water from his slicker and doffs his hat. His right hand never leaves his side clutching a pistol under the slicker.

"Pull up a stump," says Brax. "Be a mite easier to sit if you were to let go of your firearm."

"I've a mind to when you tell me who you're ridin' for," says the cowboy.

"All right. I ride for the Territory of Arizona," says Brax.

"Who? What?"

"I'm an Arizona Ranger."

"Well, why didn't you say so in the first place?" The cowboy pulls his right hand out of his slicker and reaches over to shake Brax's hand. "Name, Rory. Rory Michaels. I ride for Mr. Graham."

"My name's Braxton. Glad to meet you Rory Michaels. Mind if I get a small fire goin' to cook up some coffee?"

"That'd be real fine, Mr. Ranger. What are you doin' out in this 'toad strangler'?"

"Let me get the coffee on and we can talk about that." Brax strikes up a fire from dry kindling under the trees. He grabs his smoke-stained coffee pot from the packhorse, pours water into it from his canteen, and tosses in two handfuls of ground Arbuckles. "We'll let that boil while we jaw-jack."

"That fire feels good. Kinda' knocks the chill," says Rory as he pulls his gloves off, unbuttons his slicker, and sits on a nearby tree stump. His jeans are soaked from the knees down, and his blue shirt is wet as well.

"I'm wandering out in the weather trying to find out about a feud between your boss and Mr. Tewksbury. You know of any troubles?" Brax watches the young cowboy's expression closely.

"Mr. Ranger, I've been ridin' for the Grahams for almost two years. There's bad blood between Mister Tewksbury and us. Some folks been hurt. On bad days it looks like all hell can break loose. On other days, we tolerate each other. What are you goin' to do about it?"

"Me? I'm not going to do anything right now. I've been out here off and on for over two months trying to find out what's happening. You're the first that I've talked with about it."

"Does this conversation make up your mind one way or another?" asks Rory.

"Nope. Only one point of view don't give me a whole lot to go on."

"That coffee is smellin' about right. Can we have some?"

"Here's a cup," says Brax knocking dust from a tin cup he passes to Rory. "Take some and leave some."

Rory pours a cup and reaches the pot over to pour Brax one as well.

"Here's mud in your eye," says Rory taking a careful sip.

"Plenty of mud all around us today," says Braxton with a quick laugh.

13
NEW BEGINNING

I've been in Green Valley for months, Braxton realizes as he wakes up. *I've helped round up stray cattle, mend fences, chop wood for Becca's home, and position myself as a general handyman. In between, I'm being a lawman? Why am I still here?*

He rolls over in his hayloft bed and knows the answer.

It's Becca. I don't want to be away from her. What's going on with me? Every possible minute of the day I'm around her. We eat together, ride together, walk together, talk together, and sit on the porch together. Last night, we sat together on the back porch kissing, and when the idea of marriage came up, she didn't object.

He recalls the gentleness of the initial kiss, Becca's soft lips. His lips lingering close to

Becca's for the second, third, and more kisses. Yes, they did talk seriously of marriage.

If this isn't for better or worse, nothing is; I've got to make certain she'll have me, and, if she agrees, then talk with her parents. Real soon, I need to let Captain Jackson know I can't continue to ride the territory. Today is the day.

He shakes loose hay from his long johns, puts on his shirt and jeans, tugs on his boots, hangs his legs over the edge of the loft, and jumps down. *This morning is as good a time as ever to bring things to a head.*

He walks out of the barn toward the back porch and spots Becca emptying a pan of water from the washstand. She wears a red short-sleeved dress that hangs to her knees and tall booted Apache moccasins. Her blonde hair tied into two ponytails hangs on either side of her head. He walks to her and wraps his arms around her from behind. Laying his chin on her shoulder he whispers, "Do you love me?"

Becca smiles as she turns around in his arms. "Do you think any man can handle me this way unless I love him?"

"Oh, no. I'm sure you are more than able to deal with anyone wrestling you around." Brax raises his hands in mock defense. Kneeling, Brax takes Becca's hands in his. "I just need to know if you love me enough to really marry me?"

Throwing her arms around Braxton's neck, Becca whispers to him, "It's sure taken you long enough to ask. I didn't know if I was goin' to have to hogtie you and do the askin'." She stands with tears in her eyes. "Yes, you Arizona Ranger, I will marry you."

Braxton rises and looks at her solemnly, "What if I wasn't a Ranger? Would you still marry me?"

"Sometimes men are really thickheaded," Becca says. "Braxton Bierman, I'm marryin' YOU. Whatever you are, or wherever you go, we will do it together."

Braxton looks at his lovely woman and realizes his life will never be the same from this day forward. He smiles, places both hands on her shoulders, and says, "Where's your pa? I got work to do."

"You know he's on the front porch. I imagine what you've got to say won't come as any surprise to him, but go get it done."

Braxton steps through the doorway, passes through the kitchen and living area, and finds Maud and Billy Jewel on the bench on the porch.

Walking out he stops in front of them.

"Good morning."

Maud nods and Billy responds, "Hope ya slept well."

"Yes, I did. Folks, Becca and I've been talking, and we've agreed; well, I asked and she said, yes; I mean, I need to ask your blessing to marry your daughter." Braxton stands ramrod straight as he waits for their reply.

Bill Jewel looks up from whittling on a small stick. "It's about time, Son. I was beginnin' to think I was goin' to need my shotgun to get you to make the move."

"No shotgun necessary," replies Brax with a smile.

"I do need to know how you're plannin' on takin' care of our Becca. You're a Ranger and libel to become kilt." Billy's solemn eyes stare at Braxton.

"Yes. That's always a possibility. I don't have much to my name, that's a fact. What I do promise is to love her and give my life to her. That's the best I can offer." Brax returns the stare.

"Well, hell, Son, that's all I offered her Momma, and look what we's got now." Billy sits back on the bench with a loud, long laugh. "You'll do, Son. You'll do."

Maud looks at him with tears in her eyes, "She's my one and only. You're goin' to take good care of her, right?"

"Maud, she is my life, and I'd kill myself before I'd allow any hurt come to her."

"Well, get on with things, Son. We don't have no church or parson round about here, and I know Becca's firm on gittin' married in a church. Nearest honest to God one is down to Camp Verde. Y'all goin' to have to ride there to get hitched." Bill Jewel looks at Braxton.

"If it's all right with both of you, then that's what we'll do. I'll let Becca know and we can leave in the morning, right?" Braxton looks at the Jewels expectantly.

Billy looks at Maud, nods, then, he reaches over and shakes Brax's hand.

"Thank you," says Braxton.

"Shucks, Son, it's us thankin' you. We been rightly worried about our girl's life out here under the Tonto Rim. Then out of the clear blue, you ride into this valley and her life. Kinda like it's meant to be. Now, get. Go get ready and both of you ride tomorrow. Go with our blessing." He turns to Maud and helps her stand. "Come on, Old Girl, you can blubber in the house and keep the neighbors in the close by cabins wonderin' what's happenin'. We'll tell them directly."

Braxton finds Becca just inside the door smiling through the tears that run down her cheeks and drip off her chin.

"You spend time with your folks. I'm going to check over our horses, get my gear ready, and if you will put your things on the back porch, I'll get yours ready as well. We'll ride to Camp Verde in the morning. I love you." He takes Becca in his arms, kisses and releases her, walks past her, and out the back door.

I've got another life I need to provide for, and Captain Jackson needs to be told. The closest telegraph is in Verde.

This is the place. The canyon narrows near the top, the trail is steep and turns sharp to the right, it blocks the view to those behind, and there is cover for my warriors to hide behind. It is the right place. Now, we ambush the pony soldiers. They are close and my braves will avenge many lives.

Na-tio-tish quickly arranges the placement of his men in their ambush location. He sees they line one side of the canyon and have an open path of escape once the ambush is sprung.

We will sell our lives at great expense, if necessary, but our enemy will pay dearly. This is where we'll wait for those who stalk us.

Brax sits on his mount beside the back porch waiting for Becca to join him. Both horses are saddled and packed for the ride to Camp Verde. It is not a long ride, but traversing the Rim always has a certain amount of danger. He has also heard from some families in Green Meadow that Apaches raid near by. The morning air is clear and crisp, and smells of pine as the sun creeps over the tops of the trees surrounding the meadow.

It's a beautiful dawn below the Mogollon Rim.

Becca walks onto the porch in well-worn jeans, a red plaid, long-sleeve shirt, a denim jacket, brown mule eared boots, and a high crowned wide-brimmed rancher's hat. She hugs her mother and father, and then climbs onto her horse. She and Brax wave to her parents before riding across the meadow and into the forest beyond.

"I think we'll ride up to Pine and over to Strawberry on top of the Rim. It means we climb to the top, but the area below the Rim is really rugged ground to cover. Going up, over, and then down to Camp Verde can make for a quicker and easier trip," says Braxton.

"That's fine with me," says Becca. "I always like the view from the top of the Rim. The forest looks like a green blanket coverin' all the mountains, valleys, and hills."

"You've got quite an eye for landscape, the world seems to go forever from up there," Braxton says with a smile.

During the next few hours, they negotiate a moderately steep trail that climbs upward and weaves back and forth to traverse canyon walls. The ride changes and the trail levels out as Brax and Becca near the little village of Pine. Stopping their horses for a breather, they dismount and walk to the edge of a promontory. Before them lies the landscape of central Arizona Territory. Green changes to brown and gray where the Sonora Desert reaches up from southern Arizona. Wind whispers through the pines around them and the huge trees sway gently.

"Way over there, past all those mountains is Phoenix." Brax points out the Mazatzal Mountains. "Back that way is the Tonto Basin." He gestures to his left below the Rim. "Down that way is Tucson; can't see it from here." His hand points towards the south.

"I never get enough of seeing this. God created a special place when he made the Rim," says Becca.

"You know, the Almighty made something special in you, too." Brax hugs Becca and they kiss a long, soft, lingering kiss. "I never get enough of seeing you." He kisses her again.

"I can get real used to you, Braxton Bierman." Becca sighs laying her head against his chest.

"I hate to leave this moment, but we have a ways to go." Braxton helps Becca mount and steps into his saddle.

They ride through the village of Pine and turn their horses uphill again for the short climb to the top of the Rim.

Riding into the settlement of Strawberry, they find a café. The signboard out front reads Abigail's Fine Food. They dismount, tie their horses to a hitching rail, and enter.

Brax casts a look around. The cafe is a wood-frame building, one room with four tables and mismatched chairs. A potbelly stove sits in the middle of the room in a sandbox base. An open doorway leads to a kitchen in back. The only windows are in the front of the building on either side of the doorway. A couple of cowhands sit at one table talking to a middle-aged woman.

Brax and Becca take a seat by the window.

The woman stops her conversation and walks over to them. "Y'all are strangers around here. Don't think I've ever seen you before. I'm Abigail." She stands with one hand in her apron pocket and the other on her hip.

"Yes, we're from under the Rim in Green Valley. My pa's been through here. You may know him, William Jewel?" Becca watches Abigail's face.

"You, Billy Jewel's daughter? Why sure, Billy's been by here often. He's always out running down them mountain lions. You know, one of these days a big one's gonna turn and get that man." The lady laughs raucously enjoying her own humor. "Course, he ain't about to let it happen. Well, well, Billy's little girl. What's your name, honey?"

"I'm Rebecca Jewel, and this is my fiancé Braxton Bierman. We're on our way to Camp Verde to get married." Becca smiles at the woman.

"Well, do say. Gettin' married. Let me whip up something special for the both of you; won't take no time a'tall. But, you said Camp Verde, right? Them cow swishers over there just told me Apaches are close by Verde, somewhere on top of the rim over round Backer's Butte. You'd best talk with them about a better way of getting' there so to avoid any troubles. Let me bring you today's special and a treat." She rushes into the back room and shouts orders.

"I'm going to talk with those riders." Brax stands and walks over where both cowhands look up at him.

"Gents, hear you know something about Apaches hereabouts?"

"Friend, we know the Army has four or five companies coming together over in the vicinity of Backer's Butte. I'm hopin' they finally catch up with that murderin' Apache, Na-tio-tish. 'Bout time they killed that one," the freckled face rider says.

"Yeah, Al Sieber got his Apache scouts working overtime to bring this renegade to ground. He's out there with one of the companies

145

chasing them right now," the other skinny, blond-haired rider adds.

"You see any trouble getting to Camp Verde from here?" asks Brax.

"No, friend. You just wind your way down Fossil Creek. You should be away from any trouble. Ain't no way any Apache could stage an ambush on Fossil Creek. It's too steep and rugged to pull off any shenanigans. Just keep your footing, give your horse its head, and hang on to your saddle horn," he says and laughs. "It's all downhill from here."

"Thanks, Men. I appreciate the information." Brax nods and returns to his table.

"What'd they have to say?" asks Becca once Brax is seated.

"They said we should follow Fossil Creek into Verde. It's a steep trail, doable, but difficult. I'd planned to take Clear Creek and follow through the canyons, but guess we'll do Fossil Creek instead." Brax sees Abigail headed toward them with plates of steaming food, biscuits, and a pot of coffee. On the tray sits a muffin with a lit candle in it.

"Let's eat."

A lone Apache scout scrambles down a rocky embankment to stop Al Sieber and another scout.

"I see warriors along the upper gorge of Clear Creek near the top of Rim," says the raven black haired Apache scout. His red silk headband shimmers in the sunlight.

"Any idea how many?" asks Sieber.

"Many, maybe fifty."

"Go back and see but don't be seen. I'll let the Lieutenant know."

"Bueno, Sieber." The scout nods and runs up the canyon.

Ol' Na-tio-tish is waitin' fer us. Well, it's time to turn the tables.

Al Sieber turns his horse down the canyon to intercept the approaching troopers.

Na-tio-tish knows his ambush is lost when dismounted cavalry attack both ends of the line of warriors he's placed along one side of the gorge. The few mounted soldiers entering the canyon are a diversion. He knows the ambushers have become the ambushed.

This perfect spot to destroy my enemy becomes a killing ground of my warriors.

There are many more pony soldiers than one company, and the enemy seems to keep coming.

Rifle fire increases from across the gorge and pins his men down. Screams and shouts echo from the canyon walls. He watches in frustration, unable to effectively do anything, or escape until a rifle round buries itself in his chest. Then he worries no more.

Brax wakes up from a cool night's sleep outside of Strawberry, builds the fire, and starts coffee brewing. Becca rouses, stretches, and props on one elbow.

"Got kind of chilly last night. I had to drag the horse blanket on top of me," she says. "You sleep okay? I saw you sitting outside the fire's light beside a tree watching the night."

"Old habit, my Beauty. It's kept me alive for a while. Besides, I can nod in the saddle later today if I need to. Coffee is cookin', be ready in a minute. Also got some of Abigail's biscuits from yesterday. Can't go wrong with good biscuits." Brax rises up from beside the fire.

"I'll remember 'you can't go wrong with good biscuits.'" Becca gathers the blankets and shakes them out, then carefully places them on the ground again to roll into their bedrolls. She brushes aside pine needles as she works. Gathering the blankets, she steps over and lays them on their saddles.

"Coffee's ready," Brax pours two tin cups and hands one to Becca along with the cold biscuits wrapped in a bandana.

Wind whispers through the pines as a morning breeze sweeps across the Rim, drops over the edge into the valleys, and Camp Verde, one thousand feet below.

14
COWBOYS

Byron steps onto the porch of the Hooker ranch house. Guillo follows. The front door is open, and they enter a hallway with no exterior windows. He looks left and right down the empty hall. Across from them another open door leads to a patio. Byron steps through and into an oasis. He's in the midst of a lovely garden totally surrounded by the *hacienda*. Along the roof ridges are parapets that allow men to position themselves for defense. They're inside a fort.

"Gentlemen, welcome to my home," says Hooker. "I found it years ago. Originally, it was a Spanish *hacienda*. The Apaches burnt it down, and when I found this valley with the remains of the house, I restored it to its original appearance. I took the liberty to name it Sierra Bonita after the beautiful nearby mountains. Welcome, welcome; make yourselves at home."

Henry Hooker takes a seat at a table in the middle of the patio and points toward open chairs. A servant enters with a tray holding a pitcher of water and carafe of a caramel colored liquid. Glasses rattle on the tray as he sits it on the table.

"Thank you, Franciso," says Hooker to the departing servant. "Now, what brings you gentlemen to rustle stock from my spread?" Hooker folds his arms across his chest.

Byron grins and says, "First, Mr. Hooker, we didn't rustle anything from you or anyone; and second, if we had, you'd have never caught us."

"Touché, Mr. Bierman. I like a fella with spunk. That's what's kept me out here in this territory when others said I should just give up and ride out of here."

Guillo leans over to Byron and whispers, "What he mean, toochy?"

Byron grins at Guillo and says, "Tell you later, *Tio*."

"It appears you and my good friend John H. Slaughter pulled a good one on me in regards to the government cattle contract." Hooker sits back in his chair. "I knew John H. couldn't drive enough stock up from Mexico fast enough to supply the army's needs. Then up jumps your herd in San Simon. Quite a move. Yes sir. Quite a move. Believe me, I won't be surprised again."

"Well, Mr. Hooker, we're just businessmen like you, and when John H. made us an offer, well, we had to go with it. No hard feelings?" Byron asks.

"Oh, hell no. No hard feelings at all. I admire y'alls pluck. Given a similar situation, I'd done the same thing. Enjoy the contract. I aim to get it back."

"We will, Mr. Hooker, and we intend to keep it." Byron takes his hat off and lays it on the table.

"How are you going to increase your herd on San Simon land? Vegetation is sparse and water is even less. I don't see how you can expand without serious overgrazing, and that puts everything into jeopardy. Have you given that any thought?" Hooker steeples his fingers together.

"It's a great point, Mr. Hooker. In order to grow the herd, we're going to have to keep it near the Gila River end of the valley. There's grass and water available to sustain growth. On the south end we will keep a herd sized to fit the land. We've dug wells and built stone tanks for the south herd." Byron watches for Hooker's reaction.

"You've thought this through. Good. I like to work with someone who has planning as part of his operation. Glad you're in the Territory. Now, to more pressing problems...the Cowboys," says Hooker.

"John H. said something about them," says Byron. "Those riders today were Cowboys, I take it?"

"From the description of the horse you saw, I surmise they are working my south pastures. I'm sending Clint and my riders south to flush them out and drive them off my range. That might mean they show up on yours." Hooker points at Byron.

"Why should they come after us?" asks Guillo.

"Why do snakes go after prairie dogs? Because they're there, my friend." says Hooker. "John Slaughter has done a great job with the Cowboys and shoots them on sight. He's tied up more than he'll admit with Mexican bandits right now. With most of his herd in Mexico, he has to invest time there. The Cowboys hit with impunity on both sides of the border. Robbing, rustling, and killing are their way. Unless you're prepared, you become their victim. You'll do good to be ready." Hooker nods his head in conclusion.

"So, do you keep riders on your range with orders to shoot to kill if they see Cowboys?" Byron asks.

"Not yet, but coming close to that is my next step," replies Hooker. "I've built my ranch up from nothing, fought more than my share of Apaches to keep it, dealt with con men and the government to hold it, and by the eternal, I'm not about to lose it to murdering rustlers." Hooker's voice grows louder as he speaks.

"Sounds like they've pinched a nerve, Mr. Hooker," says Byron.

"Son, you have no idea," Hooker abruptly stands, turns around, and faces Byron and Guillo. "Gentlemen, I've got a little *fiesta* planned for this evening. You're welcome to join us over by the bunkhouses. Throw your gear on an unclaimed bed and enjoy our hospitality."

"Well, it's too late to ride back to Maley, so we accept your offer." Byron nods.

Hooker calls a servant to lead Byron and Guillo to the bunkhouses. Byron picks up his hat from the table. "We appreciate your offer Mister Hooker."

"It's my pleasure gentlemen."

With the servant, Byron and Guillo leave the *hacienda*.

Crossing the area between the main house and the bunkhouse, Byron sees a self- contained community. Barns, stables, a blacksmith forge, hay storage, and a dozen smaller casas surround the Hooker's house.

Arriving at a bunkhouse, they find their saddlebags, rifles, and sleeping rolls have already been placed on open bunks.

"Always like to deal with someone who reads my mind," says Byron.

Stepping outside onto the porch, they pour a basin of water from a pitcher to wash away the trail dust from their hands and face.

In front of the bunkhouse, they see a side of beef slowly roasting over an open fire. Ranch hands walk around and casually talk among themselves. Some have carried chairs out of the dining hall and sit around the fire.

"Sorry to treat you like we did today." Clint walks up to Byron. "Didn't know who you were and not taking any chances. You understand, right?"

"Don't worry. No harm done. Would have acted the same way myself." Byron rolls down and buttons his shirtsleeves. He finds a huge log lying in the open plaza and sits down. "Tell me about the Cowboy problem, will you?"

Clint sits down beside Byron. "Sure. We've got an active bunch of outlaws and rustlers working over the entire southeast corner of Arizona Territory. We know Ike Clanton and Curly Bill Brocius lead a group operating from Tombstone. Them and the Earps had it out a while back, and they took to hiding out for a while. Most think they just went to Mexico. They steal what they want and kill anybody who gets in the way. That pretty much sums it up."

"Have you dealt with them on Hooker's spread?" Byron glances at the beef roasting over the fire.

"Not until recently," answers Clint. "I think the Earps and John Slaughter are taking some starch out of 'em. I also heard an Arizona Ranger company began riding the border flushing the lowlifes out into the open. Most don't make it back into hiding, if you get my drift." Clint gives a quick wink.

"Are your men fixin' to reduce the number of Cowboys if they show up here?" Byron inquires.

"Yes, sir. My boys and me plan on increasing the body count. Only one way to end their rustlin' and killin', and that's to kill them first."

Clint nods his head, rises, and joins a group of men.

Families of many ranch hands drift in to join the festivities. Tables are brought from the dining hall and set up outside. Foodstuff starts to appear on the tables. Guillo wanders over and begins sampling. Those cooking the beef give a shout about being close to time to eat. Byron joins the line of people filling their plates.

Returning to the log, he begins chowing down on fresh tamales and enchiladas. Guillo walks over gnawing on beef ribs.

Henry Hooker strolls into the group smiling and waving to cowhands and families around the fire. He nods to Byron and Guillo.

Mexican ranch hands bring out guitars and start to play. Their songs are fast and exciting. Byron likes the music and thinks back to his uncle's *vaqueros'* celebrations at the *hacienda* in Animas. He watches Guillo start to sway with the music, join in the singing, and move with the rhythms.

From around a nearby building steps a young woman. She moves into the center of the open area and slowly begins a dance to the music of the guitars. The musicians notice her and change their rhythm to match her dancing. Her movements mesmerize Byron. The long flowered skirt clings to her body and below her knees it swirls as she spins. Her white cotton short-sleeved top is bunched together at the waist and tied with a crimson scarf. Her flowing black hair sparkles in the waning sunlight. Her high cheekbones, straight nose, and pouting lips are lost to her penetrating onyx eyes. Byron is captivated.

The music increases in rhythm and tempo, and the woman twirls around the gathering. Byron watches her arms reach out and up. He's lost in the sensuality and intensity of the moment. Suddenly the music stops.

She collapses to the ground.

There's a momentary pause and then thunderous applause. Byron lunges forward to help her to her feet. She reaches up and grabs his hand. Holding on to her longer than necessary, he gazes into her soft, hypnotic ebony eyes.

The young dancer stares at Byron. "*Muchas gracias, Señor.* You are new here. What is your name?"

"Byron."

She smiles. "I am Felina."

"Do you live on *Señor* Hooker's *rancho*?"

"Oh, no, Byron. *Mi hermano* works for *Hacendado* Hooker. I live in Solomonville and visit *mi familia* from time to time." She brushes off her skirt and straightens her blouse.

"Is your brother in the crowd?" asks Byron.

"*Si.* He is the *hombre* who turns the beef over the fire."

Byron looks at a short dark haired fully mustached *vaquero* talking and laughing as he minds the slowly turning meat on the spit.

Others from the crowd come by and offer their thanks to Felina for her dance. Small children run and hug her then spin away in swirls of their own. She smiles, chats, and laughs with all who stop to talk with her.

Musicians begin to play again and couples start dancing. A *vaquero* walks over and asks Felina to dance. With a smile she takes his arm and begins swirling around with him. Shortly, Hooker walks over, taps the *vaquero* on the shoulder, and replaces him as Felina's dance partner.

The music's rhythm increases and Hooker stops in front of Byron. He gestures for him to take his place. Felina stands smirking and invites his embrace. Nervously, Byron places his hand around her waist and taking her other hand in his, whirls with the other dancing couples. Her laughter is infectious. He finds himself smiling and laughing along with her.

Too soon the music stops.

Felina's friends surround her to express appreciation for her dancing. Byron is envious of those who take her attention away, but steps aside and wanders off to sit by Guillo.

"So, what you think?" Guillo nods toward Felina.

"I think she's tremendous, beautiful, and marvelous," sighs Byron.

"*Ay, yi-yi*. You have it bad *Sobrino,* nephew," Guillo shakes his head. "I can tell you of a time in Socorro when another *amigo* crashed very hard over a *señorita*. It is not a pretty story and ends when *tres muy malo hermanos*, bad brothers, of the *señorita* wanted to carve some pieces off of me."

"I know the story, *Tio*. Pa always liked to tell it. Ma got a kick out of the three brothers as well," says Byron. "But, this is different."

"It's not so different." Guillo smiles a knowing smile and tosses a stick towards the fire. "It's still a man and a woman." Standing, he moves to a group of ranch hands beginning a card game under some Sycamore trees.

The *fandango* continues into the night. Henry Hooker leaves for the main house after the sun goes down. Food is consumed all evening. After children are put to bed, the ranch hands bring out the liquor and pass bottles around.

"Just a reminder," shouts Clint above the chatter and noise. "Morning riders replace the 'night hawks' at daybreak." Cowpunchers nod their heads and nobody misses a beat with the party. Clint shrugs and sits down with his group of men.

Byron continues watching the festivities. He sees Felina move from group to group. She stops periodically and waves at him. He waves in return.

How do I see her again?

She said Solomonville. Can I go there to see her?

I forgot her brother's name. Did I get it? Will I recognize him when I see him?

I can't let her enter my life and leave again.

Two *vaqueros* walk over and sit beside Byron on the log. A jug is offered; he upends it and drinks deep.

My head hurts, he thinks, and remembers the shared jug of Mescal.

The pounding of hooves jerks Byron awake. Outside the bunkhouse a cloud of dust settles as fifteen riders gallop past toward the main gate to replace the 'night hawk' cowhands guarding the herds.

Crusted eyes seem locked shut as he rubs his hands across his face. *I just went to sleep. How did the night pass so quickly?* He looks around the bunkhouse, sees Guillo, and realizes they are the only ones still in their bunks. A whiff of coffee drifts through the open bunkhouse door.

Dragging out of bed, he slides into his boots, straightens up his shirt, walks onto the porch, pours a pan of fresh water to wash his face, and runs wet hands through his hair. He steps into the doorway and sees Guillo sitting on the edge of his bunk.

"Did you win or lose last night? Do we still have a ranch to go home to?" he asks.

"*Compañero*, the cards they start so good and then they becomes *muy malo* monsters. I hope you kept some monies to get us home because I have *no mas dinero.* I am hungry enough to eat the entire south end of a northbound cow. Let's find the cookhouse. I can smell it. *Frijoles, tortillas, chorizo,* and *huevos* all calls my name. *Si?*" Guillo steps onto the porch and splashes water on his face from the pan. Together they head for the cookhouse.

Clint rides up to the porch of the main house where Henry Hooker, Guillo, and Byron stand.

"Thanks for stopping by. Hope our hospitality is appreciated. My folks like to party from time to time and I don't discourage it," says Hooker. "It makes for a tighter family feel. Our work is tough enough and throwing a fandango from time to time makes everyone happier about working here."

"Mr. Hooker, I agree with your philosophy and am going to implement something like it on the B-Z," says Byron with a smile.

"You boys want some advice?" asks Hooker.

"Well, we've eaten your food and drank your whiskey, so the least we can do is listen to your advice," says Byron.

"Sell out now. Find a good buyer, and sell. San Simon can't support the kind of herd you're fixin' to run. It has nothin' to do with y'all. It's just the land and lack of surface water. If we hit a drought year, and we have them, you'll be left begging."

"Mr. Hooker, I value your advice and appreciate your hospitality, but you have to know, we run cattle. Given your knowledge of the Territory, we will be judicious in the way we handle our land and herd. I want to count on your friendship and offer ours in return. You're a good neighbor." Byron offers his right hand to Hooker.

"Well, at least consider this, I've been cross breeding blood lines of livestock to strengthen my herds for a while. My scraggly Texas longhorns can whip their weight in predators from grizzly bears to mountain lions, but I'm wantin' to raise better beef cattle. I'm importing Herefords to build my herd. They make better stockyard cattle as well as free range. Would you be open to do the same?" Hooker smiles and shakes Byron's right hand and says, "Give it some thought, boys. Friends and neighbors we are."

Byron and Guillo untie their horses from the hitching post, mount, wave at Hooker, and ride out of the *hacienda* compound with Clint.

"You can double back through Maley as you did on your ride to get here, or you can go a little longer route up to Fort Grant and go through the gap in the Pinaleno Range into San Simon Valley close to Solomonville. I do know Felina headed home this morning in a single horse *carreta*. She may like some company." Clint sits on his horse with his arms folded across the horn smiling at Byron.

Byron blushes under Clint's stare and replies, "Ain't seen that end of your valley yet, so might be worth a look. Thanks for everything, Clint. Come see us at the B-Z."

"May do that sometime, Neighbor. Ride careful. Don't forget about the Cowboys on this range. Tried to warn Felina this morning but she's hardheaded and didn't listen. *Hasta luego, amigos.*" He turns and rides back into the compound.

"Hey, *Sobrino*, the *Señorita* has nobody to protect her and Cowboys may be around. We should hurry, No?" Guillo grins at Byron.

"*Vámonos*, you old *bandito*. Let's go protect her." Byron spurs his horse into a lope as they ride away from Hooker's *rancho*.

Byron didn't think Felina could be far ahead but it appears her single horse rig makes good time on the well-traveled road to Fort Grant. Riding the road Byron is amazed at the belly deep grass that covers the valley. It is surprising what a little water can do to this land. Sulphur Springs Valley has the water and San Simon doesn't. Hooker's words sink into Byron's subconscious as he ponders this luxurious landscape.

Riding up a slight rise in the road, he sees figures in the distance move rapidly along.

"There she is," he says to Guillo as he motions forward.

Guillo quickly redirects his focus to the right. He points at four horsemen riding rapidly to intercept Felina's cart. Byron quickly judges their distance to be a little closer than the riders.

He spurs his horse into a gallop and knows Guillo is right behind him.

Felina seems oblivious to anyone else near her cart. As he closes the gap, he hears her singing a tune. A quick glance to his right, confirms that the riders see Guillo and him race toward Felina.

Suddenly the sound of gunfire reaches him. Riding down into a swale and back up they catch

Felina. She is huddled in the bottom of her cart lashing at her horse to run faster.

Byron rides hard past the cart and sees fear flash in Felina's eyes. He grabs the lead on the cart's horse and turns it quickly into another low swale beside the road. He slides quickly from his saddle and pulls his rifle as he dismounts. He reaches over the cart, shoves Felina down to the bottom, and steadies his rifle on the edge of the now still *carreta*.

The four riders thunder over the edge of the swale, their forward momentum throws them straight towards the cart. Byron cuts loose with his Winchester, levers another round, fires, levers, fires, jacks the lever again and fires. Beside him, he sees Guillo does the same thing from the other side of the cart.

Two horses tumble down onto the ground and begin thrashing around violently. One of the riders kicks loose from his saddle and tosses through the air landing with a sickening thud. The other rider goes down with his horse. The third horse jumps clear of Byron and charges across the grassy pasture, its rider leans forward in his saddle and lies against his horse's neck. He is quickly out of rifle range. The last rider tries to pull up and turn his horse. He manages to spin broadside of the cart when Byron cuts loose with his Winchester. The rider draws a bead on Byron with his Colt when he suddenly lurches up and out of the saddle as Byron's .45 slug slams into him. With no rider, the buckskin horse turns and trots slowly into the open plain.

Byron looks at his shirt and notices a bullet hole through the side. The slug missed him by a fraction of an inch. Taking off his hat, he sees another bullet hole shot through the crown. Guillo holds his arm awkwardly and Byron sees blood stains his sleeve from a hole in his upper right arm. Felina slowly rises from the bottom of the *carreta*.

"That was too close, *Sobrino*," says Guillo. Byron ties his bandana tightly around Guillo's arm.

"Yep. Another minute and we would all have been ground up under their hooves and full of lead," agrees Byron.

"Why would they do this," asks Felina in a small shaky voice. "I do not even know them."

"I'd say you're a victim of opportunity," Byron offers.

Guillo moves over to the wounded horse and shoots the thrashing animal in the head. Beside it lies a Cowboy, shot in the forehead.

Byron moves to the Cowboy thrown from his horse that landed hard in front of the cart. Blood seeps out of his mouth, both arms lie stretched out at awkward angles and he blinks at Byron.

"Who are you?" he whispers as blood bubbles on his lips.

"Bierman," says Byron. "Why were you chasing the cart?"

"Lookin' for a good time." He tries to smile and grimaces.

"Too bad, Cowboy. Your bad luck," replies Byron.

His eyes close and a long sigh escapes between his lips.

Byron moves carefully through the grass to the third Cowboy.

He finds him on his back; a small entry wound of the .45 slug is in the middle of his chest. Byron knows the upper half of his back is probably blown away from the exit of the bullet. He stares at Byron and watches as he moves around to check for firearms.

"You know you're a dead man, don't you," responds the mortally wounded Cowboy.

Byron almost laughs as he thinks of a sick reply about 'it takes one to know one.' Instead he kneels to look at the man. "Why," he asks.

"Ike will find you and kill you," the Cowboy replies.

"Ike who?" asks Byron.

"Ike will kill you." the dying man almost shrieks at Byron.

Blood bubbles and boils from his mouth as he gasps and lies still staring at the sky.

"What did him say?" Guillo walks quickly up to Byron.

"Somebody called Ike is going to kill me," says Byron.

"*Sobrino*, Mr. Hooker, he talks about someone named Ike, No? *Si*, a *muy malo hombre*, Ike Clanton. Yes? Is this the Ike him means?" asks Guillo.

Byron watches the speck of the fourth rider vanishing on the horizon.

15
CAMP VERDE

From the hotel front porch, Braxton considers the distant Rim and decides from here it doesn't look like a bad ride. From the saddle seat he gripped coming down, he knows it is a ride he doesn't want to make more than once. An uncontrolled shiver rattles through him.

One step away from eternity, just one step. That's what I experienced coming down Fossil Creek trail. It's beyond my better judgment I'd allow my life to be put in such a position. I know a lawman's job has risks, but to balance my life on the back of a downhill horse begging to arrive at the bottom alive doesn't make good sense.

He ponders on how situations beyond your control simply slip up and snatch life away.

Brax and Becca's ride, from Strawberry on top of the Rim, begins as a gently sloping downhill trail following Fossil Creek. Soon, the creek begins to change into waterfalls that plummet over the edge of the Rim and dash to the rocks below. The trail they ride turns into a steep slide, which hangs them over the edge of gaping canyons hundreds of feet deep. The trail switchbacks across the cliff face as it winds its way downward attempting to follow the creek. At every hairpin turn, canyons open up below Brax and Becca in sheer vertical drops. Fossil Creek continues to descend vertically in splendid waterfalls that pour into crystal pools, only to overflow and spill downward again collecting in other pools below.

Braxton leans back in his saddle, gives up his grip on the reins, and allows the horse to make safe, judicious steps. He braces himself by thrusting his stirrups forward over the horse's withers. His grip on the saddle horn is white knuckled. Glancing behind, he sees Becca recline as well and appears to enjoy the ride.

The trail is rocky at best and in many spots the gravelly scree is treacherous ground for the horses. Stepping on loose stones, many times the horses are forced to crouch on their haunches as they slide on the rolling rocks. Each time, Braxton grips the saddle to keep from shifting his weight. He fears he might overbalance his horse. He glances at the rocky projections, and craggy outcroppings that wait for them in the canyons below.

On flat ground he stops the horses for a breather. He needs one as well. Becca takes the opportunity to fish around in the creek pools for flotsam washed down from above. The stones she collects are covered with mineral deposits and look fossilized.

Resuming their ride, the hazardous descent continues. Reaching the bottom of the Rim, Braxton and Becca dismount and lead their horses downstream along Fossil Creek. In a crystal blue pool, they water the horses and hobble them, then turn them loose to graze in the tender grasses along the creek. They walk back up the creek, find another pool, strip to their long johns, and plunge into the water. Swimming and splashing around, they climb out onto flat stones along the bank to soak up the soft drying sunlight. Braxton stares at Becca stretched out on the rock. The wet, skintight long johns do nothing to disguise her femininity. He shuts his eyes to soak up the sunshine and his imagination runs rampant. He rolls onto his stomach to curb his rising desire.

The terror of the downhill ride silently and quickly oozes from his mind. Refreshed and dried, they dress, saddle, and complete their ride into Camp Verde.

Through the doorway of the hotel another guest steps onto the porch and takes a seat in a nearby rocking chair.

"Looks like it's gonna be another great day," he says aloud.

"Well, that's a good way to look at things," replies Brax.

"Name's Gus," says the guest. "August Burgdorf, from St. Louis. I'm a salesman for Anheuser-Busch Brewery Company."

A beer drummer, Brax smiles at the man. He's dressed in a dapper black business suit, white shirt, black string tie, and shiny black boots. Wears a red satin vest and wire-rimmed glasses. He is clean shaved with slightly drooping jowls and piercing blue eyes. His flat crowned wide brimmed rancher's hat sits at a jaunty angle.

"It's a good life selling for the company," the drummer adds.

"Well, I imagine you hear about everything that happens in the territory as you move from town to town and army post to post," The creaking of the rocker ceases as Brax stops to comment.

"Yes indeed, I do, sir. You hit the old nail right on the head," Gus says excitedly. "I just heard last night about a mix-up the cavalry had with some renegade Apaches just a short ways from here." Gus leans forward in his chair.

"Do tell?" says Brax.

"Yessiree, a place the army calls Big Dry Wash, up Crystal Creek. They caught the Apache at his own game. Seems, Al Sieber and his Apache Scouts sniffed out an ambush before the Injuns sprung it. Three Cavalry companies reinforced the one following the Apaches and surrounded them. Then, they surprised them Injuns. Now, if that don't beat all, why, nothin' does." Gus sits back with a smile.

"So, what happened? What's the outcome?"

"Well, the Cavalry fellers I talked with said this broke the back of Apache uprisings. They found the leader, Na-tio-tish, dead with over half his braves. The remainder skedaddled back to the reservation. They ain't got anyone else to lead them except maybe some lonesome medicine man called Geronimo and Army is keeping a close eye on him." Gus speaks with satisfaction in his voice.

"Good to hear the cavalry has finally got the Indian situation under control. Been too long coming," says Braxton.

"That's for sure. Been too many lives lost in all these Indian troubles. Why, I heard in St. Louis, the Indian situation is a main contributor that keeps this territory from becoming a state...the Injuns, along with the outlaws. One down and one to go, as they say." Gus smiles proudly at his conclusion. "Say, friend, what is it you do?"

Brax pauses, looks toward the Rim, and slowly replies, "I'm an Arizona Ranger."

"Well, Lord have mercy. Here I sit jaw-jackin' with an honest to goodness Ranger." Gus sticks out his hand to shake with Braxton.

Slowly, taking the outstretched hand, Braxton replies, "I'm Braxton Bierman. Glad to meet you Mr. Burgdorf."

"Likewise, Mr. Bierman. I've got to hustle down the street to meet with a client. Mind if I tell them I met up with you, an Arizona Ranger?" Gus looks questioningly at Brax.

"I'd rather you just keep it between us, Gus," says Braxton.

"I understand. I will endeavor to do that, but understand it might just slip out, so don't bear me no ill-will." Gus rises and quickly steps off the porch, crosses the street, and moves toward a large saloon.

Brax shakes his head and returns to his thoughts.

It's been a whirlwind couple of days. We arrive in Verde, Becca finds the Methodist pastor of the chapel at the Fort, and within twenty-four hours we're married.

She did look gorgeous in her white ankle length dress. The short jacket covered with lace and pearl buttons sparkled just like her eyes and the lace veil draped over her head took my breath away. I don't know how I ended up this fortunate.

Brax sits silently and ponders.

He remembers they passed many farms along the Verde River entering town.

This is one busy place beside the Army post with a bunch of wood-frame buildings, adobe, and new brick buildings under construction. They've got a three-storied hotel, seven saloons, telegraph, dentist, and doctor offices; businesses and mercantile stores; three bordellos, a post office, a stage depot, and marshal's office. This is a place of progress and growth.

He watches a Cavalry detachment ride the roads from the Fort around the town.

A pleasant smile wrinkles his face as he thinks, *Mr. and Mrs. Braxton Bierman currently reside in the Central Hotel, Camp Verde, Arizona Territory.*

Frowning, he knows his contact of Captain Jackson has been put off as long as possible. He knows Becca sleeps in this morning and it'll be fine if he goes to the telegraph office. He stands and straightens out his jacket. It's the suit he purchased for the wedding. He likes the hang of the coat and wearing white shirts again.

Stepping from the porch, he walks the boardwalk up Main Street to the telegraph. Across the street from the telegraph is the marshal's; he will stop there next.

A small bell above the door of the telegraph office jingles as Brax opens the door. It jingles again as the door closes.

He looks at a skinny, long haired clerk sitting behind a customer counter about eight feet from the door. The clerk's eyes are shieded by visor.

"You know, that little ding-a-ling wouldn't last long if I had to listen to it all day," he says to the clerk.

Not looking up, the clerk responds in a crisp manner, "Well, it's lucky for the bell you don't have to listen to it then. What can I help you with?"

Braxton steps to the counter, takes a pencil from a jar, and writes out a message on the pad before him.

> *To: Captain Jackson, Arizona Rangers, Tombstone, Arizona.*
> *Tonto Basin beginning blood feud. One ranger can't stop.*

In Camp Verde. If still employed,
waiting instructions.
Bierman

Scooting the pad back across the counter. Braxton waits for the clerk to step forward.

The clerk's focus is on the newspaper in front of him.

"Say, would you be able to send this message right away? I'm real interested in the reply," says Braxton.

"Can't you see I am reading this paper? It's the account of the Big Dry Wash battle. I'll get to you in a minute, mister." The clerk slowly turns a page of the paper.

Braxton sees it's just the two of them in the office and reaches to his right side; he cross draws his Colt revolver and slams it on the counter.

"Here's how it ends. We win. Now, drag your mangy butt up to the counter and send my message or you might be missing a finger or two in a minute." Brax slams his revolver on the counter again.

The clerk tumbles from his chair, rights himself, flings the paper aside, stares in wide-eyed astonishment, and races to the counter. He quickly reads over the message and glances at the Colt.

"You a Ranger?" he asks in a quivering voice.

"Why, yes. Nice of you to ask," replies Brax. "The message. Send the message, NOW."

"Yes, Ranger, Sir, you bet. Sending it now." The clerk sits quickly in a chair at the desk beside the telegraph key and rapidly begins clicking the encoded message. After a few moments, he clicks off with a flourish. "Sent and received, Mister Ranger. May I help with anything else?" A now attentive clerk waits for Brax's reply.

"Yes. You can show more respect when a customer walks into this establishment. It may be the next one isn't as polite as I am." Brax walks to the door, reaches up, yanks the bell from its hanger, and tosses it to the clerk. "It's broken. I'll be at the marshal's. Get me the reply to that message as soon as it comes in. Got it?"

"Yes, sir, Mister Ranger. I'll run it right over. Yes, sir." says the clerk.

Brax leaves the telegraph office and crosses the street. He walks into the marshal's office and sees a person sitting at a table in the middle of an open space. A potbellied stove is in the center of the room. The table is to the right of the stove. On the opposite side of the room sits a tall double-doored cabinet. Beside it, a cot. In the wall behind the table is a door with a small, barred window toward the top.

A mustached man looks up from a book that lies open before him. "Help you, mister?" he asks.

"I'm checking in with the marshal's office," says Brax. "Is the marshal in?"

"You're looking at him, mister," the man answers. "Tom Nord, Marshal of Camp Verde. I'll ask again, can I help you?"

"Marshal Nord, I'm Braxton Bierman, Arizona Ranger, I think?"

"Well, do you know or don't you?" asks the marshal.

"I'm waitin' on a telegraph reply to hopefully clear that up for me," says Brax. "In the mean time, I still carry the badge." He flips over his jacket lapel showing his badge to the marshal.

"Not proud of it. Don't want it to be a target, or just want to walk about unidentified?" asks the marshal.

"Nope, just want to make sure it doesn't get in the way of conversation." Brax smiles at the Marshal.

"Right handy way to deal with it. Pull up a chair and let's conversate a spell," says the Marshal.

Becca wakes up in the hotel room and quickly looks around for Braxton.

I knew he would be up early. Stretching luxuriously on the big brass bed, she remembers the exciting ride from Strawberry down the Rim. She recalls the beauty of the sights as they weaved back and forth along the trail. The rough, rugged, and impenetrable face of the stone escarpment still seems to mesmerize her.

I just couldn't get enough of the magnificent canyons.

She stands, runs her hands up and down her body, and giggles as she remembers how Braxton did the same thing last night. A warm sensation sweeps over her as she recalls their lingering kisses, gentle caresses, sensual touches and exploration of each other's bodies, and their innocent laughter. Their intimate joining fills her with satisfaction and sexual fulfillment. Her long slow sigh is rich with contentment of the compatible consummation of their wedding.

Quickly, she slips out of her nightgown, steps to the washstand to wash, slides on her underclothes, and finishes off with a bright blue short-sleeved dress. She buckles a wide belt around her middle. Combing her long hair, she pulls it into a ponytail and ties it with a ribbon.

Since Brax's gone out, I'll grab a bite in the dining room and go check out Camp Verde myself. She walks with confidence as she leaves the room, secures the door, and heads downstairs to the dining room.

She spots an open table by one of the front windows and takes a seat. It is well past any morning breakfast rush, and there are only two other tables out of the ten in the room with any patrons at them. She turns to look at the street in front of the hotel and catches sight of Braxton crossing from the opposite side of the street to the marshal's office. *That's where I'll find him.* She smirks to herself and signals a waiter, places her order, and sits back to await its delivery.

The waiter delivers her breakfast. As she eats, she thinks of the wedding.

It was a nice ceremony. Braxton provides the money to purchase the perfect wedding dress. I know he is short on funds, but the dress is so special. The Pastor's wife helped me dress in one of the side rooms of the chapel. I nearly choked when I stepped into the chapel and saw Braxton in a suit. My goodness, that man of mine is handsome. She grins at the thought. *The pastor did such a wonderful job with the wedding vows. I have a signed and witnessed document showing we are Mr. and Mrs. Braxton Bierman.* She smiles a big satisfied smile. *I know I can get the hang of being married.* She enjoys her thoughts and chuckles to herself.

Finished with her meal, she looks at the Marshal's office and realizes Brax must still be there. It's time to go spring him. She signs the meal bill left by the waiter and leaves the dining room. She leaves her room key with the desk clerk, exits the hotel, and crosses the street to the marshal's office.

"That's about the story, Tom. From Mesilla to Tombstone to Green Valley to here, I didn't realize there's that much to tell," says Braxton. His comfort level with Tom Nord is reassuring. Tom shares his story with Brax and together they bond like many lawmen who have limited friendships. Two men who try to do what they think is right in the face of so many who want to rape, pillage, kill, maim, or worse. "I hope the message from Captain Jackson is good news," says Brax.

"Good or bad, we know we have to go on," replies Tom.

The door opens and Becca walks into the marshal's office. Both men stand and Braxton introduces Becca to Tom.

"Becca, this is the Marshal of Camp Verde, Mr. Tom Nord," says Braxton. "Tom, I'd like you to meet my life, my wife, Rebecca." Braxton smiles a big grin during the introductions.

"Mrs. Bierman, I am really pleased to make your acquaintance," the Marshal says as he maneuvers a chair over for Becca. "Please have a seat. Your husband and I are really getting acquainted and sharing stories. They would bore the hide off a tough old Arizona steer."

"Marshal, I know all the stories my husband has to tell and there ain't one of them boring." Becca shares a knowing smile with the Marshal.

"I reckon so, Mrs. Bierman, I reckon so," he acknowledges.

The door of the office flies open again as the telegraph clerk steps into the office. Looking quickly around he spots Brax.

"Dadblamit, Jimmy. You can knock, cain't you?" Nord stares at the clerk.

"Sorry, Marshall, but the Ranger said he need the reply right away."

"Well, don't just stand there then."

"Mr. Ranger, Sir. Just received this reply from your party in Tombstone. Knew you wanted it quick, hope this is quick enough." He hands the message to Brax.

"Thank you. I appreciate your attentiveness." Braxton flips the clerk a silver dollar and a big smile.

Grinning, the clerk turns and exits the office.

"Well, I'll be. I ain't never seen Jimmy so attentive in delivering messages ever before," says the marshal. "I wonder what's got into the boy?"

"It appears nobody ever explained the need for customer service before. Maybe, he has a better understanding now," Brax winks at Becca who shakes her head and looks the other way. "Well, let's see what Captain Jackson has to say." He rips open the message envelope.

> *To: Ranger Braxton Bierman. Governor unable to arrange funds. Stop. Arizona Ranger Company disbanded. Stop.*
>
> *Clanton and gang on run. Maybe moving to Springerville. Stop.*
>
> *Do not attempt intervention in Tonto Basin. Stop.*
>
> *On your own. End.*
>
> *Captain J. Jackson*

"Well, y'all, looks like I'm unemployed," says Brax with a wistful note in his voice. "Was a good job while it lasted."

"Unbelievable," says Tom. "We need more law in this Territory, not less with the Tonto Basin fixin' to bust wide open. Wait just a dadburn minute, I got a telegram from the marshal in Phoenix a few days ago about Ike Clanton." He rummages around in a drawer in the middle of the table. "Here it is; look at this." He spreads the rumpled message out.

> *To: Marshal Camp Verde, be aware Ike Clanton gang relocating from Tombstone. Stop.*
> *Arizona Rangers, Henry Hooker, John Slaughter, and marshals make too hot to stay. Stop.*
> *Johnny Behan no longer Cochise County Sheriff. Stop.*
> *Be aware Clanton may be headed for your territory. Stop.*
> *Some say he is moving to Springerville. End.*

"Where the blazes is Springerville?" asks Brax.

"It's up the east side of the Territory," answers Becca. Both men turn and stare at her. "Well, I know stuff." she grins.

"She's right. It is due north of San Simon Valley, on the north end of the White Mountains. It's a right pretty spot of high mountain meadows and Ponderosa Pine forests. Won't be pretty if Ike Clanton and his bunch stop there."

Braxton shifts in his chair to rise, "Well, folks, I guess this man-child needs to head out job searching. Can you point me in a good direction, Tom?" He stands and straightens out his suit.

Tom leans back in his chair, and studies Braxton for a few moments. "If I were you," he begins, "I would find my way over to Prescott and ask to see the Governor. You are right knowledgeable about this feud in the Tonto Basin and I reckon he's not. A thing like that can be a blot on a politician's record, especially if they don't try to head it off."

"Keep talking, Tom. You've got my interest." Braxton sits down on the chair.

"Well, the way I look at it, you could parlay what you know into some kind of appointment. How about, Sheriff of Gila County? Talk to the Governor and tell him about the Tonto and roll into what you know about Ike Clanton's bunch and a rustler's roost in Springerville. Yep, that'll tickle his ears." With a smug smile, Tom puts both feet up on the table and leans back in his chair.

Becca, follows the conversation. "Let's go now, Brax. What Tom's sayin' makes sense."

"I agree, it is something, I, we, need to do, but I need to get you back to Green Valley." says Brax.

"How about we add to Tom's scenario and say you'll live in Green Valley while you keep an eye on the Tonto Basin. Hey. How about using Old Clute Johnson at Camp Reno as your eyes-and-ears for the Basin? My Pa always set a big store by Old Clute." Becca smiles at her addition.

"Okay, whoa. Slow down both of you. You've got me rebadged, adding accomplices, overseeing portions of the territory, and I haven't even been to Prescott yet." Braxton holds up both arms in mock surrender. "We'll load up today and be on the trail in the morning, unless y'all want to just appoint me governor right now."

Braxton laughs at his own joke as he rises from his chair. He reaches over, takes Becca's hand, and assists her to stand. Turning to Tom, he extends his right hand.

"Much obliged, lawman."

"Pleasure's been all mine, Sheriff.'" Tom smiles broadly at Brax. "Send me a message and let me know where you finally land. You know if you ever need assistance, call on me. I'll be here in Camp Verde." Tom shakes Braxton's extended hand.

Becca and Brax turn and walk through the doorway of the Marshal's office into the bright sunlight of Camp Verde.

16
PRESCOTT

They take their time on the ride from Camp Verde to Prescott along Crook's Trail. The fifty miles are covered in a leisurely three days. Brax is overjoyed Becca is as good or better a horseback rider than he. Heavy coats keep the cold breezes from cutting through their bodies. Winter is headed to the Rim and a light snowfall stays with them as they ride. Brax leads a U.S. Army mule to carry their supplies. He picked it up at the livery to return it to Fort Whipple. What waits for them in their future? Maybe Prescott will tell.

The stable owner talks his head off with details about the trail travel. It seems, according to him, when General Crook arrived in Tucson, Arizona Territory, back in '71 to deal with the Apache issues, he left Tucson and rode to Fort

Bowie, from there north to Fort Apache, turned west and rode along the edge of the Mogollon Rim marking a trail to Fort Verde, then on to Fort Whipple. The trail he blazed, all 200 miles of it, became a pack route for supplies between the forts. Over time, it's widened and improved to the point it's a wagon road from Prescott to Fort Apache.

Braxton remembers all the embellishments the stable owner adds to his story. One that sticks with Brax is how Crook wants to use mules for the cavalry because of their surefootedness and mental acuity. The officers in the cavalry were on the verge of mutiny at the thought of riding mules...jackasses. Brax can imagine the jokes made about jackasses on jackasses. Crook relents, yet his personal animal of choice is a white mule he rides everywhere throughout the territory.

Becca and Brax enjoy the easy ride and crisp weather as they take in the landscape and serenity offered in the surrounding forest. They spot Fort Whipple as they approach Prescott. Brax heads towards the post to return their wayward mule.

After he returns the government's property, they ride into town and the city square. A pink stone courthouse fills one side of the square with other businesses and offices located on the other three. The middle of the square is a large open grassy field, with a well on each corner, and a small bunch of sheep graze the field. Brax and Becca check into a hotel on the square.

"Brax, did you see all the houses we passed as we came into town?" Becca questions Brax as they wait at the registration desk. "The decorations around the eves and porches are beautiful. I think they call it Victorian style. Can you just imagine the envy a house like one of these in Green Valley would cause?"

"It sure looks like something needin' a lot of upkeep to me," says Brax. "Not sure anybody ought to worry with it. I did notice the brick buildings and construction seems non-stop."

The clerk comes to the desk. Brax registers for a room, arranges for the horses to be taken to the livery, and their belongings to be placed in their room. He notices a dining room behind the registration area and motions to Becca.

"Been a while since we had a bite, would you like to get something to eat and stare out the windows at the square?" he smirks at Becca.

Taking a swipe at Brax's arm she says, "Oh, you. You just think because I'm from Green Valley this big town overwhelms me, don't you?"

"Well, I noticed you did gawk at everything like a 'one-eyed dog in a meat house,'" says Brax smiling.

"I'll have you know, I looked because it's interesting." She flounces into the dining room and sits at an open table by the front windows.

Brax, chuckling to himself, sits across from Becca. "That pink stone building over there is the courthouse. I've been told the governor keeps an office in there. The long single-story building to the right of the square is the original territorial office. With the new courthouse, the governor relocated. After we eat, I'll go over and see his honor. The stable owner did say Governor Tritle is waiting for the new governor to arrive before he vacates. Will know more after a conversation."

After the meal, Becca goes upstairs and Byron heads across the square, walks up the steps of the new courthouse, and enters to find a desk staffed by a clerk who directs him upstairs to the governor's office.

Upstairs, Braxton opens the door and steps into a room filled with men and women seated around the walls holding books, boxes, live animals, and various gadgets. All talk at the same time, and many gesture wildly as they speak. He wonders if he is in the governor's office or a circus.

He walks up to a clerk at a small table in the middle of the chaos.

"I'm Ranger Braxton Bierman, here to see the governor," he says. "I sent a message from Camp Verde a few days ago asking for an appointment. It was accepted."

"Just a minute, wait patiently, I'll be back." The clerk stands and disappears through a doorway.

Braxton turns and looks at the zoo behind him. It amazes him how people act and interact, some sanely, many insanely. He knows this bunch falls in the later group. The clerk returns and leads him through the door as a howl of objections erupts from the waiting group.

He is led through another small office with two clerks at work over journals open on tables before them, into a larger office with four large vertical windows overlooking the square below.

"Mr. Governor, Braxton Bierman." The clerk steps out of the office.

From behind a large desk comes Governor Frederick Augustus Tritle. His frock coat, white shirt, high collar, and cravat all accentuate his narrow physique and lean face covered with a bush of whiskers and full mustache. His dark hair is combed straight back giving him an appearance of dignity and authority.

"Bierman, glad you made it, and in quick time as well. Have a seat." Braxton is directed to a soft leather covered Queen Anne chair in front of the large wooden desk. "Your message arrived and I am thrilled you are here. Marshal Tom Nord also sent a message prior to your arrival giving some of your background and credentials. He is very supportive and speaks highly of you. So, naturally, I wanted to meet you."

"Thank you, governor, I wasn't aware you were acquainted with Marshal Nord," says Brax, enjoying the soft seat.

"Oh, my, absolutely. Marshal Nord is almost a fixture in Camp Verde, a good Republican, and marshal. I've known Tom for many years, and trust his judgment implicitly. He tells me you have knowledge of a dangerous situation that needs attention and needs it now. Sounds rather melodramatic, but here you are," says Tritle.

"Governor, what Marshal Nord alludes to is the beginning of a blood feud in the Tonto Basin area. Two parties, the Tewksburys and Grahams, have begun an altercation over cattle and open rangeland. Shooting is happening and will become worse. Add to this fracas rustlers and thieves from the border and Tombstone resettling in Springerville and you have coal oil thrown onto a smoldering fire." Brax sits back in the chair.

"Well, you paint a combustible picture, Mr. Bierman, or should I address you as Ranger Bierman? I am aware you are part of Captain Jackson's command and it chagrins me funds cannot be found to maintain your ranger company. The dunderheads in the legislature would not be convinced to extend finances for ongoing rangering. They will regret their obstinacy. My Rangers, John Slaughter, and valiant marshals in the southern part of the Territory made outlawing, rustling, and banditry difficult. Many are arrested, tried, and convicted. Some are executed without trial and jury in shootout justice.

Financial discrepancies have led to ex-Sheriff Johnny Behan's arrest and he's no longer Cochise County Sheriff; I've tried to convince John Slaughter to take the job. I am concerned to hear some of the more notorious elements are relocating to Springerville.

Where do you fit into this picture, Ranger Bierman?"

"Well, Your Honor, the Tonto Basin is a powder keg just fixin' to explode and scatter accusations all over the political arena. A feud, any feud, is bad news for everyone, guilty and innocent alike. When you mix in outlaw elements like the Clantons it only goes from bad to worse. Anything happening from this point is a blot on the legacy of your administration." Braxton pitches the most plausible explanation he can put together.

Reclining in his chair, Tritle says, "Spoken like a politician, if I ever knew one. You spin a compelling case. What do you suggest?"

"Well, Sir. It seems simple to me; you would want eyes-and-ears on the situation. You need someone in the basin, who shares information with the governor's office, so you are not caught unaware and blindsided. I propose to be your eyes-and-ears." Brax states his proposition and, as with poker, he must now wait for the bet to be raised or his hand called.

"I like your suggestion, Ranger Bierman. However, there is one problem. I am waiting in Prescott until the new governor arrives. I understand Conrad Zulick has settled his debt issues with the country of Mexico and his New Jersey and Sonora Copper Mines. He is somewhere en route from Mexico City to Prescott. I'm sure he will attend receptions in Tucson, Tombstone, and Phoenix en route. He is the first Democratic governor and the Democrats plan one wingding celebration for him. Anything

I do is only 'lame duck' until he arrives." Tritle ends with a shrug.

"Will Governor Zulick understand this potential problem?" asks Brax.

"Most of those on the outlaw trail are ex-confederates and dyed-in-the-wool Democrats. Also, Zulick will be thrilled with situations which can 'back splash' on my administration. I don't think he'll even talk with you." Tritle sits pondering his response.

"Here is what we will do, my Ranger friend. I am going to appoint you as Sheriff of Gila County; you are a good Republican, aren't you?"

"As a lawman, governor, I've tried my best to be apolitical," says Braxton.

"Excellent. You will be one of my final appointments. This is my move to stop a situation from become a burning fire. If Zulick tries to replace you, he accepts the consequences. Oh, my boy, this can't be better. Now, let me get the clerk in here." Tritle moves from his desk to the door of the office. Opening it he shouts, "Glen, get in here. I need a witness and documentation." He moves quickly back to his desk and withdraws a Bible and a book of Territory statutes.

He lays the books on the edge of the desk. The clerk enters with a legal form in hand.

"Now, Braxton Bierman, ex-ranger. Stand and raise your right hand. Place your left hand on the two books. Repeat after me. I, state your name, will to the best of my ability, maintain and uphold the laws and statutes of the Territory of

Arizona and Gila County, so help me God." Braxton repeats just as Tritle states.

"By virtue as Governor of the Territory of Arizona, I appoint you as Sheriff of Gila County," he hands Braxton a silver star badge. "I would appreciate the ranger badge in return." He holds out his hand to receive the ranger badge as Braxton reluctantly surrenders it.

"Glen," Tritle looks at the clerk. "You've witnessed this swearing in, now write it up in a legal document, sign it as a witness, complete another copy, and file it in the territory records. Give Sheriff Bierman his copy as he leaves. Go, get it done." Tritle ushers the clerk out of his office.

"Sit down, Braxton," the governor says. "You'll have an unappreciated job ahead of you. I haven't done you any favor by placing you as my appointee in the opposition's administration. However, I believe your heart is in making this territory a better place to live. Go and get cracking on the job you outlined. Live up to the star and take care of Arizona. Get on out of here; I have real work to do yet." Tritle sits down and opens a large journal on his desk and pours over the pages.

Braxton stands, turns, and leaves the office.

Tritle stares at Braxton's departing back, "As my Mexican friends say, 'Via con Dios', Sheriff Bierman," he whispers and looks back at the open journal on his desk.

Braxton picks up his legal papers from the clerk and exits the courthouse heading back to the hotel and Becca.

17
FELINA

Byron walks past the cart to gather up the reins of his horse foraging in the grass. Guillo has his mount tied to the back of the *carreta*.

"I guess one of us needs to see Felina home safely," says Byron leading his horse towards Guillo.

"*Si, Compañero*, it would be best perhaps," Guillo replies. "I should go to the *rancho* and make certain Gilberto manages everything, yes?"

"That's probably the right thing to do, *Compañero*. I'll see Felina to Solomonville and you ride to the ranch. I'll be along later," Byron nods in agreement with Guillo. "You are okay to ride with your arm?"

"*Si, si, mi Compañero*. It is hurt, but nothing is broken. I will be *bueno*. You make certain *la Señorita* gets home safe."

Byron makes certain the cart is roadworthy and the horses are all right. They start towards Fort Grant.

"Are you not to do something with the bodies?" asks Felina.

Byron looks at Guillo, both shrug, stop their horses, and dismount. They gather up the bodies of the dead riders and arrange them side-by-side along the road. The horses are too heavy to move. Grabbing blankets from the dead men's bedrolls, they cover the bodies. Next, they collect all the firearms; pull saddles from the dead horses, and check pants pockets for any identification. Depositing the weapons and saddles in the cart, they remount and motion for Felina to follow them.

"Is that all you are to do for those men?" she asks.

Byron drops back to ride beside the cart.

"Yep. They came at us with every intention to leave us lying out in this valley. We can drop the saddles off at Fort Grant and let them know about the situation. If anyone comes looking, they can tell 'em where it happened. That's about it, Felina. It's a tough land and those bushwhackers knew what to expect." Byron slowly scans the land around them searching for any abnormalities.

"It is wrong to leave them out like this. Animals will get them, yes?" she flings a quick look backwards.

"*Si, Señorita*, it is hard." Guillo speaks as he drifts near the cart to hear the conversation.

"Maybe others intending to hurt peaceful people will see them and be persuaded to change their ways, maybe not. It is what it is. Now, *Vámonos.* We have ground to cover."

After another seven miles, they arrive at Fort Grant, ride past the single-story adobe buildings that comprise the camp, and locate the post headquarters. Byron dismounts and goes inside to relate the incident with the Cowboys. Guillo and Felina wait outside for his return.

"That's the long and short of it Lieutenant," Byron says stepping back through the doorway onto the porch of the headquarters building.

"I appreciate your stopping by and giving us the details," replies the Lieutenant. "You can leave the saddles and personal effects over at the stables. He points the direction. "Good day to you, Mr. Bierman." He salutes and returns into the building.

Byron mounts and leads the way to the stable where he directs soldiers to unload the saddles. He hands a bandana bundle of personal effects to a sergeant.

They leave Fort Grant and ride east through a gap in the Penaleno Range. As they exit the mountain pass they approach a wye in the road.

"I go this way, *Compañero*," Guillo indicates to the right.

"Yes, and we will go left towards Solomonville. Be careful. Are you certain your arm is all right?" asks Byron.

"The bullet goes through, *no problemo*. It is already heals, yes?"

"Okay. Take care of yourself. I will see you in a few days," says Byron.

Guillo moves down the road and waves farewell over his shoulder.

Byron is concerned because Felina has been uncharacteristically quiet since the few miles before Fort Grant. As the road moves northeast, he attempts to break her out of her solitude.

"We shouldn't have any more distractions between here and Solomonville," he says. "Will you tell me about what you do in Solomonville?"

Felina remains quiet and flicks the reins over her horse to speed it up.

"If it's about those Cowboys back there," Byron begins.

"You know nothing. You kill and get killed. You says 'it is what it is'," the spite in her voice shocks Byron.

"Look, all I'm trying to do is get you home safe. Why, if Guillo and I hadn't been behind you, you might be out there instead of those Cowboys." Byron fires back with his own indignation.

"*Gracias* for saving me. But, maybe dying is better. I am lost a long time ago. You know nothing." Felina almost spits out her words.

Byron grabs the lead lines on the cart's horse and pulls it to a stop. He steps from his mount, ties the reins to the wagon, and walks to the back. Felina already sits on the back edge of the *carreta*.

"Okay, so you tell me what I don't know. You tell me why I am so stupid. We don't move another inch until we get the air cleared." Byron stands with arms crossed glaring at Felina.

"Who are you that I should tell you anything about what is what? You don't own me. You don't keep me. *Vámonos Diablo*, leave me be." Felina buries her head in her hands and begins to sob.

Byron's resolve quickly melts as he watches Felina's sobs wrack her body.

I know I can be hard, but I didn't really cause all of this did I, he wonders? *There is more going on here than nearly being killed.*

"You have been carrying a weight for some time, it appears," Byron kneels down and takes Felina's hands in his. "I don't want to pry or ask for something you don't want to share, but my Ma always said I was a good listener."

"*Ay, Señor* Byron, you seem so good, and you seem to have some interest in me, but you don't know me. If you did, you would be far away by now." Felina continues to weep.

Byron sits quietly, *you are headed down a slippery slope and there may be no climbing back. Are you real sure you want to push this conversation?*

"Try me, Felina," he says.

Felina looks up, lunges at him, and throws her arms around his neck. She continues to cry on his shoulder.

You've done it now you estupido hombre, in for a penny in for a pound. He wonders what's next.

"Tell me, what is it that makes you so bad. All I see is a beautiful young woman who brings happiness and cheer when she dances and sings." Byron surprises himself at his words.

"*Un Querido*, my darling, my life is something shameful to me and I can never get away from it." Felina slows her weeping and hangs her head.

"All our lives have things we'd just as soon forget, but it's life and we go on. I don't mean to sound like I'm not understanding, but it is what it is." Byron quickly reflects on his own life.

"I am from Sonora, Mexico. *Un Querido. Mi familia es cinco hermanos y madre y padre.* We raise sheep. Times are hard, we starve many times." Felina pauses and stares as if in a daze. "*Mi Madre* almost dies birthing me. I am the baby. She's sick long time as I grow up. When I am girl she dies. *Muy malo.*" Felina begins to softly cry, tears run down her cheek, and drip off her chin.

She continues after gaining some composure, "When I was a girl, *Mi Padre*, comes to me at night and takes me to his bed. He takes me, enters me, hurts me over and over. I bleed, I hurt, and I heal. He comes night after night for me. When he finishes, he kicks me out of bed. I am made to serve his wishes and he blames me for killing *mi Madre*. I hate him. I service him for long time. One night he suddenly stops after entering me and says his chest hurts. He falls back on the bed and moves little. I slip from the bed and find a wooden box I keep outside the front door. I bring it in and shake out on his body all the small scorpions I have collected. In the morning he's *muerto*. He was an *el cerdo. Si*, a pig." Felina begins crying again. Byron kneels in the dirt beside the cart not fully comprehending the life story that sweeps over him.

Suddenly, grasping his arm, Felina looks in his eyes. "*Mi hermano*, Estaban, he sells me to *dos Gringos* in Bisbee across the border from Sonora. For months these animals pass me back and forth using my body as they choose. They sell me to a whorehouse in Tombstone and the *muy malo* miners come to me at all hours biting me, twisting, pulling, entering me, and abusing me in ways I can not say. One day, *mi hermano*, Roberto, finds me and brings me to Solomonville, away from Tombstone. He saves me." Felina seems totally spent and sits like a rag doll balanced on the edge of the *carreta.*

Byron stands and steps past Felina, reaches under her arms, and gently pulls her onto the *carreta* lying her down. He flicks the reins over the carthorse's back. They begin moving steadily towards Solomonville.

Byron's mind swirls with what he has heard. It is not his intent to pry into another person's life. Yet, when Felina begins to tell him, it's as if a dam gives way and so many horrible experiences flood through.

I've got my own problems, and don't need this baggage. But deep down he knows what is shared with him binds him to Felina.

Driving the cart onto the main street in Solomonville, he stops a passing Mexicano and asks if he knows Felina. The man steps around to the back of the cart and looks at the sleeping woman. He points to a large *cantina* up the road, and gestures wildly to it. Turning, he quickly runs away. Byron watches and wonders why a sleeping woman can cause such fear.

Byron drives to the *cantina*, stops, steps off the back of the *carreta*, gathers Felina up into his arms, and walks onto the boardwalk in front of the double doors of the business. With his right foot, he kicks the door to seek assistance. He steps back anticipating an answer.

Rapidly, both doors open and yank inward. Two Mexicans stand on either side of the entrance. They both wear sombreros, tapered trousers, white shirts, and elaborately decorated short jackets. Bandoliers hang from their shoulders and drape like an X across their chests and holstered revolvers hang at their sides. Glaring eyes above full drooping mustaches grab Byron's stare. Both men stand as if ready to pounce with drawn Bowie knives clenched in their hands.

"What is it you want, Gringo?" a voice hidden behind the two men at the door asks.

"I need help. A man said come here," Byron replies.

The voice quickly steps past the door guards and looks at the woman. He motions to clear the door and for Byron to enter. He turns and shoves the guards aside.

Byron follows him into the cool, dark cantina and lays Felina down on a roulette table inside.

The voice looks Felina's prostrate body over, and turns to face Byron.

"She is unharmed; that is good for you, Gringo." He smiles a charming smile. "Where was she; how did you find her?"

Byron tells the voice about the attack by the Cowboys. The voice summons a guard over, whispers in his ear, and dismisses him. The guard runs from the *cantina*. Byron looks questioningly at the guard's departure.

"Do not worry, Gringo, any remains of the *banditos y caballos* left by *el lobos y coyotes* will be disposed of. It will be as if the incident never happens. Yes?" says the Voice.

Byron looks at a middle aged, lithely built man, with a squared jawline and black eyes that seem to swallow you up. He wears an open collared, loose white cotton shirt, and tapered expensive trousers with a wide black leather belt. A gaudy, large, silver buckle secures the belt. His boots are highly polished and shine.

Byron feels totally out of place in his trail dirty blue denims, worn brown boots, and dusty red bibbed-front long sleeve shirt. His high crowned, wide brimmed rancher's hat sits comfortably on his head and his holstered Colt rides easy on his left hip.

"*Señor*, I owe you a debt," says the voice. "How can I repay you?"

"No debt incurred *Señor*," replies Byron. "However, I would like to know why I was told to bring Felina here?"

"It is simple, *Señor*. She is *mi hermana*, my sister." the voice smiles and looks as Felina stirs awake. "Let me introduce myself. I am Alberto

Antonio Hernando Peralta. Please call me, Don Alberto."

"Well, Don Alberto, you can call me Byron, Byron Bierman."

"Ah, *Si, Si*, you are maybe the Bierman of B-Z, no?" asks Alberto.

"Yep. That's me," says Byron. "If you're Felina's brother, why do you allow her to travel unescorted from here to Henry Hooker's *rancho*? She is nothing but totally lucky me and my partner came along."

"She is, how you say, stubborn. *Si*, stubborn. I ask, tell, and threaten her to not do such a thing. She says she is already hurt more than anything else that can happen to her. I don't know why she says such things, but she is determined to go see Roberto, our *hermano*, who works for *Señor* Hooker. *Ay, yi-yi*, she is so strong willed. I do not know what to do with her sometimes." Alberto shakes his head and shrugs.

Byron smirks with a little bit of understanding after dealing with her over the dead Cowboys. "Yep, I know she is strong willed."

He looks around the room and sees it's pleasantly decorated, more like a Victorian parlor than a *cantina*. The eight tables are covered with cloths and the chairs are upholstered. Large, framed, pastoral pictures are on the walls. An ornately carved bar lines one side of the room with a shelved back bar holding bottles of multicolored liquids. In the corner sits a rectangular, highly polished wooden table. Behind it is a tall backed black leather-upholstered chair. In front of the table are two low backed overstuffed cloth-covered seats.

"Ah, you are taking in the appearance of my *cantina*, no?" asks Alberto.

"Well, yes. It doesn't look like any cantina I've seen before," replies Byron.

"It is more than a *cantina*; it is my home," smiles Alberto. "The *cantina* is where I work, my home is where I live, so why not have both together. Is a good idea, no?" says Alberto.

"It's just a mite different," smiles Byron.

"Are you two finished admiring the building?" asks Felina sitting on the roulette table. "If you are done, help me down."

Byron quickly steps over and assists Felina off the table. She stands in front of Alberto.

"Don't say a thing, *hermano*. I am in no mood to listen to you rant at me about going to *Señor* Hooker's alone."

She turns to Byron. "I like the drive, the open range, the freedom, and the escape. You understand, don't you?"

Byron nods dumbly and wonders who to side with.

"Oh. You men are all the same, controlling, demanding, and dictating. Just let me alone." she stomps off through a doorway leading from the cantina's main room.

Alberto shrugs. "You see how she is? Who can get a word in edgewise?"

Byron laughs and walks toward the rectangular table. He takes a seat in one of the overstuffed chairs. Suddenly, remembering where he is, he jumps up.

"Do you mind if I have a seat, Alberto," he asks.

With a cat-like smile, Alberto moves to the chair behind the table, takes his seat, and says to Byron, "Have a seat, *amigo*."

"Don Alberto, seeing your style of living, what is it you do?" asks Byron.

"*Mi amigo*, I do many things and most of them very well," Alberto smiles. "I take care of problems and make them go away for some. For others I provide *dinero*, laborers, and materials. And for a special few I provide offers they cannot refuse."

"I hear what you say," says Byron. "But, I still don't understand WHAT you do."

"That is just as well, *mi amigo*. It is not necessary you do." Alberto finishes the questioning.

"Okay. How long have you been in Solomonville?" Byron attempts to keep conversation flowing.

"How can I say this? My people have been here forever," says Alberto. "We came with the first conquistadors, stay in spite of Apaches, droughts, pestilence, deaths, and now *gringos*. We belong to this land. Generations ago my people left Mexico and new generations have only known this land as their land. I left Mexico with my brother Roberto. Two other brothers, *mi Padre y Madre* all die in Mexico. Roberto, he finds our sister in Tombstone and brings her to me. We are *familia*, all that is left."

"Quite a story," says Byron. "So, now you are head of the family?"

"*Si*. That is why others choose to call me Don Alberto. I take care of those who take care of me and my immediate or extended family."

"Do you have other family members in Solomonville?" Byron is intrigued by Alberto's direct and indirect answers to his questions.

I should be a sheriff. This is like an investigation.

"We have one other *hermano*, Fredrico. He herds sheep in the north part of the Territory in Springerville. There are many Mexicanos from New Mexico, Albuquerque, and Santa Fe, who move to northern Arizona Territory to raise sheep. It is a good business of which I own fifty-one percent." Alberto sits with his fingers steepled as he rests his arms on the table.

"Being a cowman, I don't see much future in raising sheep, Don Alberto," says Byron.

"Oh, *mi amigo*, it takes many endeavors to make one a whole person. Sheep, farming, mining, cattle, land, and influence are all the areas I find myself involved with," says Alberto.

"Well, Don Alberto, one is enough for me right now," Byron smiles. "I'll stick with cattle."

18
PAYSON

Braxton enjoys the easy ride along Crook's wagon road on top of the Rim to Strawberry and down to Pine. *It sure beats Fossil Creek trail.*

Moving down the Rim, the road leads into Payson. While Becca and Brax were in Prescott, he finds out Green Valley receives a new name. It is now Payson, named after an Illinois Representative who arranges establishing a Post Office. As they ride into town, seven cowhands rush toward them firing their pistols in the air. As they swarm around Brax and Becca, he reaches for his Colt to return their gunfire.

Becca reaches over to stop his draw as a rider gallops beside her shouting "Rodeo's comin'."

What the bloomin' blazes is a rodeo, wonders Braxton.

They ride into town and notice a new wooden structure with a flagpole in front of it flying the American flag.

Becca slides from her horse in front of her home cabin, and touches the ground almost the same time as Maud and Billy run from the front porch. They hug, kiss, and stand back looking at each other. Brax leans forward resting his arms on the saddle horn smiling at the reunion.

"Well, Son, looks like you been takin' good care of my little girl," Billy smiles as he reaches up his right hand to Brax.

"Yes, Sir. More like she takes care of me," Brax takes Billy's outstretched hand and gives him a firm handshake. "Saw the new Post Office as we came into the Valley. Looks like we're official now. Payson. Name's got a nice ring to it."

"Most folks are happy, course a few do grumble, but that's to be expected, I reckon," says Billy. "Y'all stayin' with us, aren't ya?"

"No. There's a new house over close by the Post Office. I arranged to move in there while in Prescott. The same feller who built the Post Office built the house. We're heading over there. Come take a look." Braxton points in the direction of a cluster of new wood-framed houses under construction. He sees a horse drawn land grader scraping a roadway between the houses and out of town toward Pine.

"We'll do that, Son. Come on in, and sit a spell." Billy waves toward the cabin.

"I'll be back," says Brax. "Got to stop over at the Post Office first." He turns to leave. "Becca, gonna' check on a spot at the Post Office. Be back directly." She nods and goes inside with Billy and Maud.

The Gila County Sheriff might find a table in the Post Office to set up shop, he thinks as he steps down from his horse.

Brax ties up the reins to the hitching rail, and ascends the steps to the front door. He enters a large room with a potbelly stove in the middle of the space. Along one side is a pigeon box arrangement in a tall cabinet behind a counter with a wall of iron bars perched on top of the counter reaching almost to the eight-foot-high ceiling. Through a curved opening in the iron bars, he spots a postal clerk busily sorting through letters and slipping them into individual pigeonholes. The clerk has a bank clerk's visor on his head. His long-sleeved white cotton shirt has garters to keep the cuffs from dragging. He wears black trousers and wire-rimmed glasses.

Brax taps on the counter with his knuckles.

"Excuse me. You the Post Master?" asks Braxton.

The clerk turns around, places a handful of letters on a nearby table, and replies, "Yes Sir. Thornton Throxton at your service. How can I help?"

"Well, Thornton, my name is Braxton Bierman. I'm the Sheriff of Gila County and I need to requisition a corner of your Post Office until they get my office built across the street. You have a problem with that?"

"Why no, Sheriff. You do know this is federal property, so we'll need to work out a rental agreement for your space, seeing as how you work for the County." Thornton rummages around some paperwork on the table.

"Thornton, let's leave our people in Prescott and Globe to sort it out. That sound good to you? How about you send a note to your folks and another one to the County folks to get together? Let's make your life and mine as easy as we can." Braxton smiles at Thornton with an infectious smile.

"Strikes me just fine, Sheriff. We'll get along real well. Pick a corner and stake your claim." Thornton reaches his hand through the opening to shake with Braxton.

Braxton grabs the extended hand and gives a firm handshake. While holding his hand he asks, "Now, Thornton, what the blazes is a rodeo?"

"Why Sheriff, it's just about the most fun that a cow hand can ever imagine. Town folks get to watch the events and have fun as well." Thornton seems to light up while he describes the event to Brax.

"Bareback horse riding, tie-down roping, 'Twisters' trying to stay on broncs, and horse racing by the local cowhands will be fun to watch. I hear there's going to be some Silver Dollar pitchin' as well. There is some prize money for the winners. Some cowhands been talkin' about 'Chicken Pullin' for the fun of it too. It's bound to be a great time. They've cleared an area over by the large corral in Mid-Town

Pasture to have the event. There will be a dinner on the grounds, church singing, why it will almost be like a revival." Thornton looks almost worn out just talking about the rodeo.

Braxton shakes his head. *Sounds like just another workday for the cowhands.*

"Much obliged for the corner, Thornton. I'll have a few things brought over to get set up. I shouldn't take up much space for very long." Braxton waves as he exits the building. Out front the road grader passes tugged along by draft horses. *Progress*, thinks Braxton. *I'm hopin' we can all live through it.* He smiles to himself, steps into his saddle, and rides back to the cabin to be with Becca, Maud, and Billy.

Braxton rides from Payson towards Camp Reno along Tonto Creek. *It's been a couple of busy years. Hard to believe it's 1884, and I'm lookin' forward to seeing Clute at the mercantile in Reno.*

Leaving the pine forests behind, he descends into the Tonto Basin and watches pines change to Manzanita and chaparral, the pine needle groundcover to stones and gravel, and the sky from drifting clouds to brilliant sunshine.

It's still a picturesque view. His gaze sweeps the landscape as he rocks easily in the saddle. The stark rock strewn Mazatzal Range overlooks the Tonto Basin. Brax remembers fighting his way up and down the jagged valleys and canyons and leaving some blood and hair scratched by every thorn bush and cactus when he crossed from Phoenix to Camp Reno.

The Camp looks dusty and dirtier than before. It appears fewer people live there. He stops, dismounts, and ties his horse in front of the mercantile. It hasn't changed much, just older. Brax stretches his back, adjusting the kinks from his ride.

I don't remember having to stretch like this before. Never thought much about getting older. He shrugs off the thought and steps onto the porch, through the open doors, and into the store.

Old Clute sits behind the counter with his feet propped up on top. His flyswatter flips around him with deadly accuracy.

"Well, well, it's about time you come draggin' your scrawny butt around here again. You still rangerin'?" Clute drawls out without shifting his position on the chair.

"No, Sir," says Brax. "Not a ranger anymore. I'm the Gila County Sheriff now."

"Dad burn. First time you come wanderin' in here as a more-lost-than-a-calf-in-high-weeds-ranger. Now, you spank-it-back here as a sheriff. If'n you come back here again as the by-God governor, I'm leavin' the territory. Why cain't you pick a job and stick to it?" Clute flips the swatter and causes the demise of three flies grouped-together.

"It's good to see you too," Brax says with a smile. "Good to see some things never change."

"Change. Hell, son, it changes around here every day. What brings you my direction now?" Clute rises from his chair and saunters over to the doorway where Brax stands.

"Well, sir. The governor wants me to keep an eye on the Basin feud. I know there isn't anyone who knows more about what's going on than you. Can we pull a couple of chairs from the store and sit a spell on the porch?" Brax moves to grab a chair.

"Sure, get two. I got a mite to talk with you about," says Clute. Brax proceeds to drag two chairs onto the porch and both men settle into them.

"Well, sheriff, things are warmin' up a bit," says Clute.

"Okay, explain 'warmin' up' to me," replies Brax.

"It seems since you passed through, Jim Stinson made a deal with the Graham bunch for fifty head of cattle if they would turn state's evidence against Tewksbury. Old Graham went and filed a complaint with some old lame attorney down in Globe, the county seat, about Tewksbury rebranding rustled cattle. The complaint got throwed out of court, but some of the Tewksbury boys rode over to Stinson's and a gunfight broke out. Some were wounded, nobody kilt. Stinson is fixin' to leave the territory now he's got things stirred up, and the Graham bunch done been catched rustlin' cattle.

Now, Tewksbury is talkin' about running sheep in the Basin. And, you talk about nothing changin'. Why, Son, you stick around here and the speed of change will take your breath away." Clute flicks the flyswatter and kills two flies perched on his boot.

Brax stands up shaking his head.

"It's hard to imagine so much skunkin' around is going on in this beautiful Basin." He leans against a porch post and stares out across the Tonto Basin. "I got to ride down to Globe to file my sheriff's credentials at the county courthouse. It's gonna' be a good sixty-mile ride, so sooner I start, the sooner I'll pass by here again. Next time, I'll try to keep from being the governor." With a smile, Brax steps to his horse, unties it from the rail, mounts, and waves goodbye to Clute. "Try to keep a lid on everything till I come back, ya hear."

"Ranger, sheriff, consarnd pain-in-the-butt, you take care of yourself and keep your back covered." Clute stands up and goes back inside the mercantile.

Brax is about twenty-five miles from Camp Reno and his horse is climbing a ridge when he hears the gunfire. The report of the firearms tells him it's a rifle duel up ahead. Slipping from his saddle he pulls his Winchester, ground ties his horse, reaches in his saddlebags for his binoculars, and creeps to the top of the ridge. Lying flat on the rocky ground, he brings up the binoculars and begins to scan the area before him. In the creek valley below him, he sees an unhitched wagon, a campsite, and sheep milling around a short distance from the wagon. Puffs of smoke come from under the wagon and from behind a large rock nearby. Across the creek valley on the hillside from among boulders strewn across the slope, he sees three puffs of smoke as the rifle fire continues.

Rolling onto his back, he looks skyward. *Looks like three to two. Time to even the odds.* He rolls back over and sights his Winchester at the next puff of smoke from the boulders on the hillside. He fires and levers three shots in succession. The firing stops as all parties seem to search for where his shots came from. Then Brax sees three figures begin scrambling up the hillside as they attempt to get over the top to the other side where their horses are probably tied. He draws down on the nearest moving figure and cuts loose with three more rapid shots of his rifle. The figure drops and lies still. The other two gain the ridge top and drop over the other side of the hill.

Brax walks back to his horse, unties it, mounts, and rides over the hill toward the wagon beside the creek.

As he dismounts, a Mexican man and teenager walk slowly toward him. Both carry well-used Henry repeaters and hold them at their waist ready for use.

"*Buenos dias, amigos*," Brax raises his hand in welcome.

The older man replies, "*Buenos dias, Señor.* Were you the one firing at the *banditos*?"

"Yep, that's me. Son, would you go up and make sure my shot was true?" Brax points to where the one shooter went down. "If he's alive, signal me. If dead, drop some rocks on him after you collect everything valuable."

"Where are you fellers from?" asks Brax.

"First, *Señor*, who are you?" counters the old man.

"Sorry, *amigo*, I'm Sheriff of Gila County. Now, I'm goin' to ask again, where are you fellers from?" Brax looks directly at the older man.

"Sorry, *Señor* Sheriff. I just needed to know. Me *y mi sobrino* have drived sheeps from Fort Apache to this valley to open graze them. Yes?" the older man answers lowering his rifle. "We hear cattle boys says no sheeps is welcome here."

"Well, *Señor*, you have stepped on a nerve. Most folks here about raise cattle and sheep are unwelcome on this range." Brax looks at the wagon and gear around the campsite. "It would be best if you push your woolies back toward Fort Apache some."

"*Señor*, Sheriff, *mi jefe* says to bring sheeps here. He is *Señor* Fredrico Peralto. He lives in Springerville and moves bunches of sheeps into *norte* territory.

Well, if that doesn't touch off the dynamite, nothing will, thinks Brax.

He looks up the hillside and sees the boy move rocks around. That's one cowboy who won't have to worry about what's coming.

"*Señor*, for the safety of your son, yourself, and your sheep, I'm telling you to move back out of the basin for the time being. I've got to keep moving to Globe. I will let them know about what's happening here and about *Señor* Peralto moving sheep. You can go or stay; it's your life and your funeral." Braxton looks around the quiet, peaceful valley with sheep grazing contentedly and knows the things will get worse before there is a chance they might be better.

The boy returns from the hillside and hands Braxton a bandana with the bushwacker's personal effects. Braxton takes the bundle and stuffs it in his saddlebag. With one last look at the pastoral setting, he mounts, and turns his horse towards Globe.

Braxton sits in the Gila County Courthouse second floor jail. He knows they are figuratively trying to kill him. Every day they haggle, he feels he dies a little more.

It has been weeks since arriving in Globe and the county officials continue to haggle over Governor Tritle's appointment of Brax as a Gila County Sheriff. In order to save money, he rooms at the jail. Empty cells don't have the best bunks, but they're free.

Politicians, elected officials, and bureaucrats have all taken exception to the credentials from the Governor. Meeting after meeting questioning Brax's political affiliation, he repeatedly states he's apolitical, not satisfying their appetites.

Globe is primarily a Democratic Party town and a Republican appointment is just unpalatable.

Brax uses the Post Office to let Becca know of his delay. He receives return mail from her while delayed. Globe reminds him a lot of Tombstone. Maybe it is because they both are mining towns operating day and night; hard rock miners drift through town around the clock. More than once Brax considers sitting down to deal Faro in a nearby saloon. Ore crushers keep up a constant pounding and lives acclimate to their rhythm.

Yesterday, one bureaucrat suggests Brax is no better than a bushwhacker in the sheep incident on the way to Globe. Brax filed a full report when he arrived at the county jail and turned over the bushwhacker's personal belongings to the court. Now, the elected officials seem hell-bent on arguing wrongful death and his possible arrest. Brax recalls Governor Tritle's remarks about not doing him any favors with the appointment. Little did he know how prophetic this really was.

A county clerk stomps up the stairs to the jailer's office, opens the door, and walks into the room. Brax sits in the corner sipping coffee. The clerk walks over to him.

"Sheriff Bierman, the county commissioners would like to see you downstairs in their office right away," he says, turns around, and leaves the office. His clomping steps echo in the stairwell as he descends.

"Seems the muckity-mucks have made up their minds about what to do with you, Brax," the old jailer smiles over the edge of his coffee cup.

"Well, it's about time," Brax says in exasperation. "They've taken their old sweet time about it."

Brax sits his cup on the potbellied stove, walks through the doorway, down the stairs, and into a large office on the first floor. Three commissioners sit behind a long table waiting for him. Brax pulls up a chair.

"Sheriff Bierman, it is the decision of the County of Gila, Arizona Territory, that the credentials you've presented from the office of the Governor, Arizona Territory, are acceptable and valid. Therefore, we concur with the appointment, and further state you will stand for re-election in the next election. This statement is signed, dated, and will be filed with the county records. Do you have any questions?" asks the middle commissioner laying aside the paper he read from.

"Gentlemen, it has taken a while longer than I expected to arrive at this point. I'm glad we are here. Just to make certain I understand, I am Sheriff of Gila County and I will reside in Payson. In the next election I'm required to run for the office, and any other past issues are finished. Correct?" Brax asks as he looks at the three political hacks seated before him.

What do they know about being a sheriff? They've spent their lives behind desks, in businesses, or "boot-licking" for votes. I doubt even one of them has stood up to the likes of Virgil Earp or has half the sense of Old Clute or knows the Rim like Billy Jewel. Let it go, Brax, let it go. He tries to shut off the negative thoughts and concentrate on the meeting.

"Yes, Sheriff Bierman, that's the agreement of Gila County. In particular, given the volatile conditions of the Tonto Basin, your additional assignment is to monitor and interact in any disruption to life and property which may incur there," the middle commissioner replies.

"You mean I'm to be a Sheriff, in other words."

"Well, in a word...yes," says the commissioner. Brax smirks at his comment.

Sitting back with a frown, the middle commissioner retorts, "This is not a laughing matter, Bierman. We've debated long and hard about your appointment and have decided, for the good of the county, to honor it as long as you do your part and keep a lid on Tonto Basin. Are we clear in this regard?"

I'll be damned if I'm another Johnny Behan, playing games with outlaws or politicians; maybe they're the same. He leans forward glaring at all three men. "First, I'm a lawman, I ride for the star; second, there is no keeping a lid on something that has to blow up; and third, I'm leaving here today headed home and will do my job. If you need to be in touch, contact me in Payson." Brax abruptly stands and walks out of the office.

"Now see here, just a minute." The middle commissioner stands up shouting at Brax. The man beside him reaches up, grabs him by the arm, and pulls him down into his chair. He shakes his head, and the three commissioners sit silently as they watch Brax leave the room.

Brax rides slowly up to the dilapidated building. The mercantile sits lifeless. Tying the horse to the rail, Brax steps onto the porch and into the empty building. Nothing remains on the shelves, even the potbelly stove is gone. Brax is startled by a voice.

"He just up and died," says a whiskered, dirty, scraggle-tooth prospector following Brax inside. "I's the last one hereabouts since Clute passed, and I's leavin' in the morning."

"When did he pass?" asks Brax.

"Why, it was a couple of days after you left," says the prospector.

"We walks in, there he sits, slap stone cold dead."

"Died sitting in his chair?" questions Brax.

"Yep. And he was as cantankerous dead as he ever was alive." the prospector says shaking his head which throws dirt every direction. "We lays him gentle-like on the floor, and his feet stick up in the air. Petrification already set in, you see. Then we push his feet down, and Old Clute sits up. Why, it takes three of us to sit on him to get him flat enough to stuff in his box. The old cuss even keeps a death grip on the flyswatter of his, so we just bury it with him." The old miner wheezes out a laugh and slaps his knee. "I bet he's swatten' flies offin' Saint Peter right now."

I remember the first time I met that old merchantile clerk. Brax smiles with the remembrance. *I hope Clute's getting a look at Green Valley now.*

"Thank you, friend, for taking care of old Clute. You got everything you need for travelin'?"

"Sure, sure. Me and Bertha, she's my mule, we're just fine. Be moseyin' on towards Safford come sun up."

"Be careful traveling," says Brax stepping outside.

Untying his horse, he steps into his saddle, and follows Tonto Creek for home, Becca, and Payson.

19
THE DEAL

His coffee is warm at best. He's let it sit too long. The *Mexicanos* by the front door continue to stare at him. The one on the right has been wiping his large Bowie knife back and forth across a leather strop for too long. Sweat trickles down Byron's forehead. *When will they make their play?*

One of the doors is kicked open, a guard tumbles from his stool, the other guard leaps up holding the knife out, and Byron jumps like he is shot.

Felina stomps into the cantina from outside. She looks at the guard sprawled on the floor and the other with the knife.

"What good are you?" she shouts at the two men. The one on the floor scrambles to stand and the other hangs his head lowering the Bowie.

"Get away from me," she shouts at them, and shoves past as she walks into the *cantina*. She sees Byron sitting in the overstuffed chair before Alberto's desk. Smiling, she walks to him.

"*Mi Querido*," Felina reaches out and gently strokes Byron's cheek.

"I don't know what you're calling me, but it sure sounds nicer than what you said to the guards." Byron smiles back at Felina.

"Silly, man," says Felina. "I call you 'my darling'."

Byron blushes violently at the sentiment. The last beautiful woman who caressed him and called him something 'dear' was his Mama. Now, he sits in this frilly *cantina* as a gorgeous woman fawns over him. *Bierman, get a grip*, he thinks to himself.

Felina continues to hold Byron's head against her body and run her fingers though his hair.

Alberto steps through the open doorway at the back of the room and takes in the sight before him.

"Ahhhemm. I hate to disturb such a scene, but there is work to be done. Will you excuse us, Felina?" Alberto gestures towards the doorway. "I would like to discuss business with *Señor* Byron."

Felina shrugs her shoulders at her brother's request. Smiling at Byron she says, "You will be here later to watch me sing and dance, No? I will dance just for you."

"Felina, a team of horses couldn't drag me away. I'll be here." Byron smiles at her and watches the sway of her hips as she walks through the doorway.

Alberto walks around the table and takes a seat in the leather chair. He leans forward onto the table and steeples his fingers in front of him.

"I trust you sleep well last night in your room?" says Alberto.

"It was okay. Thanks for giving me a place to stretch out," replies Byron.

"*Amigo*, it has been quite a while since I have seen my sister so happy. She carries much troubles inside her. It has not been a nice life she lives. Whenever something or someone can lift her troubles, I pay attention for her and for the someone she likes. I do not want either to be hurt." Alberto stares his deep consuming gaze at Byron.

"I hear the words, Alberto, but I'm missing the understanding," says Byron.

"What I'm saying, *amigo*, is, Felina has a heart that is, how can I say it, burnt up. She likes and loves like a little girl because she never left that point in her life." Alberto sits shaking his head. "It is not my place to talk bad about someone I love with all my heart, but it is important you understand, no?"

"Alberto, she unburdened herself to me about what's happened to her in the past. I listened. I don't understand why those things happened, but to me she is like a wounded dove. One beautiful to look at, but may never fly again."

"*Bueno, bueno. Amigo.* You do understand. *Ay, yi-yi*, I knew I liked you the first time I saw you. We are alike, no?" says Alberto.

"No. NO. We are not alike," says Byron. "I mean, my heart goes out to your sister, and I accept she may or may never have any heart space for me, but you and I are not alike except for that." Byron leans towards Alberto to make his point clear.

"*Si. Si.* It is enough, my Anglo friend. I have my interests and ways; and you have yours. That is enough. Now, let us speak of something which may interest both of us, no?"

"Okay. Let's leave the discussion about Felina. What is this business you've got on your mind? Is it legal? Why are you willing to discuss it with me? You don't mind if I don't trust you very much, do you?" Byron sits back in his chair.

Alberto gets a grieved look on his face and clutches his hands over his heart. "*Amigo*, you cut me to the quick. What have I done to you except to befriend you?"

"All right, all right." says Byron. "Such dramatics. What is the business?"

"*Bueno.* I like a man who gets down to details," says Alberto smiling. "Here is what I have learned. North of here, outside of Springerville a *ranchero* has a small herd of five hundred cattle. Rustlers and money troubles force him to sell his herd cheap. Do you have interest in buying it?

"If he is being rustled, why would I want to buy into a mess like that?" asks Byron.

"Ay. *Banditos* can be dealt with. You miss the bigger idea. Five hundred cattle on grassy open range and a buying market that wants more beef. Are you beginning to see the big picture? When can you have another herd like this dropped in your lap? Is interesting, no?" says Alberto.

"Sure, sure, it's interesting, and I've never had five hundred head offered to me, but I'm cattle rich and cash poor," says Byron. "Besides, I need to make sure my partner is onboard with any deals."

"*Si, si,* Guillo Zapato. He is a worthy partner and a good *vaquero*." says Alberto.

"I have no idea how you know all the stuff you do, Alberto, but yes, Guillo is my partner and best friend. He rode with my Pa and now me," says Byron. "I will do nothing to harm or hurt him. Are we clear? Why do you want to do this deal with me?"

"*Mi amigo.* I am a man of honor as well. I will never suggest we do anything to harm those we love. What I would like to see us do is purchase the herd. I am cash rich and cattle poor. I will only need to own fifty-one percent of the herd because it is my money I am putting up. You can pay me back with cattle sales. Frankly, *amigo*, I need your Anglo name and brand to avoid difficulties."

"Okay, let's say Guillo and I go along. Why should we?" asks Byron.

"Because, *amigo.* It gets all of your herds away from one location. Instead of increasing your head count in the San Simon Valley, you can increase your herd in other grazing areas. How you say, 'don't keep eggs in one basket.' It makes sense, no?"

Just then a man wearing a dapper business suit, white shirt, black string tie, and shiny black boots steps through the doorway into the main room. He carries a tablet in front of him and concentrates on calculations.

"*Señor* Peralta, it appears we can discount your order...Oh. I'm sorry. I didn't realize you have a visitor. I beg your pardon, Gentlemen."

"It is all right, *Señor* Burgdorf. May I introduce my good friend, *Señor* Byron Bierman. Byron, this is *Señor* August Burgdorf from St. Louis. He sells me beer for my *cantina* from Anheuser-Busch Breweries, yes?"

"Yes, I certainly do. Pleased to meet you Mr. Bierman, call me Gus." The beer drummer stares at Byron fixated. His gaze takes in Byron's face with a questioning look.

"Have we met before? Your name is familiar. Weren't you in Camp Verde?" asks Gus.

"Never been there to my knowledge," says Byron.

"Remarkable, simply remarkable," mutters Gus extending his right hand. Byron reaches out and they exchange a firm handshake.

"I'll leave you Gentlemen to your business and see myself out. See you next month when the shipment arrives *Señor* Peralta. Good day." Burgdorf hustles quickly toward the front door. Glancing over his shoulder, he stares at Byron and shakes his head as he exits.

Burgdorf's interruption gives Byron some time to consider Alberto's offer. The proposed purchase seems plausible to Byron. He remembers the conversation with Hooker about over grazing. Water availability is another issue a new location could remedy.

Why shouldn't I make a deal? What would Pa do? Will Guillo agree? Increasing our herd in one step by twenty percent is a big jump.

"Okay, Alberto. Let's take the next step. I have to get back to the B-Z and Guillo before anything is finalized, but contact the seller and let him know there is interest in his deal."

"*Ay, yi-yi, amigo.* It is the right thing to do. We will be in the cattle business together." Alberto smiles a huge smile.

"Don't remind me of who I might be going into business with," says Byron. "It'll just ruin my day."

Guitars begin to play in front of the bar as three musicians warm up their instruments. Byron sees twenty older, well-dressed, patrician type gentlemen have quietly entered the cantina and sit at the tables in hushed conversations drinking. Alberto moves from table to table talking with each group. Byron scoots his chair around to get a better view of the open area in front of the bar. As the music begins to build, Felina steps out and starts to dance.

A long clinging blue dress envelops her body. The portion below her knees is full and flares as she turns. Her hair is combed straight back and tied with a ribbon in a long black ponytail and her eyes seem on fire, shining brightly. Her movements match the rhythm of the music perfectly. The men at the tables sit mesmerized.

Byron suddenly thinks of a wounded dove as Felina twirls.

Byron sees the ranch house as he crests the ridge. He stops his horse to watch the activities. In the corral a *vaquero* breaks horses. While watching, Byron sees the unlucky rider thrown from his horse go sailing through the air. Other activities around the barn are chores being carried out. From the south, he spots two cowhands on horseback approach the ranch house and Guillo steps out to greet them. Byron prods his horse into a gentle lope down the hill towards them.

Drawing closer, he sees Gilberto and a new ranch hand from Solomonville stop in front of Guillo.

"*Si,* Guillo, it looks like ten or fifteen head have been driven up into the mountains away from the main herd. I see four sets of hoof prints that make me think they are *banditos*," says Gilberto. "Should I takes some *vaqueros* to find out, *Jefe*?"

Guillo starts to answer and suddenly sees Byron riding down the hill. Shading his eyes with one hand raised over them, he points.

"Here comes the *Patron* now, Gilberto. Let's see what he thinks should be done." They wait patiently as Byron brings his horse to a stop beside the riders.

"*Buenos dias, caballeros.*" says Byron. "*Como estas*?"

"We are all doing well, *Compañero*," replies Guillo with nods from Gilberto and the cowhand. "I wish I could say as well for the herd."

"What seems to be the problem?"

"Cowboys, I think," replies Guillo.

"Cowboys on our range?" says Byron.

"*Si, Patron*, we have followed them for three days," Gilberto gestures toward himself and the cowhand. "They work their way north picking off *cinco o diez,* five or ten, cattle a day as they go. We find maybe *cuarenta*, forty, cattle so far is missing."

"Driving the cattle will slow them down, how about we wait for them on the north end of the valley. They have to go to water soon enough and we can be there." Byron smiles at his idea.

"That is why he is the *Patron*," says Guillo grinning under his drooping mustache. "Now, *Vámonos*, take the *vaqueros* and ride to the north end. Spot the cattle and set an ambush. You know how to do that Gilberto, yes?"

Grinning an ear splitting grin, Gilberto replies, "Do not worry, *Jefe.* They will come to my *vaqueros* and me. We will bring the cattle home." Pulling back on his reins to back his horse up, Gilberto flicks his quirt left to right slightly touching the horse's withers. He bounds away across the pasture with the cowhand riding hard to keep up.

Dismounting and tying his horse to the hitching post, Byron watches the departing ranch hands.

"He's some *vaquero*," he says out loud.

"Si, *Compañero*, he rides for this brand. That is certain. I would like many more like him," replies Guillo. "You have been a few days coming home, yes? Let's go to the cookhouse and you can tell me about Solomonville and the *Señorita*."

Both men walk the short distance to the cookhouse, where Guillo shouts to the cook to warm the coffee and bring a couple of cups. They sit at a long table by the doorway.

"Well, *Compañero*, it isn't a nice story about the *Señorita*," says Byron. "She has been hurt and abused since a child. It is too horrible to tell."

"*Madre mia*, I am so sorry to hear that, *Compañero*. It hurts my heart to imagine all you do not say. We will leave it there, yes?"

"Yes. It is best left there. I did manage to meet her *hermano* in Solomonville. His name is Alberto Peralta."

"*Ay, yi-yi, Compañero*, you saw *La Araña*, and walked away?" replies Guillo in shock.

"I saw who?" Byron is confused.

"The Spider, *Compañero*; is how the man is called. He spins webs, traps many things. Some good, some bad, but he has eyes and ears everywhere. It is what the *vaqueros* tell me, and *Compañero*, they know."

Chuckling out loud, Byron says, "That description fits him dead to rights. He knows what is happening everywhere. The Mexicans see him as some kind of Robin Hood character."

"What is a 'robbing hook carry turd' mean, *Compañero*?" asks Guillo.

Laughing aloud, Byron reaches over and slaps Guillo on the shoulder, "You are just what the doctor ordered, *Compañero*. You truly make me see what it takes to be happy. *Gracias*."

"*Si*, I think," says Guillo with a questioning smile. "What did Peralta want of you?"

"You need to take a deep breath, *Compañero*. He has a proposition for us to consider. Like you said before, 'some good, some bad.'" Byron begins to explain the cattle proposal to Guillo. He pauses while the cook sets full cups of steaming coffee on the table for them. Guillo reaches over and pours a slug of sugar into his coffee and stirs it into a syrup consistency. Byron shakes his head.

"You know coffee like that is going to rot out your teeth, don't you?" says Byron.

"Maybe, *Compañero*, but is a sweet way for it to happen, no?" answers Guillo.

"You're right. What are your thoughts about Peralta's deal?"

Guillo pauses, sips coffee, and sips again before answering.

"The idea is a good one, *Compañero*. I like new pasture and splitting up the herds. This fits with what *Señor* Hooker says to us. I am not so happy about doing it with *La Araña*."

"I'm not either, but how else can we increase by twenty percent and pick up other grazing rights at the same time?" asks Byron. "Once we sell, we pay off the debt, and part ways."

"*Compañero*, have you not ever walked into a spider's web? You know it clings to you even if you push through it. Yes? Señor Peralta, he may be a lot like that." Guillo frowns staring into his syrupy coffee, swirling it around in his cup.

"I say, make the deal. *Bueno?*"

The bawling noise drawing closer causes Byron and Guillo to rush from the cookhouse the next morning. Looking out past the ranch house, they see a dust cloud raised by driven cattle. Walking beside the herd, a rider breaks free and gallops toward them. As he nears, he pulls to a slow walk.

"Good to see you Gilberto," says Byron.

"*Ay, es muy bueno, buenos dias, El Capataz*, foreman," says Guillo.

Gilberto stops his horse and swings down from his saddle. He stands, holding the reins.

"We find the *banditos* as you thought, *Patron*. My *vaqueros* set the ambush and we surprise them good. Two no longer live. We bury them out there. *Seis o siete*, six or seven, get past us. They ride *norte* without our cattle. I have one *vaquero* wounded." Gilberto smiles a huge pearly white smile.

"Gilberto, you have done much more than expected. *Muchas gracias.* You are truly *El Capataz de la rancho*. Being our foreman means taking care of the men and animals. You've done both well. Now, see to your *vaqueros* and turn the herd out to pasture."

"*Si, Patron. Gracias.*" Gilberto remounts and rides back to the herd shouting directions as he rides.

Byron and Guillo return to the cookhouse to finish their breakfast.

"So, tomorrow, we ride to Solomonville and meet with Peralta?" asks Byron.

"*Si,* we go find out what is involved. The herd we buy is near Springerville, Yes?" asks Guillo.

"That's what Alberto said when we talked about the purchase," answers Byron.

"So, do we take *vaqueros* from this ranch to Springerville or use ranch hands at the place?" asks Guillo.

"If there are rustlers there, it stands to reason maybe some of those cowboys might be them, yes?" questions Byron. "We might to take a few hands from here until we figure out who rides for the brand there."

"Do we take Gilberto or leave him here?" asks Guillo.

"All depends if you are planning on going to Springerville, *Compañero*," says Byron. "I'm not saying you do or don't. Any thought?"

"I will stay at this *rancho*. Take Gilberto with you. He will set things straight in short order. *Si*?" says Guillo.

"We may be gone a while. Is that still okay with you?" Byron watches Guillo closely for an answer.

"Byron, we come to Arizona Territory to grow a *grande rancho.* It takes time to do this, and sometimes we cannot do it together. Go, get things started in Springerville. I will make sure this part of our *rancho* is okay. *Si?*" A smile creeps from under his drooping mustache as he answers.

"We ride in the morning to begin another chapter," says Byron with finality. The decision is made and now he will work the plan to success.

Guillo and Byron exit the cookhouse and retrieve their horses. The two men mount and ride across the pasture in front of the B-Z ranch house towards the distant mountains to check the ranch.

20
SHEPHERD

Braxton sits in his shared space at the Payson Post Office reading an article in *The Daily Courier* from Prescott.

Unbelievable. A million acres of right of way land sold to The Aztec Company of Boston by the Atlantic and Pacific Railroad. They plan to bring cattle from drought stricken Texas to Arizona and begin ranching operations. What about the small ranchers already along the railroad? What will more cattle mean when grazing the range? Any time you couple railroad, ranchers, open range, and imported cattle, you've got a combination for disaster. Braxton smells trouble, doesn't know when or exactly where, but his lawman instinct smells it coming.

He hollers at Thornton, the Post Master.

"Hey, Thornton, you read and see everything; have you heard about the Aztec Cattle Company moving into the Territory?" asks Braxton.

"Certainly, Sheriff. There's talk all over Prescott about the million acres they negotiated with the railroad. The Atlantic and Pacific need money to keep building rails, and Aztec wants land to run cattle. Looks like everything is a go. There is noise about the wranglers from Texas they will bring along with the cattle, an unsavory bunch of punchers, I understand. Their brand looks like a cook's hashknife and they've taken to calling themselves the Hashknife Outfit. How droll." says Thornton.

"Thornton, you know more about what is happening than any other three people I know," says Braxton. "So, where will the operation base itself?"

"Oh, some say Saint Joseph, but others bet on Holbrook, old Horsehead Crossing," adds Thornton.

"Forever-and-a-day." exclaims Brax. "You amaze me."

"Why, thank you Sheriff, I attempt to please," says Thornton, returning to his mail sorting.

Brax folds up his paper, tucks it under his arm, and walks out of the Post Office. Payson is busy; construction goes on non-stop since the lumber mill started operation. Billy Jewel supervises the crew shearing pines into boards. Wagons line up every morning to collect their lumber and pull off to construction sites. Brax walks down the boardwalk along Main Street to a cafe close by. Walking into the cafe he spots Becca hustling full plates to hungry patrons. He spots an empty table in the corner and makes a beeline for the chair beside it.

"Well, Sheriff, what brings you into our little establishment today," Becca says smiling at Braxton with her award-winning smile. "Mama whipped up some fine dutch oven biscuits this morning. I can slap some milk gravy over 'em if you like."

"You know I can't resist that kind of sweet talk from you, don't you," says Braxton returning Becca's grin. "I'll have some with coffee, please."

"I only do this because I love you, you know," she bends over and gives Brax a kiss. They linger for a moment then Brax watches her disappear into the kitchen.

Billy Jewel's idea of opening a cafe in Payson is paying off. Business is busy and growing.

The Payson town Marshal, Todd Salmon, walks in, sees Braxton, and comes over to sit in a chair across from him. Todd is a young, slim man in his first law job. His goal is to do the right thing and he sees Brax as a role model and mentor. Brax sees a good man that needs to keep from being shot by wild cowpunchers coming out of the saloons. He talks with Todd about using Wyatt Earp's method of whacking unruly sorts with his pistol barrel. Cold cock them before things get out of hand. Worked for Wyatt, should work for Todd.

"Morning, Brax. Looks like another great day for Payson," says Todd. "I just talked with a couple of range hands that rode in from Tonto Basin." He pauses to get Braxton's attention away from staring at the kitchen doorway.

Braxton looks at Todd, "Oh, yeah. Mornin' to you, too, Todd. What were you saying about the Basin?"

"Some cowhands rode in talking about happenings. Seems sheep are being pushed into the Basin. They told about some shepherds being worked over by cowhands, sheep herdin' dogs shot, wagons burnt, and stock killed. Doesn't sound too healthy for sheep in the Tonto," replies Todd.

"Nope, not healthy at all. Did they hear who's behind the push?" asks Brax.

"Yep, that's why I'm coming to you. Tewksbury is leading the charge. Another Mex from Springerville is close behind him. A guy named Peralta sends Mexican shepherds out with small flocks to see how far they can push," adds Todd.

"Heard about the guy before," says Brax. "Looks like they're determined to take on the cattle companies."

"Well, I've got rounds to keep, so I'll let you enjoy the cafe help...I mean your breakfast." Todd stands and with a wink walks out.

"Damn, I got to stop coming here if everyone watches what Becca and I do or don't do," mutters Brax.

Just then Becca enters and heads over to Brax with a steaming plate covered with creamy milk gravy. She sits it in front of him on the table.

"I fixed it for you myself and put just the right amount of salt and pepper on it, heavy on the pepper." She steps back and smiles at Brax. "The biscuits are under the gravy and I can bring more if you want them."

"This is fine, Becca. I just talked with Todd and there's some mixing up going on in the Basin. I've got to leave and check it out. I'll be back in a few days. Keep my 'biscuits' warm for me." He winks at Becca, and begins to eat what she placed before him. Blushing, she hurries off to take care of another customer.

It has been a week since Brax left Payson with a mule in tow carrying his gear; he still made good time across the Basin. Cattle range freely, and a few times he spots horsemen in the distance. More than likely range hands out trying to get some kind of count. Today, he rides along the edge of Sombrero Butte on the far eastside of the Basin not far from Cibeque Creek. Stopping to give his horse a breather, he hears the telltale ring of belled sheep. As he prods his horse around an outcropping of the butte, he spots a fair sized flock of sheep moving slowly along grazing on the grasses and other forage. Out in front slowly rolls a covered *carretta*, two dogs chase around the flock to keep stragglers in check and everybody moving, and beside the cart walks a man.

Brax picks up his pace and shouts at the man. "*Amigo. Amigo.* Hey, *amigo.* I'm coming in."

Suddenly, the man turns around and pulls a rifle from the *carretta*.

Brax knows the next few seconds are dangerous. He raises his hand high above his head and continues to ride toward the moving cart.

"No *enemigo, amigo*. No, *enemigo*." he continues shouting.

The rifle lowers somewhat.

"*Buenos dias, Señor*. I am Sheriff Bierman. May I get down and talk with you?" Brax slows his horse to a stop beside the cart. He looks over and sees a woman driving the wagon with two small children beside her. *Why would this man bring his family into the basin,* wonders Brax to himself? *Bullets don't care if they hit young or old.*

"*Señor*, have you had trouble driving your sheep into this valley?" asks Brax.

"No, *Señor*. I have not encountered any trouble from anyone and hopefully none from you either," says the shepherd in perfect English.

Brax leans back in his saddle and is taken aback by the shepherd's response. In the middle of the Tonto Basin an obviously well educated Mexican stops Brax flat in his tracks.

"Well, *Señor*, it appears we can be more conversant regarding your circumstances and what it is that compels you to be in this location," says Brax.

"Indeed, sir. I am grazing my flock on open range, and my family is with me in hopes of locating a suitable spot for habitation," replies the shepherd.

"You definitely have me at a disadvantage, *Señor.* I did not expect to be dialoguing with a shepherd in this manner," says Brax.

"So, am I to conclude you expect all Mexican shepherds to be ignorant monosyllabic communicators?" asks the sheepherder.

Brax just about swallows his teeth. Not only is this man intelligent he's also articulate and argumentative.

"May I dismount, *Señor,*" asks Brax.

"Make yourself at ease, sir. Dismount and find a spot for your comfort," replies the sheep man.

Dismounting and ground tying his horse, Byron steps toward the shepherd, "Where were you educated, *Señor?* Your diction and pronunciations are perfect," asks Brax in respect.

"I am a graduate of the University of Guadalajara, sir. May I ask what educational institution you graduated from?" asks the man.

"Well, sir, I graduated from a public school in Mesilla, New Mexico Territory, and have continued to educate myself by becoming well read," answers Brax.

"Very commendable for a public school graduate," says the Mexican.

Feeling his anger begin to rise, Brax changes the subject.

"Why would an educated man move into an area contested by cattle ranchers and place everything he holds dear in jeopardy?" Brax stares at the man.

"Because it is a free land. That is correct, is it not?"

"Yes, *Señor*, it is a free land as long as your gun shoots faster and straighter than the other guy."

"I must apologize, sir. My name is Fredrico Antonio Hernando Peralta, and yours is again?" the man waits for Brax's reply.

"Gila County Sheriff Braxton Bierman."

"Sheriff Bierman, let me introduce my family. This is my wife, Maria; my son Eduardo; and my daughter Juanita. Do you have a family, sir?"

"My wife, Rebecca."

"Splendid, we would like to meet her sometime."

"*Señor*, let's cut to the chase. You're fixin' to get you and yours killed. Dead. *Muerto.* Do you understand?"

"How can that be, Sheriff, now you are with us?"

"You don't get it yet. My badge doesn't stop a bullet. We have to get you and your woolies out of here, now. And, I mean now."

"I can not go back, Sheriff. I have been sending other shepherds with my sheep into this valley on a regular basis. Now a man, Tewksbury, wants to hire my business to bring more sheep here. I cannot ask people to go for me unless I come myself. Can you understand that?"

"Oh, I understand all right. You've got yourself placed squarely between a rock and a hard place. There're two feuding families and you're providing the catyl...cattt....wait a minute, I'll get this. The catalyst, yes, catalyst, that will explode this range into all-out warfare. Do you understand?"

"Perfectly, sheriff. So what's your point?"

Brax shakes his head at the misjudgment of this shepherd. He steps close and snatches the rifle from the surprised shepherd's hands.

In exasperation, Brax says, "You're going with me. Start speeding up your flock and get your dogs to work harder; we are headed west. Now. I am the law and you are under arrest."

"For what crime, Sheriff? I have done nothing illegal."

"I'm arresting you for stupidity. Now get moving or by all that is holy, I will hog-tie you and throw you in the wagon."

The shepherd calls loudly to the dogs and quickens their pace around the flock. Brax points the direction they are to head, and the shepherd directs the dogs to start moving the flock.

Brax goes back to his horse and mounts. He turns to the shepherd.

"With any luck and the good Lord on our side, we might, just might, make it to Payson without having a gunfight. Educated Mexican, you can walk, run, or ride in your cart, but let's move. Daylight is burning and I'm not wanting to stop any stray bullets."

The shepherd turns and talks rapidly to his family in the cart. He turns back to Brax.

"Lead the way, Sheriff. We are off on a new adventure."

New adventure, my butt; I've got to keep them alive to Payson, somehow.

The two small black and white dogs work their ways back and forth behind the flock of sheep yipping and snapping at the feet of slow movers. Brax sits in his saddle and marvels at how both dogs react to whistles and hand signals from Fredrico.

I've never seen any cattle move like this. The shepherd walks along and the dogs do all the work. If I had to herd something, this looks like the animal to herd if only it wasn't for the smell.

It is three days since turning toward Payson and Brax knows they are on borrowed time. He tells Fredrico to move the flock along the base of the Rim if possible. He wants to avoid the open range area where it is more likely to run into trouble. The last big risk is now before them, Pleasant Valley. Brax knows they are almost home, but they must cross this valley and it seems to bristle with livestock. He calls Fredrico to him.

"*Amigo*, as you drive your woolies into this valley, keep moving, don't stop. The grass and water will tend to slow your flock, but your dogs will have to work harder to get them across and into the hills beyond. Do you understand?" says Brax.

The shepherd stands beside Brax's horse and surveys the lush valley stretched before him.

"Certainly, I understand, Sheriff. The setting is lovely here. I may want to stay and live in this valley," says the Shepherd.

Brax laughs a short snort, "Not in this lifetime, *Amigo.* Not herding sheep. This valley is the heart of cattledom. There's no going around it, so we have to go through just as fast as we can. *Vámonos, amigo.*"

The shepherd whistles and waves his hands; both dogs stop, perk up their ears, and start yipping and moving the sheep forward.

The flock seems to flow like water into the valley. Brax watches the animals.

Away from the Rim toward the center of the valley he sees a large herd of cattle slowly grazing. He sees four specks trailing along behind the cattle. If he can see them, he knows they can see him.

Damn. So close, but not close enough to Payson.

He rides over to Fredrico, dismounts, and says, "There." Brax points at the four specks. "They'll see us, if they haven't already. If you want to save everything, you have to go faster. I'll be back. I hope." Swinging back into his saddle, Brax turns toward the specks, now grouped together, headed his direction.

Fredrico is right. This is about the best place on earth, thinks Brax as he rides through grass belly deep to his horse. The valley is edged with pine forests and there are scattered islands of trees in the sea of grass across the valley. The land rises and falls in gently rolling hills. He loses sight of the riders in the swales only to see them when they crest a ridge top riding steadily toward him.

He glances over his shoulder, and sees Fredrico is making good progress, just not fast enough. Looking forward, the specks begin to take shape. Brax can make out four cowpunchers riding abreast.

What's the right way to play this hand, he wonders. *I've spent many times figuring the odds at the Faro table. What are my odds here? How about slim and none,* he answers himself. *Well, it's a good place to die.*

Brax moves into the middle of the valley, pulls his Winchester and lays it across his horse's withers against the saddle pommel. He reaches into his saddlebag and fishes out his spare Colt and shoves it under his holster belt. Pulling his holstered revolver he checks the cylinder and returns it to his hip. He sits patiently waiting for the riders.

The sun beats down warmly on Brax. A breeze springs up sweeping down from the Rim and sends slow ripples through the grass across the valley. He glances back to check on the flock's progress.

Fredrico is moving along real well.

Brax's horse quivers and twitches as insects buzz around. He looks toward the riders and sees four cowhands with red and blue plaid shirts, bandanas tied around their necks, tall crowned wide-brimmed felt hats, gloves, and chaps flapping as they ride. They all carry holstered side arms.

Won't be long now.

Brax awaits their arrival. One more glance at the flock assures Brax they are over half way across.

As the riders close their gap to shouting distance, one on Brax's left calls to him. "Hey. Hey. What are you doin' on this range? This is Graham's range."

"Thought it was open range, cowboy," shouts Brax.

"Thought wrong, Mister," says the cowboy.

"Well, sorry. Too late to change now," Brax says.

"What are you drivin' across our range?" asks the cowboy.

The riders quickly close the gap.

"I'm moving across the valley. Not stopping," says Brax.

"By God, them's woolies, ain't they?" shouts the cowboy.

"Yep, moving them farther along the Rim," Brax sits easy in his saddle watching each rider closely.

The riders pull their mounts and stop a short distance from Brax.

"Who are you, Mister, and what gives you the right to drive sheep here?" The speaking cowboy has a drooping blond mustache and long blonde hair hanging out from under his hat. He stares at Brax with a look of hatred in his eyes.

"Well, cowboy, I'm Sheriff of Gila County, and that gives me the right to go anywhere, with anybody, and at any time I choose." Brax slowly raises his Winchester and rests it on his leg pointing skyward. "You have a problem with that?"

"Them's sheep yonder, Nate. We can take this Jasper. There's four of us." The cowboy on the right end of the line looks at the rider on the left end.

"Yep, Nate." Brax looks at the blonde haired cowboy. "Them is sheep, and there are four of you. That's one smart feller you have riding with you."

"Why, you cur dog. I'm gonna' kill you myself," shouts the rider on the right end of the line.

"Shut up, Bud. Sit still and leave your gun alone," shouts Nate. "Okay, Sheriff of Gila County, it's your move."

"You're a wise cowboy, Nate. Here's my play. You and your boys just mosey back down the valley to your herd. Those sheep will be out of your territory right quick, and we all part peaceable like, or we can commence to shootin' each other. Now, while I'm a God-awful great shot, there are four of you. So, I'll just take my old Winchester here and lay it across my arm like this, to kind of steady it, and make sure it points directly at your middle." Brax slowly lowers his Winchester and points it at the cowboy. "This way, when the shooting starts, I can blow you clear out of your saddle." Brax stops and gives the cowboys a big smile. "Now, it's your move."

"I can drop him right now, Nate. He cain't get the Winchester around fast enough to get me. I can get him, now," the rider on the right end shouts.

The two cowboys in the middle are fidgety in their saddles and quickly look from left to right. Brax knows they are no problem. The one on the right can possibly get a shot off, but Brax stays focused on Nate.

"Shut up, Bud. His Winchester ain't pointed at you, it's pointed at ME, you moron. Shut up, now." Nate sees the middle two riders want to be anywhere but where they are.

"So, you're overseein' those sheep leave the valley?" Nate asks.

"Yep, soon as they hit the tree line across the valley they're gone," says Brax hoping this can give Nate a chance to save face.

"Well, see to it you're gone from here, Mister Sheriff, and take the sheep stink with you." Nate says with a look of relief on his face.

"I can drop the law dog, Nate. I can do it," shouts Bud.

"If you don't shut up and sit still, I'm comin' over there to pistol whip the hell out of you, you moron. Shut up." Nate shouts at Bud. He looks back at Brax. "Get goin', get off our range."

"I'll just sit here a spell as y'all head back to your herd," says Brax.

"Well, suit yourself. Just be gone right quick," says Nate turning his horse. The middle two riders are already turned and trotting away. Bud sits still, staring at Brax.

"Ride away or make your play, boy. It don't make no never mind to me," says Brax. He watches the rider's muscles bunch as his face contorts with rage.

"You're lucky Nate is ramrod, Mister Sheriff of Gila County. Next time we meet there won't be no Nate around. You're a dead man."

"Boy, if I've heard that once, I've heard it a hundred times," says Brax. "Now, run along."

Bud violently yanks the reins of his horse almost twisting it into falling, digs in his spurs, and leaps to follow the disappearing riders.

Brax slides his Winchester back into its boot, puts his spare Colt back into his saddlebag, and shakes violently. A cold sweat sweeps over him and he chills in the breeze. Turning his horse around, he sees Fredrico is almost at the tree line.

"This is one hell-of-a-way to earn a living," he mutters to himself as he spurs his horse to catch up with the flock.

21
SPRINGERVILLE

"It's done, *amigo*, you now own five hundred cattle near Springerville," says Alberto handing Byron the bill of sale. "When you sell somes of the cattles, you repay your debt, yes?"

"That's the deal," agrees Byron. "Now, all I need to do is keep them from grizzly bears, mountain lions, and rustlers. Sounds simple to me."

"*Si*, is so simple, *amigo*," agrees Alberto. "Oh, there is one little thing I need to tell you. Felina, she goes with you to Springerville."

"What? Have you lost your mind? You know what it is like there. I am not taking her there. You are *loco en la cabeza, amigo*," shouts Byron as he walks around waving his arms.

"*Si*, that is what I thought you would say, *amigo*. You know how she gets when she wants to go visit a brother. I cannot keep her here; she goes anyway. It is better with you than if she wanders around by herself. No?" Alberto throws his arms up in the air and walks around. "I have picked fifteen *vaqueros* to go with you. I think your man, Gilberto, is a good *capataz*."

"I don't know if I will need that many cowhands, but if they are not needed, I will send them back to you. Gilberto is the finest foreman around and will have the ranch squared away in no time," says Byron. "Since you've shoved Felina on me, you better have a coach for her travel. I'm not dragging some *carreta* along for her to ride in."

"*Si, si,* I have a coach arranged and loaded already. Two drivers will take care of her wishes so you don't have to worry. Yes?" Alberto offers.

"Yes, is right. Do you have any more surprises?" asks Byron.

"Well, *amigo,* only one more little one," says Alberto. "Another *ranchero* claims some of our cattles belong to them. They call themselves a 'hasher knife outfits' or something like that."

"Oh, great. Now you've got me involved in rustling? You gave me a bill of sale; is this a clean bill?"

What kind of mess am I getting into?

"*Si, si,* it is a clean bill, but you still have the *gringo ranchero* who disputes the clean bill. I know you can work it out, *amigo*." Alberto flashes a big grin to reassure Byron.

"I plan to head out, avoid San Carlos Res, to Fort Apache, keep out of the White Mountains, and get to Springerville north of there. This gives us a road to follow to make good time. Since I have this sparkling clean bill of sale, I better get there quick before we lose all our cattle. Are you ready for Felina to travel? I have pack mules loaded and ready to go."

"*Si, si, amigo*. The coach is from the livery and the drivers they bring it here as we speak," says Alberto. "All you have to do is get Felina on it."

"All I have to do? Why do I have to get Felina on it?" asks Byron.

"She wants to drive herself. She does not think she is entitled to be driven. Go make some sense to her, *Amigo*. I cannot deal with another running away episode, *por favor*." Alberto shakes his head and shrugs.

Frustrated by the turn of events, Byron stomps out of the *cantina*, through the doorway, and stops in front of a door in the hallway. He pounds on the door and waits for an answer.

"*Si, entrar.*" Felina says.

Opening the door, Byron steps into the room, and sees Felina sitting on her canopied bed surrounded by pillows. Latticework covers the windows letting soft, filtered light into the room. A large dresser stands against one wall and a shorter one is on the opposite side. Two large leather covered chairs sit beside a round wooden table inside the door. Multicolored rugs lie scattered on the floor.

"It's time to ride, Felina," says Byron. "Alberto says you are going to Springerville with me."

"*Si.* I look forward to the trip," says Felina.

"Good, let's get moving. Are you packed?" asks Byron.

"Oh, *si, si*, everything is in the coach. I will be happy to drive it."

"Whoa, there are two drivers taking care of that," says Byron.

"Then, I no go." says Felina. "No one should have to drive me."

"Felina, these men want to drive you, not have to drive you." shares Byron hoping he is right.

"No. I drive or not go."

Byron can see a small child's fit being wound up about to release.

"Okay. You drive." Byron throws up his arms and walks toward the door. "Let's go. We're burning daylight." He walks from the room with Felina following closely behind.

Walking through the *cantina*, they step out front and find the coach waiting. Alberto is talking with the drivers and turns as they exit.

"*Bueno, bueno*. It is time to go," he says while opening the coach door for Felina.

Felina motions to one of the drivers to climb down. He steps down and stands in front of her.

"Have a seat," she says to the driver pointing to the coach door being held open by Alberto.

Felina steps past the men, climbs into the driver's seat, and takes the reins from the other driver. Alberto looks sharply at Byron.

"Who can control her, *amigo*?" says Byron as he shrugs his shoulders and quickly mounts his horse.

The coach jerks forward with a lurch followed by Byron and the riders. They head for Springerville as Alberto stands shaking his head in disbelief.

"*Via con Dios, amigo,*" he shouts at the disappearing caravan.

"You will need it."

The caravan makes good time. Leaving Solomonville they head north to Fort Apache skirting the San Carlos reservation. From Fort Apache they continue on edging past the White Mountains, and turn east to Springerville.

Entering the small town, Byron views what there is to offer: Springer's Trading Post, four saloons, two bordellos, two livery stables, a few framed business structures, and a small hotel. It appears a stage stop is at the hotel. The saloons and bordellos are doing a lively daytime business with cowboys' horses tied to hitching rails along both sides of the main street. Town inhabitants walk in the street and along a few sections of boardwalks.

The entrance of twenty riders and the coach cause enough interest the townspeople stop to watch the caravan. Cowboys hang out of the batwing doors and gawk as they arrive. Byron pays particular interest to the attention from the saloons.

A few drunken cowboys saunter on the bar's porch making disgusting comments to the *vaqueros* riding with Byron. Some laugh and make obscene gestures towards Felina as she drives the coach. Some are so drunk they can't stand upright and fall down laughing.

Yep, just the place I want to live, thinks Byron.

He leans over to Gilberto who rides beside him.

"Make sure the men keep to themselves and no fights start. Take the men and coach to the livery stables. See Felina stays with the carriage until I figure out what is going on. I've got to look for the guy we bought the cattle from. Can you handle this?" asks Byron.

"*Si, Patron.* I make sure no trouble starts and will take care of *Señorita* Felina," Gilberto replies as he turns and gives directions to the riders.

Byron pulls up in front of a saloon, steps down from his horse, ties it to the rail, and walks up on the porch. Drunk and curious cowboys watch his approach.

"Hey, Stranger, how's come you ridin' with a bunch of Mex?" one drunk slurs.

"Is that filly with y'all takin' care of everybody?" another drunk cowboy doubles over laughing at his own sick joke.

It takes all of Byron's self control to push his way through the crowd to the bat-wing doors and enter the saloon. He walks over to the bartender.

"Nice place you have here," Byron says in a tone that drips sarcasm.

"Ain't bad, if you don't stay long, Stranger," snarls back the bartender. "Course you over stay and it could be permanent."

"Not planning on over staying. Wouldn't be here if I could avoid it," snaps Byron.

"State your business, or get the hell out," the bartender bites back.

"Here it is then," says Byron. "Where can I find George Markwell?"

"Georgie. Georgie. This stranger's lookin' for you," the bartender shouts towards the back corner of the saloon.

A disheveled middle-aged man raises his head from the table he sits at. His eyes are bloodshot; he wears a greasy buckskin jacket, worn blue denim pants, a head full of short cut tousled brown hair. He looks like he's slept in the chair at the table for days.

"What'cha want," hollers George.

Byron walks over to the wreck of a man and sits in the chair across from him. The noise and activity in the saloon returns to normal volume as the interest in Byron quickly dissipates.

"I'm Bierman. Bought your herd. Need to know where you have it bunched up," states Byron.

"Ha, Ha, that's rich, that is," says Markwell. He waves his arm around in a semicircle. "They're out there, Mr. Bierman. I've been run down and run out by outlaws, rustlers, and Hashknife riders who have scattered my, nope, YOUR herd all over this hell's half acre. Ha, Ha, that's rich."

"Where are your riders? Didn't they keep the herd together?" asks Byron.

"Good God, boy. Don't you get it? They were in on it. This is the biggest outlaw rustler Hell Hole in the Territory," says Markwell, staring at Byron.

"So, what about this bill of sale for the cattle?" asks Byron.

"Oh. It's good, providing you can convince the Hashknife Outift my cattle weren't rustled from them," says Markwell. "I can't be absolutely sure because of the thieving pack of riders that were supposed to work for me."

"Why are you still here, then?" asks Byron. "When you got the money from my partner in Solomonville, why didn't you keep riding?"

"My foreman got wind of the sale and rode with me along with two others to get the money to make sure they were paid," says George Markwell. "When we got back and settled up, some others bushwhacked me and cleaned me out. Now, I'm busted flat as last night's aces-and-eights," said Markwell. "I'm looking for a job. Do you need a rider?"

Byron sits back to consider all he's just heard.

What kind of mess have I walked into? Alberto assures me the cattle are here, and sent men to confirm everything before making the deal. It must have been a huge cover up to steal at this level. What can I do? What should I do? What would Guillo and Pa do?

"All right, Markwell, we're going to get them back. All of them." says Byron. Markwell sits up and pays attention to the steel in Byron's voice. "Get your gear and be down at the livery, end of the street, in one hour. We're going to work. Today."

"Everything I own is on my horse out front tied to the rail," said Markwell. "I'm ready to ride right now."

"Let's get out of here and go to work." Byron stands and moves quickly through the saloon and out to his horse. Markwell moves rapidly to keep up.

Both men step into their saddles.

"Lead the way to MY ranch house, Markwell," says Byron. "They did leave the house, didn't they?"

"Yes, Mr. Bierman," Markwell smirks at the question. "Let's head out of town going west."

"We'll go by the livery, end of the street, and pick up my riders. *Vámonos.*"

Both men trot their horses down the main street of Springerville.

The road heads due west from town almost to Green's Peak. Markwell waves the caravan off the road onto a well-used trail leading toward Blue Springs and they soon come upon Markwell's ranch, now owned by Byron, Guillo, and Alberto minus the five hundred head of cattle listed on the bill of sale.

"Home, sweet home," says George Markwell pointing at a long low single story house of stacked stone walls with a cedar shake roof. Two large barns and bunkhouses sit behind the house; a cookhouse, and large corral complete the picture.

"There's a smithy set up on the other side of the first barn," says Markwell. "It's been a good spread for a long time."

"It's going to be good again, George," says Byron. "Bet on it."

Byron calls Gilberto over and introduces him to Markwell. Byron watches while both men size each other up and seem to accept the measurements.

"Gilberto, turn some of our *vaqueros* loose on the range to flush out every head of cattle they can. Drive them close to the ranch. We'll sort out brands once they are here. Markwell, go with Gilberto and show him the lay of the land."

"*Si, Patron.* Come, Mr. Markwell, show me the lands," says Gilberto, turning his horse around.

"Gilberto, it's just George, okay?" says Markwell. "We're goin' to get along real well."

Byron dismounts and walks toward the ranch house as two riders come thundering down the trail towards the house. Byron turns to face the arrivals. Gilberto and Markwell stop as the riders pull up in front of Byron.

Both riders straddle lathered horses and wear leather chaps over blue denim pants, red plaid shirts, leather vests, gloves, and tall crowned wide brimmed felt hats. The larger of the two shouts at Markwell.

"Thought you cleared out of these parts."

"You're mistaken, boys. I'm showing the new owner around a bit," says George pointing to Byron.

"What can I help you with, Gentlemen? My name's Bierman," says Byron.

"Bierman, Steerman, don't make no difference. You're on Hashknife Outfit range, pilgrim. Best if you clear out, and take Markwell with you," sneers the tallest rider.

"No, boys, y'all are on Bierman property, and you've got about one minute to claw your ragged asses and scrawny nags off this property. Tell whoever sent you to send men next time to talk to me." Byron turns to walk towards the house.

Both riders dig for the holstered Colts they wear, and suddenly freeze when they hear Winchesters levered at one time. Looking up they see six *vaqueros* step around the corner of the house with rifles leveled at them. Byron turns and motions with his hands as he says, "Shoo, go away."

Yanking their horses' reins around, they thunder back up the trail away from the ranch house.

"Mr. Bierman, we're cooked now," says Markwell. "The Hashknife Outfit works for Aztec Cattle Company. They're leasing up to a million acres north along the railroad, shipping in cattle from Texas, and flooding our range with their stock. Those boys that showed up here are the tip of a wave heading this way. I don't mean to tell you your business, but the Hashknife is a bunch of thugs, killers, rustlers, and Texas trash that came along with the cattle."

"George, I didn't come here to be run off my range or run out of my ranch. Hashknife wants a fight. We'll give it. They want to be friendly, can't find a better friend than us. Gilberto, what do you think we should do?"

Gilberto sits still for a moment taking in the fact the *Patron* asks his opinion. "If the *Patron* says stay, *Señor* George, then we damn well stay. *Gracias, Patron*, we have work to do. *Vámonos, Jorge*, George." He spurs his horse gently and moves at a trot away from the ranch house.

"Well, I'll be," says George. "With riders like Gilberto and the others, I think the Hashknife is in for a tussle. Mind if I ride for your brand, Byron?"

"Be pleased to have you with us, George. Now, get out there and work with Gilberto, and thanks." Markwell hurries away to catch Gilberto.

Byron suddenly turns toward a ruckus at the end of the ranch house as Felina races around the corner with a Winchester in her hands.

"Where are the *pendejos,* assholes, *mi Querido?*" shouts Felina at Byron.

Smiling, Byron steps up to her and gently removes the rifle from her grip.

"Everything is fine, they're gone. Where were you during their visit?" asks Byron.

"*Ay, yi-yi.* Those drivers, they shove me inside the coach and hold the doors closed so I no can get out." She huffs her answer at Byron. "I find a horsewhip and use it on them."

Laughing out loud, Byron reaches and takes her by the hand.

"They did exactly what I want them to do, Felina. They looked out for your safety. Let's go check out this place. I'm sure it's going to take some work to set in order. No. You will not horsewhip anyone," says Byron as they step up on the porch of the ranch house.

"When I find a whip and those drivers, a little lashing will help them, I think," mutters Felina quietly.

Exhaling slowly, his finger tightens on the Winchester resting across the fallen pine tree; a blue eye aligns the target with the bead on the end of the barrel. It has been a long hunt, a lot of hiding and waiting, but now, one more step will determine life or death.

Now.

The rifle belches its slug across the mountain meadow, and the wolf leaps with the impact and collapses.

Been too long coming, thinks Byron standing from behind the warren of tree branches that hid him. *No more calves for you El Lobo.*

As he walks through the woods to where his horse is tied, Byron views the tall pine forests that patchwork the landscape interspersed with mountain meadows alive with flowers and new grasses.

It's been a tough winter, but we've made it and have managed to scrape together most of the herd Markwell sold us. He kicks at a clump of wet, slushy snow still hiding under overhanging pine branches. *It is hard to believe snow and ice accumulate as deep in these mountains as it does. Guillo will never believe it.*

Mounting his horse, he reboots his rifle, and rides to the downed wolf. He uses all his muscle power to heft the carcass behind the saddle. "Glad you aren't full grown," Byron grunts between clinched teeth. The horse prances around not liking its grisly and onerous load. Byron stokes his horse's jaw and muzzle to settle it.

"Got to take *lobo* back and skin it," he says to the horse stepping into the stirrup. Across the meadow on the horizon, Byron sees three riders. "Heard the rifle, probably," he mutters. "Don't think they're my riders."

Byron turns his horse back into the pine trees, dismounts, pulls his rifle, and walks to the front of the stand opening onto the meadow. Levering his Winchester, he leans against a tall pine and waits for his visitors.

The riders continue to advance becoming more visible. Byron sees cowboys clad in denim pants, leather chaps, heavy coats, wool scarves, gloves, and slouch felt hats.

Working cowboys?

The riders slow down from a quick lope to a slow walk. The middle rider shouts to Byron as they come to a stop.

"Heard a shot, just checkin' to make sure everything's okay."

"Its all good here, cowboy," says Byron. "Just bagged a wolf that's been stalking my herd for months."

"Good for you. Means it won't be any trouble for us either," replies the rider.

"Looks like you boys are riding for the Hashknife outfit," says Byron, now getting a better look at the riders.

"Yes, sir. We ride for that brand," the cowboy replies. "Been doin' it for a while, since we moved stock south from the railroad. Been a lot of work, but this range is mighty fine for runnin' cattle."

"Yep, run my own here too," says Byron.

"What's your outfit, Sir," inquires the cowboy.

"B-Z," says Byron.

All three riders stiffen in their saddles and quickly look around.

"We just come to see if there was trouble Mister, that's all," says the cowboy.

"So you said," replies Byron.

"We ain't fixin' to tangle with you any. We heard about what the B-Z done to those other Hashknife riders. Course they was outlaws and rustlers, and that ain't us, Mister." The two outside riders continue to look around for any movement in the meadow.

"Good to know, men," says Byron. "Those other boys stole stock from me and it was time to end their erring ways, permanently. You can't stay healthy on this range stealing from others. Why does your outfit put up with their kind?" asks Byron.

"Don't know, Mister. There ain't many of them, but like they say, one rotten apple messes up a bunch, don't it? I think some of them boys drifted from Texas when the cattle shipped here. I know some work with Ike Clanton over to Springerville. Me and my crew keep ourselves between Holbrook and the 'Pache Res," says the rider. "We did get direction to start pushin' stock towards Tonto Basin along the Rim, so we're fixin' to go that direction."

"That's a good piece to drift with cattle," says Byron.

"Yes, sir, but they keep unloadin' more cattle along the railroad and shovin' them our direction. It's sure stirring up a fit with the small ranchers." The cowboy shrugs. "A feller named Graham is havin' a tussle with a Tewksbury guy. Seems to go back a ways, but some of our boys have been ridin' with them Grahams. The Tewksbury guy is fixin' to bring sheep onto the range. Different Mex families been drivin' sheep onto range between here and the Tonto for a while. Been some talk about drawin' a deadline on the edge of the Rim, top for sheep and below for cattle."

"Cowboy, you are a regular fount of information," says Byron.

"Heck, mister, all I got to talk to are these Jaspers and cows;" he smiles, pointing at the riders beside him, and shrugs.

"Well, are we good here, cowboy?" asks Byron.

"We're fine, Mister B-Z. Be seein' you around." The three riders pull the reins of their horses, turn around and move into a steady lope across the meadow.

Byron slowly uncocks his rifle, turns, and walks back into the woods to retrieve his horse. He thinks about the information shared by the cowboy.

More Aztec cattle pushing onto this range means more conflict and troubles with the Hashknife Outfit. Outlaws in Springerville, potential troubles with Aztec, and God-awful snowy cold winters. Time to talk with Gilberto and Markwell, he realizes.

Swinging into his saddle, he spurs his horse towards the ranch house.

22
CALCULATED MOVE

"That's the gamble. I can't paint the picture any better or worse. Either we stay and die, or we go and risk living," says Byron. "Time to decide now while we can, before it's forced on us. Decide."

"I have." says Felina. "I am going. *Mexicano* shepherd they tell me *mi hermano*, Fredrico, takes his sheeps and goes that direction. I go there also." She sits with crossed arms staring at Byron, Gilberto, and Markwell around the dining table in the ranch house.

"Well, that's one," smirks Markwell.

"Does any of this make sense with y'all," asks Byron. "If we stay put, the pressure coming down from up along the Atlantic and Pacific railroad by Aztec is going to make stock raising a more difficult business. We already contend with nature and cantankerous cattle without getting into arguments, or worse being ambushed by Hashknife outlaws."

"*Si, Patron.* My *vaqueros* say they see more and more Hashknife riders on our range. Since we have shootout to gets our cattle back, they don't rides too close, but many more can make them very brave. No?" says Gilberto.

"I sure hate to ride off and leave all this luxury behind," Markwell says with a smirk gesturing around the house. "If we can save the herd, get to a lower elevation for better winters, and keep from bein' chopped up by Hashknife, it seems worth it."

"Okay, we're resolved then," says Byron. "I'll write a letter to Guillo letting him know our plans. Gilberto, we're relying on you to get the letter to Guillo and return with his answer. Everything hinges on Guillo's reply. Are you good with this Gilberto? A lot is riding on you."

"*Patron*, I will not let you or B-Z down. I will be ready to ride in the morning. No?"

"*Si*, I will write the letter and have it ready to go in the morning. Thank you, *mi Capataz. Via con Dios.*"

"*Si,* I too will be ready in the morning. I will go and clean up the coach and find those *dos valer nada*, two worthless, drivers who need a whipping," says Felina.

"Holy Smoke, Girl. Give it a rest, will you," says Markwell. "She's been houndin' those two drivers since we got here."

"Felina, we will get things ready when they need to be prepared. Main thing now is hearing from Guillo." Byron smiles as he looks deeply into Felina's eyes. "Everything in its time. Yes?"

Guillo,

This is a letter I never thought I would write. Hope all is well with you. Things here are getting a mite dicey. An outlaw outfit, the Hashknife, well most of them are all right cowboys, is crowding the range and already had a shootout or two with them. A huge eastern company is leasing millions of acres while shipping cattle and flooding the range with stock rubbing out small ranches. And Compañero, you won't believe how deep the snow is in the winter. All said, we want to move the herd to better range before we find ourselves in a fight with no winner. So, I'm asking you for your decision. I would like to take Henry Hooker up on his offer and sell most of our San Simon herd to him. I would need you to drive around eight hundred head from home to Fort Apache then along Crook's Road to near Cibeque Creek, gentle the stock down the Rim into the Tonto Basin and head west to a location called Pleasant Valley. When this is done, we should have about fourteen to fifteen hundred head in a well-watered and healthy pastured open range. Yes, less cattle, but better location more suited to what Hooker warned about happening, drought and other things. Besides it gets me out of the cold, icy, and snowy winters – good golly it was cold, Guillo.

It's a long hazardous drive I'm asking of you. I know we will lose stock to some crossing and Apaches; they're starving on the Res. If you're willing to undertake this risk, the other letter is for Mr. Hooker. It is my proposal to sell the rest of the herd to him. Review the details and make any changes you think are right. Gilberto will deliver the proposal to Hooker and return with your reply.

I know this is asking a lot Compañero, but in the long run I'm banking on it being the right thing to do. You and Pa were always ones to take a risk. I wait for your reply.

Sincerely
Byron

The light from the lamp flickers in a sudden draft. Byron lays down his steel tipped pen and stoppers the bottle of ink.

Now, it's all in Guillo's hands. Some decisions aren't made easy, and some once made are irreversible. This is one of those.

Reaching over he turns down the wick and extinguishes the lamp.

A hot dusty wind whips through the San Simon Valley threatening to snatch away the letter. Slowly, Guillo sits down on the edge of the front porch continuing to read. He looks up at the *vaquero* in front of him with mud splotched trousers and denim jacket, a faded blue cotton shirt with flap pockets, a sweat stained well worn sombrero, and dirt caked face cracked at the corners of his mouth and eyes. He's ridden hard and long. His horse looks the worse for wear as well.

"You know what's in this letter, *El Capataz*?" asks Guillo.

"*Si, Jefe*. The *Patron* talks about all the possibilities before he writes it to you," answers Gilberto. "He asks my ideas about it too. I think it is something we must do."

Guillo stands and begins to walk in a circle talking aloud. "He wants to sell the herd. Miguel has cattle shipped to him from here. Byron fights gunfights on the range with *banditos*. Hooker may not want to buy herd. Drive cattle across Res to a Rim somewhere *norte* of here. Water and open range. Leave all this behind."

"*Jefe*, I will be here to wait for an answer. The *Patron* waits for your decision."

"*Si, si, Capataz*. I know you will ride with instruction. First, go, clean up, get a good meal in you, and then come see me." Guillo turns around, steps on the porch, and goes into the house.

Walking over to a secretary desk, he drags over a chair, pulls out paper, a bottle of ink, and a steel tipped pen. *I hope I can make letters still. It has been a long time since I write.* Guillo puts pen to paper.

> *Byron,*
> *We come.*
> *Guillo*

He folds up the letter and slips it into an envelope. Putting the ink and pen away, stands, and goes onto the porch. Leaning against a post, he looks across the San Simon Valley before him, remembers Zep, Chihuahua, Allie, Manolito, Miguel, the Mogollon Mountains, Socorro, Las Cruces, Mesilla, Braxton, Billy, and Adeline.

One more time, vaquero. Mi Sabrino needs me. I go.

Straightening up, he walks into the house.

Gilberto waits with his horse in front of the ranch house before dawn. The horse softly nickers and nervously paws the ground. He remembers coming to the house yesterday evening and talking at length with Guillo about what lies ahead. He thinks his *Jefe* is trying to drain his brain with all the questions about land, route, hazards, roads, crossings, Indians, Anglos, and distances. It surprises him how much he can answer. He's sure he knows his *Jefe's* answer to

Byron. Guillo steps out on the porch with two envelopes.

"Gilberto, you are *el major Capataz y vaquero*. Take this letter to Mister Hooker and the other one to the *Patron*. Tell him we come.

Gilberto feels his heart take a jump. Saluting Guillo, he pulls the reins on his horse, and spurs him into a gallop heading south to take the pass to Maley and on to Hooker's Sierra Blanca *hacienda*. It doesn't feel like the horse's hooves are even connecting with the ground. *Ay, yi-yi.*

Since Gilberto's return, the ranch is in constant chaos. Everything not nailed down is prepared for travel. Felina's coach is stuffed with furniture and fixtures from the house, bunkhouse, cookhouse and barns. Another wagon carries spare tack, the smithy forge, spare wagon parts, and farming equipment. Byron marvels there is so much stuff. He walks through the ranch grounds watching all hands pitch in to make ready for the move. Two riders come galloping into the yard in front of the house and motion to him.

"*Patron*, Gilberto says to let you know the herd is pulled together and ready to move," says one rider.

"Good, go back and let him know to move them in the morning. He knows the way we are going. *Muchas gracias*." says Byron.

Both riders salute, turn their horses, and spur into a gallop returning the way they came. Byron walks over to George Markwell who supervises the loading.

"George, you going to miss this place?" asks Byron.

"Not one bit, Boss. Not one bit. Lookin' forward to seein' Tonto Basin. Sounds like a great place," replies Markwell.

"Herd is moving in the morning, and you ready to roll?" asks Byron looking around at all the activity.

"Yep, Boss, we'll be ready to roll first thing in the mornin'. Should make some good miles tomorrow; we'll be headin' downhill." Markwell smiles at Byron.

"Okay, make sure everyone has a ride." Byron walks back to the house. He stands leaning again a porch post.

If this idea is a bust, we're done.

The noise of packing is shattered by gunfire. Byron jumps, races to his horse, and throws himself into his saddle. He sees Markwell do the same.

"George, stop. Stay here. Get everyone undercover. This may be a feint to draw us away. Get ready for an attack." He turns and gallops to the sound of gunfire.

Hanging on, at full gallop, he sees two riders head toward him. He slows the horse to a lope and pulls out his rifle. Both are B-Z men.

"*Patron*, raiders hit the herd. They tries to scatter the cattle. Gilberto, he is ready for something like this, and stops them quick," shouts one rider as he circles around to ride beside Byron.

The second rider says, "I saw other riders go down when Gilberto sends us to you. His little knife may have some answers when we get there."

Shortly, they ride into a meadow with milling cattle as *vaqueros* move around quieting everything down. Dangling from an oak tree, a cowboy twists from a rope pulling his arms above his head so his feet barely touch the ground. Gilberto stands in front of the cowboy who has blood running down his cheek and an oozing bullet hole in his thigh.

"*Patron*, this man says he and his *amigos* work for Ike Clanton. Sometimes he rides for Hashknife," says Gilberto. The cowboy's left cheek is sliced open and a steady stream of blood runs down his face, dripping off his chin.

"Put the knife away, *Capataz*," says Byron.

"It is a quick, easy way to loosen the tongue, *Patron*," replies Gilberto as he wipes the Bowie knife on the cowboy's chaps and slides the blade back into its sheath on his belt.

"It's very effective," says Byron. "Did we lose any *vaqueros*?"

"No, *Patron*, I thinks the drunk Anglo outlaws would try somethings before we leave. They did not disappoint me," answers Gilberto. "There are three who will not move no more over there." He points to a small grove. *Vaqueros* drag three bodies by their feet toward the trees.

"How many were there?" asks Byron.

"I think there were eight or ten, *Patron.* It happens very fast. Yes?" answers Gilberto.

"That means the others are beating a path back to Springerville," says Byron. "I know it's midday, but we need to move now, Gilberto. Can you get our men to start moving the herd, now?"

"*Si, Patron*, we will move and watch at the same time. *Bueno?*"

"*Bueno, El Capataz. Muy bueno.*" Byron points his horse back toward the house. Turning around in the saddle he says, "Cut down the outlaw, wrap something on his cheek, and turn him loose. He's not going to bother us any time soon. *Bueno?*"

"*Si, Patron,*" Gilberto answers reluctantly. Under his breath, he whispers to the outlaw, "Today is your lucky day, *pendejo.*" Gilberto yanks out his knife and slices the rope holding the cowboy who collapses in a heap. He shouts orders to take care of the man and turn him loose. Replacing his knife in the scabbard, he rides away to join the *vaqueros* and the herd.

Byron shivers, realizing the anger and efficiency his foreman is capable of. It's time to get the others moving. He rides quickly back to the house.

23
ON THE MOVE

Clint leads Henry Hooker's cowboys up to the ranch house of B-Z. Guillo watches their approach and stands up as Clint's horse comes to a stop in front of the porch. Guillo leans on the porch post. *Today's the day, and I wonder what Hooker's men think about the deal?*

Clint leans forward crossing his arms on his saddle horn.

"You're giving it up?" he asks.

"*Si, amigo*. Going north to start again. Starting again is okay, no?" says Guillo.

"Well, Pard, it ain't to my liking, but if'n it fits you, go for it." Clint smiles.

"*Señor* Hooker, he shares from Byron's letter with you, no?" asks Guillo.

"Yep, he read all the details. So, how do you want to start?" replies Clint.

"The *vaqueros* have the range stock rounded up just south of here. Is good to go there and count. Everything else, she will be loaded up on wagons and ready to leave by end of week. Have your cowboys put their belongings in the bunkhouse." Guillo points to a close-by bunkhouse. "Let's ride out to begin the count." A stable hand brings Guillo's horse and both men ride to the south.

The dust, noise, and commotion of driving over eight hundred cattle stirs up interest in Solomonville, and the *vaqueros* are careful to avoid the ditches and irrigated fields as they drive the cattle beside the roadway. People along the way stop and watch the cattle move past. At the edge of town, a crowd gathers as townsfolk stop their buckboards, buggies, and horses to watch the trail drive. Guillo tirelessly oversees the steady progress and the *vaqueros* encircle the herd to keep it as compact as possible until they pass the town. When everything is in order, he turns away and rides into Solomonville.

Ah, it must be the place, Guillo smiles to himself. *For someone who doesn't seek attention, La Araña is not difficult to locate.*

He looks at a single-story adobe building with no exterior windows facing the street. In the middle of the wall is a large recessed heavy wooden double door. On both sides of the door sit *Mexicanos* draped with *serapes* and their chins resting on their chests under their *sombreros.*

Guillo rides past the doorway, dismounts, and ties his horse to a hitching rail four buildings away. Walking quietly, he steps to the recessed doorway. Creeping up on the drowsing guards, he kicks the tilted chair out from under the sentry closest to him. The man collapses as the other watchman springs from his chair, drawing his pistol.

"Ah, ah, ah," says Guillo smiling at both men with his Colt pointed at the fallen guard. "It is not a good time to *siesta.* You never know when guests they can come calling, no."

Both men glare at Guillo who gestures for them to unload their firearms and throw them in the street.

"Now, *amigos.* No harm's done. *Si?*" He smiles at both men. "It would be a nice time to go to another *cantina* for something to drink. No? *Vámonos.*"

Both guards reluctantly begin to move across the street; they never remove their stare from Guillo.

"*Si, amigos, es muy bueno.*" Guillo steps to the double door, placing his back against the door, and opens it inward never taking his eyes from the guards now standing in the middle of the roadway. Swiftly, he opens the door, steps inside, slams it shut, and stands with his back to the double door looking into Alberto's *cantina.*

"What is the meaning of this intrusion, *Señor.*" demands Alberto rising from his table in the corner. Alberto reaches towards a drawer to his right.

"Ah, ah, ah, *amigo*. Do you not see my *pistola*? She points at your bellybutton. No?" says Guillo. Alberto slowly stands upright. Guillo deftly slips a bolt on the door effectively locking it. He walks to the table and sits in an overstuffed chair. He motions with his revolver and Alberto sits with a thud.

There's banging on the front door. Alberto looks at the door and then the man holding the revolver. Guillo nods his head and shrugs.

"*Silencio, estupidos. Silencio.*" Alberto shouts at the top of his voice. The hammering on the door stops.

"*Es* much nicer to talk when quiet, no?" asks Guillo.

"What do you want, *amigo*. I have money, *mucho dinero*, take some and leave." says Alberto.

"*Señor*, let me introduce myself. *Me llama es Guillo Zapato*," says Guillo.

A flicker of acknowledgement glimmers in Alberto's eyes.

"*Si, si*, we are *Compañeros, Señor* Zapato," says Alberto with excitement in his voice. "We together own a cattle herd, no?"

"*Ay, yi-yi, Señor* Peralta, we are no *Compañeros.* Do you know what I do when I see *La Araña*? I takes *mi grande zapato*, big shoe, and squashes it." Guillo taps the barrel of this revolver on the edge of the table.

"What is your point, *Señor.* We can talk threats all day long if you wish," says Alberto.

"*Si*, my point. I like a man who comes to the point." Guillo watches Alberto's face closely. "For almost a year you have been toying with *mi Sabrino*, Byron Bierman, yes?

"We have been business partners as you say," replies Alberto.

"Ha, business partners. You have found ways to use my young *Patron* to achieve what you want."

"I have done only what he would permit, nothing more."

"*La Araña*, it is over, today."

"We have a cattle deal that is not over. He owes me."

"Ah, yes, you arranged a purchase of cattle with *mi Sabrino*, as a Anglo front man. You no can do the deal because Anglos will not easily complete big deals with *Mexicanos.* No?"

"Let's say, making the deal was easier with an Anglo and I needed *Señor* Bierman for his name and brand. Yes?"

"Well, *amigo*, it almost gets *mi Sabrino* killed, and this, *el ladron*, you thief, makes me a little angry. *Si*, thief fits you well," says Guillo.

"How can I argue with a man holding a gun?" says Alberto.

"There is no need to argue, *amigo.* Today is another deal day. Here is your deal," says Guillo." At the rancho B-Z you will find two hundred heads of cattles. *Señor* Hooker, he is rounding up his cattles now, and yours will be there if you do not delay. These cattles make our deal over, *al finales.* We no longer will be bothered by you, *comprender, amigo?*"

"*Tengo entendido que*, I understand that, *Señor* Zapato," says Alberto. "But, *Señor* Bierman, he has *mi hermana.*"

"Oh, *Señor* Peralta. I know your *hermana*, Felina, and you *Señor* have never had your *hermana.* She always does what she wants, when she wants, no?" says Guillo smiling. "Now, we are *al finales, si?*"

Knowing the character of the man sitting across from him, eyeing the Colt, Alberto calculates cutting his losses, and replies, "*Al finales, Señor, si.*"

Rising from his chair, Guillo says, "*Bueno, bueno, amigo.* It is a good morning to be alive. I will find my way out the back. Do not bothers to open the front door for me." Looking around the *cantina* he says, "*Ay, caramba*, this is no *cantina, amigo. Es burdelo*, bordello, *si.*"

Rapidly, Guillo walks through the doorway in the back wall, down the hallway, and through the door leading outside. In the alleyway, he quickly turns towards where his horse is tied. Without confrontation he gets to his horse, mounts, and heads out of town. Passing the double front doors of Alberto's *cantina*, he sees they are flung wide open and he hears Alberto screaming at the guards inside the building.

Guillo catches up with the herd well past Solomonville, and urges his *vaqueros* to push the cattle along faster.

Yes, today is a good day to be alive.

The coach lurches again, this time it almost throws Brax over the side. He grabs the rail around to the top of the coach and hangs on.

"Can't you hit EVERY hole in this excuse for a road, Henry?" He shouts vehemently at the driver. The 'whip' sways with the rocking of the Concord stagecoach. A master "six-in-hand" driver, he tugs on the reins woven between his fingers directing the six-horse hitch pulling the coach.

"Sheriff, it don't get no more fun than running this stretch from Rye Creek to Annie's Orchard. These horses want to run some, so quit your bellyaching and enjoy the ride. Sure beats walkin'," Henry shouts back.

Brax clings to the shotgun seat of the stagecoach that runs its route between Globe and Payson. He doesn't want to be here, but the ballot boxes riding in the boot of this coach make the ride necessary. As Sheriff of Gila County, he has to make certain they reach the county seat in Globe. Glancing to his right, Brax watches Henry Smoot pull on each rein just enough to guide the six horses thundering down the road in front of him. Henry's black duster jacket is brown from trail dust while the bandana tied across his face keeps him from breathing dirt and only lets his eyes peep over the top. A dome-crowned wide-brimmed felt hat is pulled low across his brow and dangling hat strings tie it securely to his head. Brax is friends with Henry; they have been since he rolled the first Concord stagecoach into Payson.

The ride down the Rim from Payson takes on a different view from the shotgun seat instead of being horseback. Henry masterfully directs the six horses through the switchbacks weaving the road back and forth down Rye Creek hill. Brax holds his breath in many spots. Now, Henry lets his team run as the road levels out somewhat and winds through growths of Piñon pines, oak trees, and manzanita along the roadway. Annie's Orchard is coming up shortly and Brax knows he can jump down for some stability as the team takes a breather, is watered, and cooled down.

"Henry, if you'll allow me a little steadiness, I'd like to roll me a smoke," says Brax fishing around in his vest pockets for cigarette paper and his bag of Bull Durham. "It'll help steady my nerves while I'm watchin' your driving."

"Cain't guarantee nothin' steady, Brax. This here stretch of road's been washed out a bunch from rains, so hang onto your noggin." Henry watches Brax try to pour tobacco onto the creased paper in his fingers spilling most of it. "Might be waitin' till we get to Annie's would be better," he says with a wink.

In disgust, Brax gives up, returns his cigarette makings to his vest pockets, and rides along in a sullen mood. "Didn't want a smoke anyway," he mutters under his breath.

The Concord coach continues swaying and jolting along the road.

"Hey, Brax, look at it this way," shouts Henry, "At least you ain't havin' to ride every trip with me and my 'girls.'"

"Just because you feel so all fired special about driving a six-horse team of all mares, don't make them your 'girls,' Henry," Brax shouts back. "What's riding every trip got to do with things?"

"Why, them 'whips' that drive the Black Canyon route from Wickenburg to Prescott has sheriffs ridin' every trip with them. Them highwaymen are thick as fleas, holdin' up stages at almost every turn in the road."

"Henry, if they was to start that malarkey on this route, I'd just stay home and let them shoot you," Brax says smiling a big grin at Henry. "Look there, Annie's Orchard at last. Slow this bucket down, Henry. I got to get off and stretch before my butt is shoved up my backbone."

Henry expertly guides his team into the open area in front of a ranch house set among rows and rows of apple trees.

A short, white haired, past middle-aged woman, wearing a long blue dress covered with a white, bib-topped apron stands on the porch. She has one corner of the apron pulled up wiping her hands on it.

"Hello, Henry. Pull your team up yonder; you know where. The boys will help you," she shouts at the driver. "Howdy, Brax, what brings you down our way? I thought you and Becca would spend all your time with your two younguns'."

Climbing down from the stopped coach, Brax turns and greets Annie with a big hug. He holds her back at arms' length, and says, "Had to get away, Annie. Those two cryin', whining babies can drive a man crazy. Why, I'd rather deal with rustlers and outlaws." He smiles at the diminutive woman.

She slaps him lightly on the shoulder. "You are as bad a man as those you chase down. Is Becca doing okay after birthin' those twins?"

"She's just fine as a fiddle, Annie. We named 'em Mike and Maudie. Has a nice ring to the names, don't it?" Brax says with a smile.

"You ain't namin' mules, you Galoot. Go on, get inside, and grab some apple pie before it gets cold. I gotta check on the paying passengers," Annie asserts while she attempts another slap on Brax's shoulder.

He skips out of reach and goes into the house where Annie's husband, Caleb, is slicing half a dozen pies, cooling on a long table.

"Brax. Good to see the law down this way. Heared Annie chewin' on you out there on the porch. Glad Becca and your kids are okay," he says.

Brax watches the older man deftly slice pie after pie. He stands at the table in his bib overalls, red flannel shirt, and brogans, slipping pie slices onto the plates stacked beside him.

"Here go. Give a bite. I think it's one of Annie's best. She's been bakin' since dawn," Caleb says handing Brax a plate of pie and a fork.

"Only thing that could make it better would be a big slice of cheese on this, Caleb," Brax laughs knowing the old man's secret to pie eating that his wife hates.

"You know talkin' like that in Annie's hearing is gonna get you and me in trouble, don't you, Sonny." Caleb joins in with laughter.

Annie and the other passengers step into the room and they help themselves to slices of pie.

Henry arrives, grabs some pie, and stands with Annie, Caleb, and Brax.

"You know, you never rightly said why you was heading to Globe today."

"Well, you know the ballot boxes loaded in the boot of your buggy?" says Brax. "As Sheriff, I have to accompany them to Globe. County officials need the documents to finalize the election results."

"Well, the telegraph sent the results in already, didn't it?" asks Annie.

"Yep, but the County needs the ballots to confirm the telegrams," says Brax.

"You know we voted for you, Sonny," says Caleb.

"I know some folks did, and I appreciate your vote," answers Brax. "If I win or if I don't, it's fine by me. I never ever expect to take a party side, can't say I really did. Just had to have a label to run under. Mainly, I'm just a Sheriff."

A Republican, whoever would have thought I would be a Republican. I just know I want to be the opposite of those mouthy jerks that questioned my appointment as Sheriff. Although, I might be out of a job again once the final count is finished.

"Load up folks, Globe's awaitin'," shouts Henry. He puts his plate down and thanks Annie and Caleb. Stepping out the door, he begins hollering to the boys helping hitch the team.

Brax sits his plate down on the table, shakes hands with Caleb, and gives Annie a hug. "Be seein' y'all. Let me know if you need me." He steps out the door and up on the stagecoach into the shotgun seat. The passengers clamber aboard; Henry snaps the reins across the backs of the 'girls' and the coach is Globe bound.

The herd is trailing well from Green's Peak west across the face of the Mogollon Rim. After weaving through the forests, the drive skirts the edge of the White Mountain Apache reservation, passes Apache Springs, crosses Crook's Road, slides down the Rim along Bitter Creek, and crosses the Cibeque, into Tonto Basin. Some cattle are lost to Indian thefts but Byron is content to look the other way. Now, the range begins to open up and more grassy expanses with rolling hills and valleys stretch in front of the trail drive. It's been a difficult drive but he sees an end to their journey. Markwell keeps talking about a valley up ahead, Pleasant Valley. God's spot in Arizona, he keeps calling it.

The herd grazes along the face of the Rim and keeps moving westerly. The last big barrier is Canon Creek, cross a couple of small ridges, and drop into Pleasant Valley. Byron is ready for it to arrive. He spots Gilberto loping toward him.

"*Patron*, up ahead, *mi vaqueros* say Canon Creek it is there." Gilberto points forward while slowing to a walk beside Byron's horse.

"All right, *Capataz*, form up the herd for another crossing. I will ride back to the wagons and let them know to prepare."

"*Patron*, there is *un poco problemo*," says Gilberto. "It is the sheeps. Two flocks, they are in front of us to makes the crossing too."

"Sheep, crossing into Pleasant Valley. Find Markwell for me, *pronto, por favor*." Byron's expression displays concern and frustration. Gilberto turns his horse and gallops toward the herd shouting as he rides. A drag rider turns and rides toward Gilberto. Byron sees him shouting and gesturing, and the rider adjusts his direction to intersect with Byron.

George Markwell gallops up to Byron.

"Yeah, Boss. What's the deal?"

"Sheep, George. They are in front of us crossing Canon Creek before our herd. Tell me again about the deadline you heard about." asks Byron.

"Well, them Hashknifers were sayin' they's agreed on a line drawn along the top of the Rim to separate sheep grazin' from cattle graze land. That's about it," says Markwell.

"Who's the 'they' that agreed," asks Byron.

"Beats me, Boss. I'm just repeatin' what I heard," says Markwell.

"So, give me your opinion on sheep crossing into Pleasant Valley below the Rim," says Byron.

Markwell slides his hat back on his head and scratches at his forehead before answering.

"Well, Boss. I'm just glad I don't own them sheep," says Markwell.

"How messy do you think it might get?" asks Byron.

"Knowin' them Hashknife boys, it can be dicey. I heared the Graham outfit is dead set on no sheep comin' into Tonto," replies Markwell.

"Find Gilberto, and tell him to swing the herd south. I'm not fixin' to walk into something not of my own makin'," says Byron. "We can strike the south end of Pleasant Valley and overflow into Tonto. Let's see what that does for us. Ride."

Markwell spurs his horse in search of Gilberto to deliver the message.

How can it be we've come this far only to have troubles find us?

Have I just swapped pockets, one set of troubles for another?

There's got to be somewhere I can just raise cattle and not fight battles.

He shakes his head in disgust.

Guillo is past Fort Apache and moves along the northern edge of the reservation following Crook's Road. The point *vaqueros* tell him there are signs another herd cut across the road in front of them and snaked its way down the face of the Rim following Bitter Creek. It looks like they crossed maybe three days ago.

What other herd of this size would be moving east to west in mass? It has to be Byron.

Guillo signals for the point man. A *vaquero* pulls away from the herd and gallops up to Guillo.

"The *Patron* takes his herd down the creek ahead of us. Can you do the same?" asks Guillo.

"*Jefe*, I will takes these cattles wherever you wants them to go. *Si*." answers the point man.

"*Bueno, muy bueno*. Take us down the Rim to join up with the *Patron*. Send *dos vaqueros* ahead to make contact. *Vámonos*." says Guillo.

Last night, I lose diez, ten, cattle to indios. I do not want to lose more. We need to get into the Tonto Basin to put a stop to thievery. It will be muy bueno to see mi Sabrino again. It is a hard drive and one I would not like to do again.

He turns and rides to the wagon to tell them to prepare for descending into the Basin.

Brax stretches out on the jail bunk in the County Jail in Globe. A couple of days ago he delivered ballot boxes from the north end of Gila County to the county seat. He hears whooping and hollering coming up the stairway into the jail and swings his feet off the bunk to await the noisy runner. The door flies open and the new younger jailer shouts at him.

"You done it, by crackers, Brax, you gone and done it," he says.

"Slow down, slow down. Just what have I gone and done?" asks Brax.

"You done been reelected Sheriff for Gila County." the jailer dances a made-up jig around the open area of the jail. "You showed those Jaspers on the council good Sheriffin' pays off."

"Well, I'll be. I thought for sure I was comin' for my termination," says Brax. "I better go downstairs and see the smiles on their perky faces."

Brax quickly slides into his boots, stands up, walks through the jail area, and down the steps to the council chamber. Stepping inside he sees tables set up all around the room, clerks run back and forth, opened ballot boxes, and ballots scattered on all tables fall onto the floor. A voice addresses him from his right side.

"Seems you really put their tail in a twist, Sheriff," says the voice.

"Well, sir. I was upstairs and heard about winning the election," replies Brax.

"That you did, Sheriff. That you did. Well, more precisely, your constituents did it for you," says the voice. "Allow me to introduce myself, I'm Judge Samuels, County Judge for Gila County." He extends his hand while sitting in a chair beside the door. Brax reaches out and clasps his hand returning a firm handshake. "Pull up a chair, Sheriff. It is quite a circus to watch."

Brax spots a near-by chair and pulls it up beside the Judge. He sees a distinguished looking white haired gentleman wearing a dark business suit, white shirt, bowtie, and shiny black boots. He looks to Brax to be fairly fit and tall, but sitting down makes it hard to determine.

"Yes, sir, Sheriff, you flung them into a tailspin. Votes from Globe proper came in and had you long gone. Then some boxes came in from the area outside of Globe and your status began to climb. More areas outside of Globe sent boxes and soon you had them sweating bullets. The 'coup de gras' came with the ballots you brought in from the northern half of the County. Your name came up four to one over your challenger. They confirmed what some claimed was an error in the telegraphed messages. Your opponent is a Democratic political hack anyway. Never saw much in the jerk in the first place, but I'm the Judge and impartial."

"Well, Judge, I didn't go out and do a lick of campaigning. I just ride for the badge," says Braxton.

"That's what makes you so irresistible, Sheriff. A good man, doing the job the only way he knows, the right way." says the Judge smiling. "You can't beat that with an ore crusher."

"Thank you, Judge. I appreciate your kind words," says Brax.

"Oh, they had their minutes in this room," says the Judge. "That commissioner," he points to a skinny plain man standing with clerks looking over lists. "He intimated the boxes you brought in were tampered with and the votes stuffed."

Brax's cheeks immediately flush and he knows his anger is rising. The Judge senses his reaction.

"Tut, tut, tut, Sheriff. As the watchdog over these official events, I simply asked that bright young man how the votes could be stuffed with the boxes locked and no other access. He stared at me with his frog-like eyes and didn't reply. Of course, I couldn't leave it there. I had to add the keys for the locks were mailed to this office in Globe, so you carried no means to open the boxes." The Judge wears a huge grin. "It was absolutely droll, I couldn't hardly contain myself. 'Hoist on their own petard', as it were."

"Judge, I fairly would have given a month's pay to have seen their faces when you rained all over their parade," says Brax.

"Yes, yes, well, Sheriff, my advice is to get out of Globe. Go do what you do so well. Rest assured, I will see everything is handled correctly and entered into County records. By the way, thanks." The Judge stands up and moves forward talking to clerks and commissioners.

Brax slips quietly through the doorway, exits the room, heads upstairs, and collects his belongings.

Time to go home.

Brax enjoys the belly-deep grasses north of Greenback Valley, and the rocking motion of being in the saddle as opposed to the jolting ride of the stagecoach. The borrowed livery gelding is a good ride.

Suddenly, a scorching sensation scratches across the skin on his neck. Slapping at the annoyance, he pulls his hand away with blood on it. He hears the report of a rifle and quickly drops from his saddle falling on his face beside his horse.

Brax slowly moves his hand, pulls his revolver, and slides it underneath his body.

He waits.

It seems like an eternity to Brax as he lies face down in the grassy field. His horse commences to graze and walks away from him.

He waits.

Brax wonders, *who shot at me? Did they mean to shoot me? A rifle could mean hunting. Is someone hunting the range? Why don't they come?*

He waits.

After a long delay, he feels slight tremors in the ground and knows someone on horseback is approaching.

He waits.

A horseman rides up beside Brax's horse and sounds like he is checking the saddle and bags. The rider steps down. Brax hears the jangle of spur rowels and jingle bobs. The boots walk around his horse and stop beside Brax's body. He feels his body   roughly nudged by the barrel of a rifle.

"I told you, you were a dead man, Sheriff of Gila County," says the rider.

I know the voice, thinks Brax. *Where have I heard it before?*

"I think I'll shoot you between the eyes just for good measure," says the rider using his rifle barrel to prod Brax's body to roll over.

As Brax is slowly rolled over he quietly cocks his Colt. Balancing on his side, he suddenly flips onto his back, snaps his Colt upward, squeezes the trigger, and sends a .45 slug into the rider's forehead.

With a completely stunned look on his face, Bud drops to his knees, and sits on his spurs. The rifle in his right hand swings in front of the body and acts as a prop against his chest, keeping his torso upright and unable to fall.

Brax quickly scrambles up and walks around the leaning corpse.

"Graham's cowboy, Bud." whispers Braxton. Talking out loud to himself he quickly looks up at the landscape around him. "Last time there were three others."

Not seeing other movement on the range, he looks back at the dead man. The tall crowned hat with wide brim shades the corpse's open eyes.

Brax steps back.

What a stupid loss of life. This ignorant boy, who has so much to live for, thinks a gun makes everything better. Stupid, stupid, no, damned stupid.

Brax shrugs off the incident.

It is what it is, I can't change it, and neither can he.

He walks over to Bud's horse and shakes out a blanket from the bedroll behind the saddle. He comes back and wraps the body in the blanket, picks it up, carries it to the horse, and hefts it up to lie over the saddle. It takes all his muscle power to get the body up, and he walks around the prancing horse, grabs Bud's arms and pulls his body to a balanced position. Rummaging around in the saddlebag, he finds a pigging string, places a loop around one dangling boot and ties the other end to a hand. Tightening the rope, he cinches the body down to the saddle, and straightens out the blanket covering the corpse.

Hell of a job, Braxton thinks picking up Bud's rifle, hat, and his own hat. The rifle slides into its scabbard on the dead man's horse, and Brax shoves the hat under the blanket. He gathers up the reins of the cowboy's horse, walks to his own, and steps into his saddle.

If I turn east, I'm bound to run across riders.

Brax settles his hat on his head and spurs his horse into a steady walk.

24
REUNION

It has been a day since spotting the dust cloud behind them. It seems to grow larger and higher today. Byron sits on the hillside watching the remuda run past him as the horses follow the herd. It's been almost two hours since Gilberto sent two *vaqueros* behind to check out the cloud of dust.

He hears shouts. Looking back along the trail of the herd, he sees two riders galloping toward him. Both stand in their stirrups and wave their *sombreros* as they ride.

Fearing the worst, Byron shouts at Markwell who`s driving the remuda, "George, tell Gilberto to get some rifles back here. Pronto."

He pulls his rifle from it`s scabbard and races down the hill on his horse towards the shouting *vaqueros.*

Got to get closer to make out what they're shouting. Byron spurs his horse.

Suddenly his hearing makes out their shouts, *"Esta GUILLO. Patron. Esta Guillo.* Good God, it's Guillo registers with Byron.

Slipping his rifle back into the scabbard, he flicks the reins back and forth across his horse's withers to increase his speed. He races past both *vaqueros* who yank their horses around and gallop to catch up with him. Dashing forward he spots another herd plodding along guided by experienced *vaqueros.* Charging by the point rider he sees Guillo.

It's Byron's turn to gallop standing up in his stirrups, waving his hat in the air, and shouting.

The fire burns bright when more dead wood is piled on it. The meal is finished and the coffee pot makes a third round. *Vaqueros* recline on bedrolls beside their saddles. They laugh, reminisce, and share stories of recent events. The 'night hawks' slowly ride the perimeter of the combined herds singing softly. Guillo and Byron sit together at the edge of the fire lit circle.

"I'm glad you made it safely, *mi Tio,*" says Byron.

"*Si, mi Sobrino*, it has been a long drive," responds Guillo. "Is the snow really as deep as your *vaqueros* say?"

With a laugh, Byron responds, "It may not have been that deep, but it sure felt that way. The cold is what I didn't care for."

"*Si*, I imagine it can be cold," Guillo agrees. "You have done well. Your *Padre* is proud, I'm sure. I am."

"There were many times I wished you or Pa could have been with me to make the decisions," says Byron. "I made 'em thinkin' like you might and hopin' they were right."

"Byron, we are here, No? It looks like some right decisions they are made, yes?" Guillo responds with a smile. "Sending you north was a right decision though at the time it troubles me *mucho. Su Padre*, he tells me to take care of you."

"Troubled you. It terrified me," responds Byron.

"*Si*, but now you are the *Patron*. The *vaqueros*, they respect you and call you *Patron* because you earned it, Byron. That no could happen if I was with you. No, you must earn it alone, and you have," says Guillo with a sound of satisfaction in his voice. "Look at them," he gestures to the men around the fire. "They follow you without questions now."

"Just the same, I'm glad we are together once again," says Byron. "Let's keep it this way, *por favor.*"

"*Si, mi Sobrino*, together is much better, *bueno, muy bueno*," says Guillo with a big grin exploding under his drooping mustache.

Constant gunfire in the distance brings Gilberto at a gallop, "*Patron*, you hears the guns, yes?" he asks with agitation in his voice.

"Yes, Gilberto, it doesn't sound like it's letting up," answers Byron.

"Do I take the *vaqueros* and ride to the gunfire, *Patron*?"

"No, it may be something to draw us away from the herd. Make sure our *vaqueros* are ready for an attack. It can come from any direction. Bunch up a few in case we need to rush some reinforcements one direction or another. *Si?*" says Byron.

"I will put some *vaqueros* with rifles in the chuckwagon *carretta* and have it ready to use where needed, *Patron*." Gilberto replies.

"*Bueno, bueno*. Now, go get our men ready; trouble may be on us before we know it," says Byron.

Gilberto sinks spurs into his horse sending it into a one-leap gallop. As he rides toward the herd, Byron turns to the noise coming up behind him. Felina races the coach toward him. She slows down as she nears. Guillo rides beside the coach.

"What is all the gunfire, *mi Querido*," she asks. "I am hearing it for some time. Is troubles coming our way?"

"Don't know, Felina. We'll prepare for anything. Why are you up here? You should be with the other wagons," Byron remarks.

"I will be with you, no?" she smiles at Byron.

"I give up. Do what you're going to do, Felina. I think Alberto is the lucky one since you came with me," says Byron.

"Oh no, *mi Querido*. You are much more the lucky one." She smiles again at Byron and throws a kiss.

Guillo watches the exchange between Felina and Byron. A knowing smile creeps across his face.

"*Sobrino*, what is it? What goes on?" asks Guillo

The gunfire slackens then stops. The herd keeps moving. The cattle flow up and over a rise as Byron watches their progress.

Any moment now, whatever is coming our way is bound to hit.

The cattle climb the next ridge and he sees them start milling around not readily going down the other side.

"I'm not sure, *Compañero*," answers Byron. "Will you stay here to make sure we are safe? I must ride to them." He points to *vaqueros* on their horses on the ridge standing in their stirrups signaling for him.

"*Si, si,* go find out." Guillo waves Byron away.

Cattle keep moving up the hill to pile up with the others along the top ridge. Byron pulls to a stop with the *vaqueros* who point into the valley below.

Before him, the ground is littered with dead and dying sheep. It looks like snow covers the ground. The coppery smell of blood hangs in the air and spooks the cattle. Gilberto rides up beside Byron.

"Who could do such a thing, *Patron*?" He asks in shock. "I no likes sheeps, but *madre mia*, these is murder. No?"

"Yes, Gilberto, this is murder. Cold-blooded, soulless, brutal, wasteful murder," says Byron his eyes swim in tears. How could anyone, anyone, wantonly kill this many animals, he wonders? Two *vaqueros* ride up to Gilberto and exchange in rapid fired Spanish.

"*Patron, mi vaqueros* say the men who do this ride west. They thinks it is fifteen of them maybe. They are not far away. Should I find them and shoots them too?" asks Gilberto.

"No. Stay with the herd. Ask Guillo to catch up with me. I'm riding after the murderers to see where they go." Byron says.

"That is not such a good idea, *Patron*. They may see you and without *vaqueros*, they might kill you," says Gilberto.

"*Muchas gracias,* Gilberto. I appreciate your concern, but the herd is most important. I'm not going to follow too close, just close enough to not lose them. Send *dos vaqueros* behind me in about an hour, *bueno*?" says Byron.

"*Bueno, Patron*. I don't likes it, but I will do it. *Bueno*," answers Gilberto as he turns his horse toward the herd to drive them down from the ridge avoiding the slaughtered sheep.

Byron hears a familiar rattle approach him on the ridge top and knows Felina drives the coach up beside him.

She stares at the gruesome sight and looks at Byron with tears streaming down her cheeks and dripping off her chin.

"Why? How? Who could do such a thing," she asks. "I will find them and shoot them down like they did them innocent sheeps." Felina pulls a rifle from under the coach seat and begins to drive the coach down the hillside. Byron quickly reaches over, grabs the lead reins, and yanks the horses to a stop.

"I've told you once to go back with the other wagons, I'll not tell you again." says Byron. His blue eyes glare into the dark pools of Felina's eyes. For a moment their wills clash, then the dark pools soften under Byron's relentless stare.

Felina drops the rifle into the area under the seat and slowly turns the coach, rolling it back towards the other wagons.

Guillo gallops up the opposite side of the hill, and yanks his horse to a stop beside Byron. "This is one unholy mess. I've never seen this before. What would make someone do this?" he asks Byron.

"I have no idea, Guillo, but here is what must happen. Make sure this herd gets to the southern end of Pleasant Valley, and don't let Gilberto be swayed to follow me with all the *vaqueros*," says Byron.

"*Si, si, Sobrino.* But, where do you head?" asks Guillo.

"I've got to find out what kind of monsters did this." Byron says pointing at the sheep kill.

"*Si*, but you better come back. I no wants to take over this herd without you." He yanks the reins of his horse and reluctantly heads down the hill at a lope.

Byron watches the herd sidestep the bloody grounds and move up and over another ridge further west.

He rides straight ahead through the dead sheep and picks up the trail of the fifteen murderers.

Two *vaqueros* sit on the ridge and watch their *Patron* ride west. They wait just long enough before they begin following him.

Brax spends most of the day riding east. It's strange he hasn't seen one cowboy on the range. He passes any number of cattle wondering and grazing as normal, but not to see one rider is strange. He rides up onto the crest of a hill and looking east spies a group of cowboys in the hazy distance. It appears to be a large group. Two or three riders can mean good conversation. Four or more means there is an issue to deal with. This many says nothing good is going to come from meeting them. Since he's seen them, he knows they have seen him. He still has Bud in tow, and the body needs to go back to Graham.

Brax looks around and sees he is in miles of grass. *Never a good tree around when you need one. No sense tiring my horse, I'll just wait for them.*

Kicking one boot free of its stirrup, he lifts his leg up and wraps his knee around the saddle horn. Reaching into his vest pockets, Brax pulls out cigarette paper and his Bull Durham. Easily, he pours tobacco onto the creased paper, licks the edge of the wrapper, and rolls a smoke. Holding the cigarette between his lips, he slips the fixings back into his pockets, pulls out a box of stick matches, strikes one, lights his smoke, and takes a drag. Slowly exhaling, he wonders what Becca and the twins might be doing right now.

Byron trails the fifteen that wantonly massacred an entire flock of helpless sheep. He forgot to ask about any shepherds and is afraid for their fate. It's been a few hours of riding across the Tonto Basin through patches of pine and oaks, hedgerows of manzanita and chaparral, and miles of grass. He has no idea where the riders are headed, but knows eventually they should come to the south end of Pleasant Valley. That may be their destination.

As he crests a rise leading into another large open grassy area, he spots the group of riders and in the distance a hazy figure on horseback looks to be leading a pack animal. Byron realizes in his haste, he's closed the gap with the fifteen riders considerably. If any of them glance over their shoulders, he would be very visible. There is nowhere to hide, so he slows his pace to fall back from the group.

The group of fifteen riders spreads out in a line and move toward the lone figure waiting for them. The riders slow from a steady lope to a slow walk and finally stop within shouting distance of the lone rider. Three riders separate from the middle of the pack and move toward the lone rider, who hasn't changed his position. Byron watches transfixed and wonders what the single rider hopes to accomplish in stopping this group of murderers. It's inconceivable to Byron one man can face this group of killers.

Wait. Maybe he is one of them. That would explain why he hasn't moved.

Braxton watches the three cowboys. They look like working cowhands with chaps, blue denims; plaid shirts with button flap pockets, bandanas, gloves, boots with spurs, various hats, and two wear denim jackets. As they ride up slowly toward Braxton, the middle cowboy starts speaking.

"You lost, Stranger?"

"Nope. I know exactly where I am," answers Braxton. "Where you boys bound?"

"None of your business," the middle cowboy responds. "You blocking our way or just sight seeing?"

"Oh, far be it from me to block your way, Cowboy," says Brax. "I would like to know what brand you're riding for; I've got a package for the Graham bunch."

"It's your lucky day, Stranger. We ride for Graham. What's the package?"

Brax turns loose of Bud's horse's reins, "This here is one of your boys." He slaps the horse's rump and it jumps and trots, with its corpse, toward the line of cowboys."

One of the cowboys from the lineup lopes forward and grabs the horse's reins, looks at the blanket covered package, lifts one end, and shouts to the middle cowboy in front of Braxton.

"It's Bud, Slim. He's deader than hammered hell."

Slim turns granite eyes toward Braxton.

"Seems you saw fit to kill one of my riders, stranger. That ain't healthy in these parts."

"Well, Slim. It is Slim, isn't it?" asks Brax. "Your swell cowboy saw fit to try to bushwhack me a ways back, and Gila County doesn't take kindly to their Sheriffs being bushwhacked."

"My, my, Lordy, boys, we have a high and mighty Gila County Sheriff sitting right here in front of us. What do you boys think about that?" shouts Slim.

Whistles, jeers, catcalls, and slurs burst from the line of riders.

"Don't appear my boys think too highly of Gila County Sheriffs," says Slim. "You know what? Neither do I."

"That's a shame, Slim, seeing as how you are the closet one to me and the first one something will happen to if any of your boys get a crazy notion," says Brax.

Slim's eyes flicker and register concern and fear as Braxton sits staring at his face.

"Sheriff, you plan on doing anything to us?" asks Slim.

"You done anything that should cause me to do something to you?" replies Brax. "My goal was to return a bushwhacker to you. I've done that. You got more to talk about?"

Byron sits on his horse hoping to blend into the range grasses and that the cowboys' attention remains on the lone rider in front of them. He faintly hears bits and pieces of the conversation as the words carry on the breeze. In his mind he becomes convinced the lone rider is one of the gang of Cowboys.

The lone rider turns loose the pack animal, and another Cowboy picks it up, looks under the cover, and acts strangely about the load on the horse's back.

Byron suddenly hears the word, Sheriff.

The lone rider is a sheriff? What good is one sheriff against fifteen riders? It looks like things are winding down.

If the sheriff rides away, the massacred flock and shepherds will never be discovered.

Byron makes up his mind. It's such a stupid thought, it amazes him he is going to do it.

"I've got to ride through the line of cowboys and reach the sheriff," Byron says out loud to build up courage to do the deed. Gathering his horse's reins to keep its head up, Byron digs his spurs into horseflesh and bolts toward the line of cowboys.

He races down the hillside and tears through the line of riders scattering four of them as he bursts through. Everyone gets real antsy real quick, but no shots are fired as he races up to Braxton. Spinning his horse around, he faces Slim.

"They slaughtered an entire herd of sheep a few miles back," gasps Byron pointing east. "There may be a dead shepherd or two as well. Who would kill helpless animals like that? What's wrong with you? What kind of beast are you?"

"Whoa, Stranger, I don't know who you are but your mouth is going to get you kilt," says Slim staring at Byron. "My boys and me been out cleaning up the range. We ran across some woolies that were messing things up. They won't no more." Slim sits back in his saddle laughing out loud and is joined by the other cowboys.

Looking over at the sheriff, Byron experiences a shock that almost knocks him off his horse.

"Braxton? Braxton? Is that you?" asks Byron in total disbelief.

"What the hell are YOU doing here?" Braxton shouts at Byron.

"What the hell are YOU doing here?" Byron shouts at Braxton.

"When you two figure out what you're doing here, you let us know. In the mean time, we're riding through, sheriff," says Slim raising his hand to wave the riders past. Suddenly, he rocks back in his saddle, his right-hand shoving his hat back up on his forehead. "I must be seeing double. Boys, take a look. These Jaspers are two peas in a pod."

Braxton and Byron stare back at Slim.

"Whoa, whoa, whoa, Big Dog," says Braxton getting back on track.

"I want to hear what this fella has to say," pointing at Byron. "Since I already heard your version,"

"What's he know? He's just rode up," shouts Slim.

"Killing livestock and sheep herders is against the law in Gila County. We might just need to ride over yonder and take a peek at what he claims."

"Sheriff, I'll just save you the time. Here's the lowdown. Sheep is bein' moved on this range. The boys and me used up about a month's worth of cartridges making sure no woolies ever live here. If a shepherd steps in the way of our shooting, that's a shame. That's it, end of story. Now, we'll be riding through." He turns to the cowboys.

"Don't think so, Slim. You see, in my business, what you just said is called a confession. You're going with me to Payson jail. Which ones of your riders do we need to take with us?" asks Brax.

Slim sits back in his saddle, throws back his head, and laughs aloud. He slaps his thigh and says to the two riders beside him. "He's takin' us to Payson jail, boys." He throws back his head and laughs again.

Byron looks at Brax like he's lost his mind, and he looks at Slim and knows he's lost his.

"Time to ride, Boys." shouts Slim grabbing for his revolver.

Brax kicks his other boot loose from his stirrup, reaches over and grabs Byron's arm, and both tumble backwards off their horses. Brax knows he is going to hit the ground hard, but hard is better than dead.

Immediately, three slugs slam into Braxton's horse and two hit Byron's killing them instantly. Both horses drop into a heap. Braxton drags Byron up behind the warm horse carcasses and begins to return pistol fire at the now charging cowboys.

Slim takes a slug to the middle of his body from Braxton. Byron shoots one of the three close cowboys in the shoulder spinning him off his horse. The third cowboy yanks his horse back to join the line of cowhands now rushing towards Braxton and Byron while firing their revolvers.

Suddenly, on the hillside, across from the downed brothers, two rifles begin steady, rhythmic firing. Brax and Byron look over their dead mounts to see accurate rifle shots knocking riders from their saddles.

As suddenly as the fracas begins, it ends. The line of riders is decimated by the accuracy of the rifle fire. Four riders break off charging forward and escape to the west, and three others to the east.

Brax stares across the field to see two *vaqueros* stand, leap onto their horses, and ride toward them.

Rising, Brax pulls Byron up from the ground, and throws a bear hug around him.

He steps back, holds Byron at arm's length, and says, "Brother, have I got a lot to tell you."

AFTERWORD

Thank you for purchasing this book. If you enjoyed reading it, please consider leaving a review online at Goodreads or at your favorite online retailer.

For more information about Dr. Wm. A. Burgdorf and his books, you may want to visit the author's websites:
www.waburgdorf.com,
Dr. Billy's Book Blog -
http://bgbcreative.wordpress.com,
Adventures of Bocephus & Becca -
http://learningaboutabunch.wordpress.com,
and email: **DrBilly@waburgdorf.com**.

NEW RELEASE

Humps & Hooves
By
William A. Burgdorf

1

Arrival

Two cavalry soldiers sit on stacks of crates on Indianola's wharf. Both wear dark blue waist length jackets with a single row of brass buttons and light blue trousers with a gold stripe down the outside of both trouser legs. Their pants are tucked into tall, stovepipe black boots. White belts crisscross their chests; one holds a cartridge pouch and the other a small haversack. Slouch hats with gold tassels keep the sun from their faces. Midway on both sleeves of the soldiers' jackets, two gold chevrons pointing down identify these men as corporals.

 William Roberts sits on a stack of tarp-covered crates watching the gray-black clouds roll across Matagorda Bay as they tumble and convulse crashing into one another. *If it would just stop storming,* Billy gazes at the clouds, *we could get our ship docked and complete this detail.*

Beside him, a block and tackle hoists a cargo net of large barrels out of the hold of a ship and swings its yardarm over the wharf to unload. Its line snaps and the cargo careens to the dock. Barrels holding crockery shatter and scatter shards of wood and porcelain flying in every direction.

"Damn near hit me," shouts Samuel Adams rising from behind a large crate. "Billy, you all right?"

From behind the tarp-covered pile comes a reply, "Don't look like I'm hurt."

The Corporals stand as the crowd of people rises from many hiding places and stumbles through the debris of the crushed barrels.

Sun beats down on the dock where people gather watching sailing and steam-powered vessels cruise the bay. They join the shoving, jostling, pushing, and shouting people who fill the open spaces between stacks of crates, barrels, boxes, and tarpaulin-covered piles.

Mercantile goods, hides, foodstuff, furniture, plows, and items from all over the world accumulate on the docks.

"Damn it's hot, Billy," says Sam as he removes his hat and mops his sweating brow with his kerchief. "You know a guy could get killed around here."

"Yep," mutters Corporal Roberts. "These people are thick as fleas on this wharf, not to mention all the cargo. It's only May, Sam. What'd you think it's goin' to feel like when summer gets here?"

"Ovens of hell gonna open for sure then," replies Sam. "It felt like that last year."

Sam watches stevedores tie the lines thrown to them from the ships. They lash them to the wharf and move wagons, dollies, and handcarts around preparing to receive their cargos. The extended dock is a madhouse of activity. Nets of crates swing overhead, carts and wagons rumble along the dock carrying merchandise, random tarpaulin-covered piles obstruct strollers, handcarts navigate the dock, and crowds continue to hinder and frustrate the stevedores. White, black, and brown workers churn about, stripped to the waist, sweating profusely, and spewing profanity in multiple languages as they wrestle with unloading one ship after another.

"Bein' in the Army ain't no bed of roses," says Sam. "But, I don't think I'd trade with these fellers workin' here."

"Yep. Can't beat being in the army," mutters Billy with a sarcastic snort. "You see the *U.S.S. Supply* in the line up along the dock? That's the boat we have to find."

"We've waited two weeks for that ship; it's bound to be here," says Sam. "'Course the storms didn't help its timely arrival."

"Well, here's hopin' today ends our wait in Indianola."

****

It all stinks: the people, the ship, the quarters, the food, the animals...especially those camels. Everything is wet. Constantly wet. Katrina holds her hand to her face trying to block the odors. She is eighteen and halfway around the world from her home in Mainz, Germany, aboard a ship carrying her family to the new and distant land called Texas.

Why would Papa want to move us from our comfortable home to come to this 'end of the world' place? For years, he's read letters from those who moved earlier with the Adelsverein Society. The letters share glowing tales of the land, animals, and rivers. Nothing can be that grand. Katrina walks along the ship's passageway. *Finally, Papa sells everything in Germany and books us passage on a ship to New Orleans in some place called Louisiana. He says a town named New Braunfels in Texas will be our home. We are all forced to leave what we know for this savage frontier.*

Katrina slowly climbs the narrow companionway ladder, gripping tightly onto the handrail as the ship lurches from one rolling wave into another.

How cruel, how thoughtless, how just like Papa to do this to us. It's all Ernst Gruene's fault. His letters convinced Papa to move to Texas and grow cotton. What does Papa know about cotton? Nothing; absolutely, nothing. Gruene farms acres and needs strong backs, and Papa's willing to join him. Oh, I'm beyond help.

Stepping onto the open deck, the steady wind whips Katrina's hair about, undoing any hope she had of holding it secure. Looking up, she sees the sails billowing and straining against the masts as ropes creak and groan under the stress. To her left, she sees low clinging clouds rapidly approaching the ship, dumping rain as they sweep along above the waters.

More rain. It's been days of rain since leaving New Orleans. I overheard the Captain tell Papa it's keeping us from our destination. What was the name? Oh, yes. Indianola. The soldier in the blue uniform, a Major, yes, a Major, keeps telling Papa this is where he is taking his stinking camels.

****

From the vantage point of the quarterdeck, a pockmarked, weasel-faced man lingers beside the ship's rail, watching Katrina walk the main deck. Stringy, greasy hair protrudes from under his stocking cap, and his cotton knee-length pants, blue plaid shirt, and leather vest are filthy with rope tar and grime. His gaze sweeps over her long brunette hair flowing in the wind, her small mouth, and deep blue eyes. He's watched her move about the ship ever since leaving New Orleans. His lecherous stare consumes her curvaceous body barely concealed by the grey ankle length high collared dress that clings to her in the sea spray and wind.

Oui, this is a girl for Pierre LeMains to take; he absentmindedly licks his lips. *Those fools in the Quarter only thought they catch LeMains. Sacre bleu, those buffoons could not lay a trap worth springing. This ship was ready to sail, and I was ready to leave behind those I killed. An affair of honor, ha, an affair, oui. What an affair with Angelica. But her stupid husband and brother, they were no match for my blade.*

A sharp blow to the side of his head yanks Pierre back to reality as he instinctively grabs the handle of the butcher knife at his belt. His ear aches from the cuffing. He spins around to face the Chief Mate whose hand is clutching his boning knife's handle.

"Get off the quarterdeck, you Frenchie rat," the Mate says. "Get below or into the rigging. You've got no business on this deck."

Rubbing his ear, Pierre slowly removes his hand from his knife. "*Oui, mon capitaine*, I am moving."

"Hold. Get aloft. The Captain wants us to haul in the sheets. There's more gale brewin'."

Pierre deftly swings himself up and onto the rope ladder rigging. He begins climbing to the yardarms holding the aft sails.

"Do not sleep too soundly, *mon capitaine*; hammocks have ways of becoming shrouds," he mutters as he climbs. His new vantage allows him to continue his salacious gaze of Katrina until she turns and leaves the deck.

****

In the ship Captain's cabin, two men engage in a heated discussion.

"Yes, Major. I know, Major. You don't want to be ashore any worse than I want you and your camels ashore," says the Captain standing beside the table. He is shorter in height and has to look up at the man across from him. His blue uniform jacket is stained with salt from the ocean's spray. The Army Major has been with him since the Mediterranean, across the Atlantic, stopping in New Orleans, and completing the journey to Texas where the cargo of camels can be unloaded. The Major's steely eyes and assured mannerism is quietly insistent and resolute. The Captain knows he is driven to complete the delivery of his responsibility, and that he carries authorization from Secretary of War Jefferson Davis.

"Captain, we have been delayed and delayed. What keeps us from landing in Indianola?" asks Major Wayne.

"Weather and sandbars, Major. We've had this discussion already."

"Surely, there's more that can be done. We are so close to port."

"The only thing more we can accomplish is to run aground. I don't think that's agreeable for either of us. Later today, after the squalls pass, I'll send a boat ashore to arrange for a tow across the sandbars blocking the harbor entrance. With good weather, we'll be able to land tomorrow."

"Very well, Captain. I'll make arrangements with my herdsmen, and alert the passengers to prepare to disembark."

"Thank you, Major. Please assure those thirty German families we'll get them ashore safely."

"It was fortunate you were able to accommodate them after their ship floundered."

"Indeed."

"The failing pumps on their ship rendered them useless to keep up with the seepage flooding the lower decks. They were in imminent peril of sinking. Only your quick action of coming alongside and taking off the ship's crew and passengers saved lives."

"We had the room, and on the seas, one Captain assists another."

"Still, your quick response saved the people."

"Now, if you'll be so kind, I must get back to running my ship?"

"Certainly, Captain. I would never presume to take you away from your duties."

With an obvious harrumph, the Captain holds the door open for the Major's departure. He follows and makes straightaway for the companionway ladder leading topside. He brushes past Katrina as she descends. He acknowledges her with a quick nod.

****

"The Captain seems in a hurry." Katrina watches the officer rush to the deck.

"Yes," smiles the Major. "I believe we have journeyed too long, and he wants to be rid of me and my charges."

"Well, Major, I understand his urgency. I, too, want to be done with ships and seas. Will it be long now? From my observations on deck, I see the coast is nearby."

"With any luck, we should be offloading tomorrow. So says the Captain."

"Splendid. Not soon enough for me. Would you tell my father? He'll want to tell the others."

"I would be happy to do that."

They walk along the cabin passageway toward midship.

Katrina sees her father. "Papa, Papa, the Major has good news."

A patriarchal German gentleman stands from the box where he is sitting. His silver white hair shines in the darkness of the ship's interior. He wears a full beard, a black frock coat, and dark trousers. Tapping out his pipe, he carefully extinguishes the embers and tucks it into his vest pocket.

"*Willkommen*! Major. *Vas* you say, Katrina?"

"Mister Baum," the Major interrupts, "please let your people know we should be disembarking tomorrow. Prepare yourselves to leave the ship."

"*Ja, das goot. Wir bereit sei zu gehen.*"

"Papa says we will be ready to go, Major."

"You've been a definite help in communicating with your group during this trip, Miss Baum."

"Papa said we have to be prepared. I've

learned English, Fritz is fluent in French, and Louis in Spanish. Albert and Collet are still too small to learn another language.

"Well, Louis and you will be called upon quite a bit once ashore, I'm sure. I've got to check on my men. Please excuse me." The Major touches the brim of his hat and continues to walk toward the bow of the ship.

Katrina watches his departure as she anticipates tomorrow.

Finally. We're off this wretched, stinking, tossing excuse for travel. Ashore. No more waves, but steady ground and whatever this new land brings. Papa, Papa, what have you gotten us into? Katrina busies herself rolling up the quilt *Großmutter* Baum gave her when she left Mainz.

****

High above the deck in the building storm, Pierre's bare feet grasp the rope stretching from one end to the other of the sail spar. It's his only perch while his body lies prone against the sail sheets that he and other sailors beside him pull on. Hand-over-hand they gather up and reef the sail into bundles to prevent the wind from catching it and billowing it open.

"Hey, Frenchie, what are you doin' with us?" asks a rail-thin, hawk-nosed sailor reaching for another grasp of sail. "You sure seemed in a hell-fired hurry to get out of New Orleans by signing on for any open berth."

"*Mon ami*, sometimes it is better to just go, *oui*?"

"Been in a port or two like that myself. Lucky we need men. Lost some good ones crossin' the Atlantic."

"I've been all over, *mon ami*, from Dominica, Guadalupe, Haiti, to the Florida Keys. Long enough in New Orleans, *cherchez la femme* causes me to leave. Now, I'm on to the next port."

"Whoa, Frenchie, you signed on with the U.S. Navy comin' aboard this ship. It ain't no merchant vessel. You can't just up and leave."

"Pierre LeMains comes and goes as he pleases. Who's to stop me?"

"The Chief Mate for starters, then the Officers. Anybody caught deserting gets the Cat-O-Nines. I only seen one man Catted, and it ain't a pretty sight. His back was chewed up something fierce."

"LeMains will never feel *Le Cat*, *mon ami*. He will just leave and not be found."

"What if someone tells the Mate about your plannin' to jump ship?"

Pierre turns his head to look directly at the sailor. "Then that man will no longer have a tongue to speak with, *mon ami*."

A rogue wave suddenly smashes into the *U.S.S. Supply* heeling the ship far over onto its starboard. All the sailors in the rigging grasp firm holds to keep from being flung overboard or onto the deck far below. Pierre continues to look at the other sailor as a sinister grin spreads across his face. "Besides, *mon ami, un jeune femme*, the young woman, leaves this ship at Indianola. She needs LeMains to go with her."

****

After a long morning, the *U.S.S. Supply* is finally warped to the dock in Indianola. Katrina stands on deck, watching the sailors scramble to secure the ship for arrival and set up block and tackle to transfer cargo. They remove tarp coverings from the cargo bays and lower ropes to extract goods from the ship's hold. Sweating sailors trudge around the capstan, taking in and letting out ropes to raise crates, barrels, farm implements, and stacked boxes out of the hold. They swing the yardarm to the dock. Other seamen hold firm to guide ropes lowering items onto the wharf. Katrina is spellbound watching the work.

"Katrina, Katrina," calls her mother. "*Ve* are leaving. *Ja.*"

Katrina turns and joins the other German families trudging down the gangway carrying their possessions in bundles, bags, and boxes.

2

Indianola

The corporals lean against the wharf pilings as they survey the ships securing to Indianola's dock.

"I think it's tied up at the far end," replies Sam. "That's what I hear'd that fellar, you know, the wharf master, just shout."

"Take a look at the chalkboard over there on that shed, and make sure it's our ship. If it's on the board, then the wharf fellar is probably right." Billy points at a large chalkboard mounted under the shed's overhang.

Sam takes a slow walk over to the board, scans the writing, and reads out loud, "May 14, 1856, arrivals. The *S.S. Carpathian* from Bristol, England; the *S.S. Raven* from New York; the *S.S. Patricia* from Le Havre, France; the *U.S.S. Supply* from...that's it. It's here." Sam shouts at Billy.

"Yep. That's her. Finally."

"Well, it's about time. Let's walk the dock and see who comes down the gangway," says Billy. "The Colonel says we are to meet an officer and follow his directions."

"I'm gittin' tired of sleeping in that room over the saloon," said Sam. "There ain't much sleeping especially when two or three other fellars pile in on the bed and start snoring and squirmin' around.

"Still beats sleeping on the ground, bedbugs and all," says Billy.

Both soldiers make their way through the crowd of people along the wharf. Easing past struggling workmen, edging around sightseers, and dodging wagons and dollies, as they sidestep rushing passengers.

****

On the dock, Katrina and her family quickly intermingle with the crowds scrambling along the wharf. They shove and stumble their way toward the land end. Grasping hands reach out to snatch their bundles and bags from them. Tenaciously, Katrina clings to her goods and shuffles along.

Midway along the dock, Katrina collides with a blue uniformed soldier and stumbles forward into his arms.

"Ahhhh, I'm so sorry, Sir."

"Well, I never," begins Billy. He stops and gazes intently at Katrina. "It's my fault, Ma'am. I'm sorrrrry." Billy clutches the woman to keep her from falling.

"You may let me go now. I'm recovered," says Katrina. She looks into the deep blue eyes of the soldier.

Billy observes her long gray dress, sunbonnet, and bundles dangling from each arm.

"Yes, Ma'am. Let me make sure you're all right." Billy quickly steadies himself and unhands Katrina. Her appearance, brunette curls, blue eyes, and attractive figure stun him. He stutters, "I, I, I, didn't pay attention. My apologies."

Suddenly, Sam grabs Billy's arm and pulls him down the wharf. Billy's eyes remain locked on Katrina's until the crowd swallows him.

****

"Soldiers. Soldiers. Hey, you there." A uniformed man standing by the top of the gangway on the ship shouts to get their attention.

"Did you see her, Sam? Did you see her? She's beautiful, a vision, who is she?"

"Didn't see anybody, but you better see him,"

says Sam indicating the officer pointing at them.

"Look sharp, Sam," says Billy snapping to attention. "Yes, sir. Corporals Roberts and Adams at your disposal, Sir."

"Gentlemen, I'm Major Wayne. I'm to meet my escorts to Fort Mason. Are you two part of that detail? "

"Yes, Sir," both reply. "We're to guide the Major and his party."

"Very well, very well indeed. How many men have been dispatched to assist with transportation to Fort Mason?"

"Sir, our detail is five men."

"Good Lord. Doesn't your commander realize what we have to deliver?"

"Yes, Sir. Our Colonel was very emphatic y'all be escorted safe and sound. He's particularly interested in your arrival though he wasn't all that clear on details," says Billy.

"And, just who is this very interested Colonel, Corporal?"

"Colonel Robert E. Lee, Sir," says Billy, with a smile. "He's one of them West Point officers and a fine commander."

With a snort of derision, Major Wayne responds, "We've travelled half-way around the world to deliver our cargo, and your Colonel only dispatches five troops to assure our safe arrival?"

"Well, Sir, our detail will do everything possible...," begins Sam.

"Stand back, stand back, gangway, clear the wharf," shouts a seaman racing down the gangplank. "Them animals is off loadin'. Clear away." He runs across the dock and cowers behind a stack of crates.

Billy and Sam's ears are assaulted by the most God-awful noises they've ever heard. Groaning, squealing, snorting, bellowing, and grunting roars assail all those on the wharf. The block and tackle ropes strain taut winding around the capstan. Slowly, the load inches upward.

Eight short, swarthy men with towels wrapped around their heads like hats, wearing long robes, spill from the hold onto the deck and rush down the gangplank. Two of them hold guide ropes and shout, "Hut. Hut. Hut."

Billy watches as a wild eyed, drooling, spitting, humped animal rises from the ship's hold and swings suspended. Its four leg thrash the air in a slow run. Billy sees its body is wrapped in a cloth sling. The two men with guide ropes swing the animal over to the dock.

"What is that?" shouts Sam.

While lowering, the animal snaps and snorts

at anyone in reach. A flailing hoof catches a man in robes and kicks him off the wharf into the water. Two of his friends quickly pull him back onto the dock. Another man has his towel hat snatched from his head by the snapping animal.

"That, gentlemen, is what you are taking delivery of." The Major stands with his arms folded across his chest.

"Yes, sir. Just exactly what is it?" repeats Sam.

"Corporal, you are standing at a moment in history," replies the Major breaking into a smile. "The beginnings of this experiment can revolutionize the movement of supplies and communications across the Southwest."

"Yes, Sir. But, what is it?" Sam flicks a quick questioning glance at Billy.

"Camels, Corporal. Camels."

Billy and Sam stare at each other.

The animal is gently lowered onto the dock. Gaining the firm footing, the animal spits on spectators and snaps at those near by, while continuing to bellow. The robed men quickly surround it. They unharness the beast and immediately set to work calming it down. The hoist returns to the hold to extract another animal.

"What the hell do we know about camels?"

whispers Sam. Billy slowly shakes his head.

"I only ever seen pictures of camels," replies Billy.

****

Turning from her encounter with the soldier, Katrina continues to the end of the wharf and sees her father approach two other German men standing beside a small shed. They are in deep conversation.

Passing the shed, the crowds thin considerably, and the German families congregate in an open area. The men and boys surround the women and children. Katrina's father joins the group.

"The men have arranged *vagons* for us. *Ve* go *vith zem* to the nearby village of Karlshaven. *Ve vill vait* there for our property from the ship. *Ve* go, *ja*."

****

"Gentlemen," says the Major, "we'll have to wait for our cargo to be unloaded and then we'll prepare to march. Please show me where the boarding house is for my stay."

"Yes, Sir." Both Corporals respond.

"First, a tavern would be appreciated."

"Yes, Sir," snaps Billy. "A respectable tavern is

close by. Arrangements have been made for you at Mrs. Wilson's. A superior boarding house," " Both corporals remain at attention.

Noticing their stance, the Major says, "At ease, gentlemen. Show me the tavern."

"We'd be happy to, Major. Let's walk back up the wharf. I have a hack arranged for your transportation," says Billy.

"Splendid. Lead the way, Corporal."

Together, the three men dodge their way to the waiting hackney carriage.

Stepping into the carriage, the Corporals sit across from the Major. Billy volunteers that Indianola is a thriving seaport rivaling Galveston in the shipping it handles.

"The town really came into its own when Germans began to use this as a point of entry into Texas back in 1844. A Prince named Braunfels set up some immigrants in a settlement close by called Karlshafen. Then they used Indianola as their port for more and more of them to arrive."

"Interesting," replied the Major.

"Them Germans have spread out into the Hill Country all around Fredericksburg," added Sam not wanting to be outdone.

"I see," said the Major.

"'Course oxcarts carry goods to and from Indianola to San Antonio and Chihuahua, Mexico. Them freighters do a good bit of business from these parts," Sam continues.

"During the war with Mexico, Indianola grew because of all the shipping to supply the troops. General Taylor's boys were equipped from a depot set up here."

"Sound logistics," says the Major.

"A new post office, stagecoach service, hotels, restaurants, saloons, maybe a few bawdy houses, cantinas, and a hospital are here. The town stretches almost two miles along the shore plumb to Powderhorn Bayou," says Billy

"You've got some place here," replies the Major watching the town displayed in their passing. The carriage stops in front of the tavern, the Major climbs out, and enters.

The hack driver leans in and says to Billy and Sam, "Y'all gittin' out here with that other soldier boy or you headed somewheres else? I ain't waiting around forever. Pay up or git out."

Jarred out of their state of shock, both corporals climb out; pay the driver, and the hack rolls away.

"Do you think we need to roust out the rest of

our detail and let them know what we've got ourselves into?" asks Sam. "I know ain't none of them boys ever did see a camel."

"We need to go to the livery and find our troopers,

 tell them, and then come back to the dock and see what we've got to shepherd," says Billy.

Both Corporals begin walking toward the livery to find the other soldiers of their detachment.